L. A. JONES

THE NIGHTMARE FACTORY

ORCHARD BOOKS
338 Euston Road, London NW1 3BH
Orchard Books Australia
Level 17/207 Kent Street, Sydney, NSW 2000

First published in the UK in 2012 by Orchard Books

ISBN 978 1 40831 470 8
Text © L. A. Jones 2012

A CIP catalogue record for this book is
available from the British Library.

1 3 5 7 9 10 8 6 4 2
Printed in Great Britain

Orchard Books is a division of Hachette Children's Books,
an Hachette UK company.
www.hachette.co.uk

For my parents, Gill and Dave

L. A. JONES

THE NIGHTMARE FACTORY

ORCHARD

PROLOGUE

Andrew raced down the alleyway, heart thudding against his chest. He could hear the blood pumping through his head as he panted for breath, throat dry and aching. He stopped running, clutching at the searing pain in his side as he turned to get a better look at the figure chasing him.

It was an elderly man, frail and wrinkly, with an emaciated body cloaked in shadows. His grey face and long straggly hair was illuminated in the pale moonlight, but his hungry black eyes were as dark as ever, burning into Andrew's with a deep loathing.

'Who are you?' Andrew yelled. 'What do you want with me?'

The mysterious figure did not reply. Instead, his lips parted into a disturbing smile, revealing a set of rotten teeth. More shadowy figures crept out of the darkness, spilling out from every direction, edging closer towards him like a black carpet unrolling. Andrew stared at their hooded skull-like faces and yellow bony hands, and shivered, suddenly wrapped in an unbearable cold.

The old man stepped into the moonlight and Andrew could see every crack and crevice on his skin. He was so tall; he towered over Andrew like a statue. He was dressed in an old-fashioned suit and top hat, and was holding a walking stick, which had a small human skull on the top. Slowly, his pale hands reached out.

He grabbed Andrew's wrist, and as he did so, Andrew could feel cold shooting through his veins. 'At last,' the man said in a rasping voice.

But then he let go. He put his hands to his ears as a ringing noise blasted out from every corner of the alleyway, so high-pitched that it cut through the air like a knife. The hooded figures retreated into the darkness, disappearing into the black abyss of shadows as quickly as they had appeared. The old man cursed furiously as he too began fading into the darkness. Slowly Andrew felt his surroundings drifting further and further away from him.

It was over. For now.

But these strange creatures wanted something from Andrew. The only question was, *when would they be back to get it?*

1

Andrew woke up gasping for air, the sound of his alarm clock ringing incessantly in his ears.

He put his hands to his head, mind spinning with confusion. *Had that been a dream?* He stared around his bedroom. *Why had it felt so real?*

He noticed a bright red hand mark on his wrist, scorched there as if it had somehow been burned onto his skin. He reeled backwards, shivering as he ran his fingers over the wound. It looked like a burn, so why did it feel icy cold?

How could something that had happened in his dream transfer into the real world? Unless…unless he'd somehow done it to himself, in his sleep. That had to be the reason…

…*didn't it?*

The door burst open, making Andrew jump. His mum stormed inside, and picked up the buzzing alarm clock.

'Aren't you going to turn this thing off?' she said.

'Get out of my room!' Andrew yelled. He jumped

out of bed, hustled his mum out and kicked the door shut.

He sat back down, taking deep breaths.

'OK, just keep calm,' he told himself. 'Act normal, and everything will be alright.'

He quickly pulled on some jeans and a long-sleeved T-shirt and hurried downstairs.

His mum was sitting at the kitchen table, still in her dressing gown and slippers, and scanning the morning paper. Poppy, his twin sister, was sat eating a slice of toast.

She smiled. 'Hey, bro.'

'Morning,' he said, then turned to his mum. 'Sorry about that. I didn't sleep well.'

She looked at him, sweeping a hand wearily through her silvery hair. She smiled.

'Not to worry, love. Sit down and have some breakfast.'

'What's that smell?' he said, tensing at the stench of smoke in the air. He put his hand over his nose. Ever since the fire, the smell of smoke made him want to gag.

His mum cringed. 'Sorry, I burnt the toast.' She handed him a mug of tea. 'What are you doing up so early? Usually I have to drag you out of bed.'

Poppy grinned. 'Err, that's when we have school, Mum, but it's the holidays, remember?'

Mum slapped a hand on her forehead. 'That's right. How could I forget? Pass me my purse will you?'

Andrew looked at her oddly, and then handed her the purse. She took out two slightly creased twenty-pound notes.

'Here, go and have some fun for once.'

Poppy stopped eating and looked up.

'Err, are you feeling alright?' Andrew said, grinning.

'Yes, now take it before I change my mind.'

'Wow, thanks, Mum,' Poppy said, taking the money. 'Come on, Andrew,' she said as she jumped down from the table. 'Let's go spend it.'

They hurried outside, but as soon as they had reached the end of their road, Andrew pulled her to one side.

'Poppy, listen, I need to tell you something.'

She paused, frowning. 'What is it?'

He showed her the strange mark on his arm, explaining about the nightmare.

'Hmm,' she said, examining it. 'That is weird. But you must have done it in your sleep somehow. Maybe you were tossing and turning, and lashed out at yourself.'

Andrew nodded, relieved.

'You're right. That's what I thought too. Come on, let's head into town.'

A muggy heat hung over London, and the local outdoor market was bustling with people. Row after row of stalls filled the cobbled square, selling anything from knock-off handbags to antiques. Poppy rushed straight to the second-hand bookstall, while Andrew made his way over to the stand that sold video games and DVDs. He was just handing over his money for a new horror film, when a muffled scream made him spin around.

He scanned the busy crowd. A tall kid with broad shoulders and thick biceps had Poppy cornered up against the back of the fish stall.

'Let me go,' Poppy shrieked.

A nasty grin spread over the boy's face. 'Not until you hand over that twenty I won't,' he said, holding her by the arm.

Anger surged in Andrew's stomach. He began to push through the crowd to reach her.

'No way. Get lost you big idiot,' Poppy yelled, trying to squirm away from the boy.

'Feisty for a girl, aren't you? Well, if you won't give it

to me, I'll just have to take it.' He snatched the money from Poppy's hand.

'Oi! Give that back to her,' Andrew shouted.

The boy turned, scowling. 'Oh yeah? And what are you gonna do about it?'

Andrew whipped the twenty-pound note from his hand. 'That,' he said, shoving it in his pocket.

The boy stared at Andrew, his cheek twitching irritably. Then he let out a sarcastic laugh.

'That wasn't a smart move, jerk,' he said, and grabbed Andrew by the collar of his T-shirt. Andrew gasped for breath. A crowd had started to form. The boy lifted his tight fist up to Andrew's face.

Andrew braced himself for the pain.

And then something really strange happened. The fist began to move towards him in slow motion. Andrew peered around at the frozen faces of horror in the crowd. Time seemed to be passing by unnaturally slowly, the words coming from the bully's mouth in a sluggish groan.

What's happening?

Every tiny action Andrew saw was broken up into a million fragments. He didn't know what was going on, but he wasn't about to waste his chance. He grabbed the bully's arm and twisted it around the back of his neck. Then he pushed him hard in the chest.

Time returned to normal and Andrew watched, stunned, as the boy went flying across the square. The horrified faces switched to ones of bewilderment. A few shocked gasps echoed around the market, but none as loud as the one that came from his own mouth. *How did I do that?* he thought, staring at the huge boy who was picking himself up from a dirty puddle. The boy wrapped his hands around his bruised ankle. His cheeks were flushed red with embarrassment. He glared up at Andrew with narrow lizard eyes that shone with a mixture of fear and hatred.

Everyone was staring at Andrew. A few of the market sellers nearby had even begun to clap and cheer. Poppy just stood there, her forehead creased into a frown. She tucked her mousy brown hair behind her ears and grabbed his arm.

'What just happened?' she whispered.

Andrew shook his head. 'I-I don't know. I only gave him a small push.'

Poppy frowned. 'There was nothing small about it. You pushed him halfway across the street. How'd you *do* that?'

I have no idea, thought Andrew. He had never done anything like that before…

'Perhaps it was —'

He stopped talking, noticing a woman close beside them. She was in her twenties, but had long dark hair with thick grey streaks running through it. Despite the hot weather, she was dressed from head to toe in black clothes, and even though Andrew came to the market all the time, he had never seen her here before.

'Err, can I help you?'

The woman smiled. 'Fast reactions you've got there. You're a lot stronger than you look.' Her eyes trailed down his skinny frame. 'I must say, that was very brave of you, standing up to a thug like that. Almost…fearless, you might say?'

'He is,' Poppy said, jumping in between them. 'He's known for it at school. My brother's not afraid of anything.'

Andrew felt himself blush. 'Poppy, shut up!' he said, digging his elbow into her side.

The woman's painted red lips formed a smile. 'Is that so? Why don't you come back to my stall? There's someone I'd like you to meet.'

'You have a stall here?' Poppy said. 'How come we've never seen you before?'

The woman smiled again. 'I'm new here. This is my first week at the market. Follow me,' she said.

Andrew opened his mouth to refuse, but she was already hurrying back to her stall, and he felt strangely compelled to follow.

There was a table full of tarot cards and candles for sale. Behind that was a gypsy wagon. It stood on four golden wheels, each one nearly three feet high. The main part was made from oak and covered with intricate carvings of fairies and elves. Andrew couldn't help but think that it seemed almost magical. Along the top of the wagon was a wooden bar with lots of strange looking circular objects hanging from it. They were made from willow, with their insides woven into loose webs, and decorated with feathers and beads. Andrew stroked them, wondering what they could be for.

'So who did you want us to meet?' Poppy asked, reminding him why they were there.

'An old friend,' the woman said. She turned and knocked three times on the door of the cart. 'He'll be here in a minute. My name's Tiffany Grey.' She reached out her hand. Andrew was just about to shake it, when the cart began to shudder like an earthquake had hit it. A few seconds later, a man with long grey hair clambered out, banging his head on the roof as he did so. The man towered over Andrew, rubbing his scalp. He was at least seven feet tall, and he had long white hair and a stubbly beard.

An uneasy feeling crept over Andrew as he stared at the man in front of him. Remembering his nightmare, he realised who it was.

2

Andrew gulped and backed away.

'What's the matter?' the man asked, frowning. He was dressed in a lime green suit, and wore a purple top hat covered in yellow stars. A couple of the market sellers were staring at him curiously.

'I've seen you in my nightmares!' Andrew said, pointing his finger at him.

Tiffany Grey and the old man exchanged worried glances.

'Your nightmares? What do you mean?' the old man said.

Andrew kept his eyes fixed on the man's face. 'I've dreamt about you,' he said, moving closer. 'You keep chasing me.'

'You've never met this guy before.' Poppy said. 'Are you sure it's him?'

'Yes, it's him! I'm certain of it!'

The old man's frown deepened, and Tiffany Grey, who was already pale, grew as white as a porcelain doll.

'Did this man look exactly like me?' he asked.

There was a sense of urgency in his voice, and Andrew paused, surprised by the man's reaction. He stared into his crystal blue eyes, full of sincerity, and a shadow of doubt crept into his mind. 'Well yeah… Except…'

'Except what?' Tiffany urged, leaning closer.

'Well the guy from my nightmare…his eyes were black, not blue like yours,' Andrew said. He looked at the man's brightly coloured suit and purple hat. 'And he didn't have such a crazy fashion sense. In fact, he was wearing a cloak and top hat and had a weird stick with this skull thing on top of it.'

Tiffany gasped, and turned to face the old man. 'Oran, didn't I tell you? Andrew's the boy from my prophecy. He has to be.'

'Excuse me,' Andrew said. 'What prophecy?'

Oran ignored him. He sighed, his face solemn. 'I fear you may be right,' he said to Tiffany. 'But if Andrew really is the Releaser, it means we can stop Vesuvius before he steals him. We can —'

'What are you two going on about?' Andrew cut in, annoyed. 'What prophecy? What Releaser? And are you the man from my nightmares, or what?'

Oran shook his head. 'No.'

'But then who…?'

The old man sighed deeply and stroked his stubbly beard. 'You mustn't worry about that. Here, take one of these.' He lifted one of the strange looking circular objects down from the stall and handed it to Andrew, who studied it suspiciously. Attached to it were pieces of cord, with beads and vibrant purple feathers hanging from them. 'As long as you use it, you'll be safe.'

'Safe from what?' Andrew asked. *None of this made any sense…*

'What is it?' Poppy asked.

'It's a dreamcatcher,' Oran said. 'It'll stop you from having any more nightmares. Hang it above your bed and it will allow all the good dreams to slip through the net, while any nightmares get caught up in the web.'

Andrew burst out laughing. 'Yeah, right,' he said. 'Nice sales pitch but I haven't got any money.' He handed the dreamcatcher back and folded his arms. 'Besides, a bad dream can't scare me.' He tried to act casual, but he could hear his voice cracking as he said it. This whole thing was just plain weird – the nightmares, these people, the dreamcatchers. *Everything.* And it was beginning to freak him out.

Oran's eyes narrowed. 'That's what worries me.' His gaze fell over the bag in Andrew's hands.

'What have you got there? May I?' he asked, peering into it.

Andrew stepped back, pulling the bag away, but it slipped out of his hands and onto the floor.

He reached to pick it up, but Oran got there first, grabbing the DVD and studying its cover.

'*Back from the Dead 2.*'

Andrew nodded. 'Yeah, it's been banned in fifteen countries. It's going to be awesome.'

Oran stroked his beard again. 'I see. So you're really not afraid of anything then?' He looked at Tiffany, frowning. Then he placed the DVD back in the carrier, along with two of the dreamcatchers from the stall.

'Please take these. They're free.'

Andrew took the bag back. 'Free…? I don't get it. Why are they free?'

'Because it's imperative that you use them,' Tiffany said, raising her voice. 'Think of them as a gift. Hang them up above your bed as soon as you get home, not a moment later. Do you understand?'

Andrew nodded, confused. But he didn't understand. He didn't understand any of this, nor why they were being so insistent.

'Come on, Andrew,' Poppy said, nudging him. 'We've got to get back, *remember*?'

'Remember what?' he said. She nudged him harder in the ribs. 'Ouch! Oh yeah, 'cause. Well...thanks for the dream thingies.' He turned to walk away.

'Take heed of what I've said, Andrew. You will use them, won't you?' Oran called after him.

Andrew shrugged. 'Yeah, I suppose.' He was pretty sure he would have agreed to anything if it meant he could get away.

'Good. You will be in great danger if you do not.'

Danger? thought Andrew. For not hanging up a few strange looking feathery things? It was ridiculous. He pulled on Poppy's arm and they hurried away, but when they reached the corner of the market, Poppy stopped, eyes wide. 'Andrew, what the hell was that all about?'

'I dunno,' he admitted. 'It was weird, wasn't it? He looked exactly like the guy from my nightmares only...only different somehow.'

'Weird? It was a little more than weird. That guy was a complete fruit loop, and as for the woman... Well, wearing black in the middle of summer? It isn't exactly normal, is it?' She sighed. 'I don't trust them. The way they reacted to your nightmare – it wasn't right. It was as if…as if they were hiding something.'

Andrew nodded. He felt the same way. There was definitely more to this than Tiffany and Oran were letting on.

Poppy took out the dreamcatchers and held them up, studying them carefully. 'Do you think these things are cursed?'

Andrew laughed. 'How could they be? They're just a load of junk.'

She put a finger to her lips. 'You're probably right, but let's not take them home; they creep me out.' She walked over to a bin on the corner and chucked them in. She slapped her hands together as if she was glad to be rid of them.

Andrew didn't see any point in trying to stop her. After all, they were just a bunch of twigs and feathers. But as he walked home, a troubling thought played on his mind. He had never told the man his name, yet he had called him Andrew from the very start…

Later that night, a fierce storm was raging outside and the wind rattled against the window frames of Andrew's bedroom like an invisible beast trying to break in. Andrew pulled his clothes off, catching sight of the scars on his back that were left from the fire. He swallowed hard, guilt gnawing away at him. He turned away from the mirror. Every time he saw them, it was a painful reminder of a night he had survived and one that his father hadn't. He sighed, tugging on his pyjamas. He couldn't bear to think about it any more.

He slid his new horror film into the DVD player and switched off the light. He was settled into bed, enjoying the movie, when the television crackled and the screen turned into a mass of black and white dots.

'Stupid cheap television,' he muttered, whacking the top of it.

A face appeared within the fuzzy dots, with long white hair, soulless black eyes and gappy yellow teeth...

Andrew blinked, certain he was seeing things.

'I'm coming for you, Andrew. You can't hide from me. You have to fall asleep eventually, and when you do, I'll be waiting,' the man said in a hoarse, breathless voice.

Andrew sat upright, staring at the TV. 'What?' he whispered into the darkness.

There was a crack of thunder from outside and the TV screen began to flash and break up again until it was completely blank. Andrew rubbed his eyes.

A long mischievous cackle filled the room.

'Who's there?' Andrew said in a loud voice. He wondered if it was the man from the market. Perhaps he had followed him home?

But there was no reply. The rain lashed down outside, the wind roared, but the house was completely still. Andrew got up to check that the window was still locked, and then switched off the movie. He crept back into bed, and pulled the duvet all the way up to his neck.

When he closed his eyes, his mind started to drift. He wasn't sure if he had imagined it or not, but earlier, time had seemed to slow right down. He'd managed to push a boy over who was twice his size. Then there were the strange people at the market with the dreamcatchers, and the fact that Oran looked so similar to the man from his nightmares. He couldn't shake the feeling that somehow all of these things were connected. But how, and why? Nothing seemed to add up.

He yawned, unable to stay awake. Soon, his eyelids grew heavy and he slipped into a troubled sleep, pulled slowly beneath the blankets of dream world.

In the depth of his sleep, Andrew dreamt that he was at the beach playing football with his friends – he'd just scored a goal. The violent sea crackled against the rocks as if in applause. The squawks of seagulls carried through the salty air, and Andrew ran towards the goalposts again, the hot sand pressed between his toes, as he lined the ball up for another shot.

Suddenly, he was submerged in darkness. It was like someone had turned off the light in his head, as if he had become blind. He wrapped his arms around his body, realising the air had turned icy cold.

From out of the gloom, the man from Andrew's nightmare's appeared. He was walking slowly towards him, laughing menacingly, but there was someone else there too... *Oran.*

'Why didn't you use the dreamcatcher?' Oran rasped as he struggled to hold the man back.

Andrew stared at them, wondering how this dream could feel so real. Confused at how these two men could look so alike.

The shadows broke apart and he saw five dark figures creeping out. Their ghostly faces were the only things visible in the pale moonlight that leaked over the horizon.

They prowled towards Andrew, gazing at him with big black eyes marked by fiercely red pupils. Each one had a skeletal body, draped in a black hooded cloak, as if they were woven from smoke. They floated inches above the ground, chilling the air with every breath.

'Andrew,' they whispered in eerie, croaky voices. 'Come with us.'

'Quickly, Andrew, get out of here,' Oran yelled, face red with panic. 'You need to wake up.' He was losing his grip on the old man.

Snapping back to life, Andrew tried to run, but the cold in the air was overpowering, and his legs, stiff as wood, refused to move. The old man let out a terrible, ear-piercing cackle as the creatures in black cloaks crept ever closer.

'Yes,' he cried, eyes glistening like two black marbles. 'Grab him. Bring him to me.'

Andrew tried to force himself to wake up, but it was no use. Finally giving in, unable to do anything else, he felt the creatures' bony arms encircle him, and then...

Blackness.

3

Andrew's eyes shot open, his clammy skin stuck to the bed as if by glue. Confusion rippled through him.

'No way,' he breathed. *This isn't my bedroom.* He shivered as he noticed the thick brick walls and a steel door. There were no windows, just a dim light bulb shining down from above, casting ominous shadows over the room. Then he realised that he wasn't in a bed, but on a hard white table. He rubbed his eyes, wondering where on earth he could be. There was a lot of strange machinery around the room, and a trolley with syringes and scalpels lying on top of it.

OK, you're obviously still dreaming. All you've got to do is wake up, he told himself, shutting his eyes and pinching himself hard on the arm.

'Wake up, wake up,' he said, digging his nails in harder with every word. He opened his eyes again.

Nothing had changed. He took a deep breath, coughing at the awful stench that lingered in the air, redolent of damp and mould and tinged with the overpowering smell of antiseptic. Was he in a hospital? No. Hospitals were clean and hygienic. This place looked like something out of one of his horror films.

A throbbing pain shot through his head.

'Ow!' he winced, reaching around to try and find the cause. He ran his fingers over a small metal object in his scalp.

'What the…?' It had a hole in the middle of it. The hair around it was warm and sticky. He pulled his hand back and saw that it was covered in blood.

He grabbed onto the edges of the table, heart pounding and head swimming with dizziness. Someone must have kidnapped him, but he couldn't understand how, or more importantly, why. The last thing he remembered was being asleep. His mind raced back to his nightmare. Oran had tried to protect him. If Andrew and Poppy hadn't thrown away the dreamcatchers, would none of this be happening now?

There was a groan from behind him and he spun around, fists in the air.

'Who's there?' he said, scanning the room anxiously. At the far end of the room was a table, similar to the one he was on. He thought he could see somebody lying on top of it. He squinted into the darkness at familiar red and pink pyjamas…

'Poppy?' he said, his voice cracking. 'Is that you?' He jumped down from the table and raced over to her. His legs felt like jelly, and for a moment he thought they might collapse beneath him. He shook her frantically.

'Poppy. Wake up!'

She looked up at him with half-open blue eyes, heavy with confusion.

'Andrew, what are you doing in my roo —' She stopped dead as she noticed her surroundings, terror glazing over her face. Her eyes widened.

'Help!'

'No, don't!' Andrew said, putting a hand over her mouth. 'They'll hear you.' He wasn't sure who, but he didn't want to find out. 'It's OK. It's going to be all right,' he said, putting his arm around her, wishing he could believe his own words.

She swallowed, blinking back tears.

'Where are we?' she asked, putting her hand to the back of her head and wincing. 'Ouch. What is that? It feels like metal.'

She's got one too, Andrew thought. He parted Poppy's hair. There was a metal disk in her head, with a hole in the middle. It looked a bit like a washer, except bigger. But why was there a hole?

'I don't know what it is,' Andrew said, frowning. 'It might be some sort of plug.'

She stared at him, lips trembling. 'Why would it be a plug? I don't understand. What's it for?'

'I have no idea.' He hesitated. 'We'll be fine, Poppy, don't worry.'

'How do you know that? We've got some strange thing in our heads and the last thing I remember was being asleep and having a terrible nightmare.'

Nightmare? Andrew thought. *Had they had the very same dream?*

'I had a nightmare too. What happened in yours?'

But she wasn't listening. She was staring down at his wrist. 'What is that thing?'

'Huh? What thing?' Andrew said. He glanced down. A thick metal band was wrapped around his wrist. It had a small padlock and a red flashing light on it and something engraved on the front.

3091. Property of the N.F.

He pulled back, shuddering. What did N.F. stand for?

'I've got one too,' Poppy whispered, her face crumpled with panic. 'Except mine says "Three Zero

Nine Two". She yanked at it. 'It won't come off. God, what is it?'

'I don't know,' Andrew said. 'But I don't like it.'

A noise from the hallway snapped his focus back to the room. He froze, listening intently.

'What was that?' came a rasping voice from the other side of the door.

'What was what?' came another.

'I hear something. I'm going to go in and check on them.'

'Quickly,' Andrew said. 'I think they're coming back.' Whoever *they* are. 'Pretend you're still asleep.' He clambered onto the table he had woken up on and shut his eyes, trying to keep as silent as possible. He could feel his heart beating rapidly against his chest. A loud creaking sound filled the room as the huge metal door swung open. Andrew felt his skin prickle with goosebumps in a sudden gush of icy air. The closer they got, the colder he felt.

'They're both asleep, see?' said the deep, rasping voice.

It didn't sound human.

'I know. But I heard something,' the other voice insisted.

Andrew dared to open one eye just enough to catch

a glimpse of his kidnappers. He bit down hard on his lip, stifling a scream. They were the same creatures from his nightmare, with a cloak of shadows pulled over their pale, skeletal bodies. Andrew swallowed, throat dry. *How is that even possible?* He closed his eyes again.

'Kritchen,' the first one sighed. 'I heard nothing. It was probably just your imagination. You gave them both the sleep-inducer prior to their operation I presume?'

Operation? Andrew thought with a rush of terror. Then he remembered the metal thing in the back of his head.

'Yes, Ghould, one dose for the girl, two for the boy. But it worries me – he doesn't seem to emit much fear. Can you feel that? Nothing…'

'Yes, and Master Vesuvius is aware of that,' replied Ghould. 'He believes this boy may be the one we have been searching for. So naturally, we must be extra vigilant with him. But they are asleep, Kritchen, any fool can see that.'

The one they'd been searching for. Andrew recalled these words over and over. So, they'd been looking for him for some time…but why? He stayed absolutely still until he felt the temperature in the room rise again. When he was certain that it was safe, he sat up.

'Poppy,' he said, climbing down from the table. 'Hey, Poppy, it's OK. They've gone.'

She looked at him, eyes wide with terror.

'Andrew,' she whispered. 'I dreamt about those creatures last night. They were in my nightmare.'

Andrew shivered, but not from the cold.

'I dreamt about them too,' he said and then paused, not sure how to go on. 'I know this might sound crazy, Poppy, but I think they stole us from our dreams.'

'Why would they do that?' she asked. '*How* could they do that? It's…it's…'

Andrew nodded. 'Crazy, right? Impossible? But it's the only explanation. I think the people at the market were trying to protect us. You know, by giving us those dreamcatchers.'

She frowned. 'You mean the ones I threw away?'

'That doesn't matter now.'

'But it does. This is all my fault,' she said, eyes starting to well up.

'No. If anything, it's my fault. Didn't you hear what they said about me being the one they've been searching for?'

'What do you think they meant by that?' she asked, wiping away the tears with her pyjama sleeve.

34

'I have no idea,' Andrew said. He couldn't imagine what these creatures could possibly want with him. He was just a normal thirteen-year-old boy. 'Perhaps they mistook me for somebody el —'

He stopped. The words died on his tongue. The huge metal door burst open and the two creatures floated into the room. They moved silently over to where Andrew and Poppy stood, their shadowy cloaks sweeping along the floor like silk.

Kritchen turned to Ghould. As he spoke, his bones protruded from his hollow cheeks. 'I told you he was awake. What shall we do with him now?'

4

Andrew stood pinned to the spot, glancing from his twin to the shadowy creatures. They could run, but they would almost certainly be caught, or he could try and reason with them. Both options seemed utterly hopeless.

'How long have you been awake?' Ghould rasped. When he spoke, rotten teeth were exposed in his skull-like face, making him appear even uglier than Andrew had first thought possible.

'Not long,' Poppy said, in a dry whisper.

The creature eyed her suspiciously, and then turned to Andrew. 'And you?'

'I just woke up,' he said. 'We both did.'

'And how much did you hear?'

'What?' Andrew said. 'Nothing. We didn't hear anything.'

The creature's red eyes flashed from Andrew to Kritchen. 'Are you sure you double-dosed the boy? He seems unusually lucid.'

Kritchen's grotesque face contorted into a frown.

Andrew couldn't take his eyes off the awful scar running down the left side of his cheek. 'I suppose I could have got it wrong. Perhaps I gave him too little.'

'We should inform Vesuvius at once,' said Ghould. 'If he knows anything…'

Kritchen shook his head.

'No,' he pleaded. 'Not the master.' There was more than a hint of desperation in his voice. Kritchen cleared his throat. 'I mean, he would not be pleased. And it would be pointless. You heard the boy, he didn't hear anything.'

So what I heard is important, Andrew thought, mind whirling. He looked at the two ghostly figures standing in front of him. It was hard to imagine them being terrified of anything. Yet they were. What could possibly be so awful about this man, Vesuvius, that it frightened even them?

Ghould paused, apparently thinking. 'You are right. We shall keep this to ourselves. I shall go and alert Vesuvius that they are ready.' The steel door slid open and he floated through it.

Andrew got up, heart thumping. A mixture of anxiety and anger was surging through his veins. 'Ready for what?' he asked, glaring at Kritchen. 'What are you going to do to us now?'

The creature turned his head towards Andrew and he felt a rush of cold wash over him.

'Silence,' Kritchen growled. 'Do not speak unless spoken to.'

Andrew leaned back against the table. It was no use trying to communicate with these creatures. They were as icy cold on the inside as they were on the outside – as if they had no emotions at all. He looked at Poppy, who was fingering her metal bracelet. Andrew knew she was terrified. She was shaking, causing beads of sweat to drip from her brow.

'Don't worry,' he whispered. 'I'm going to get us out of here.'

Kritchen moved closer towards them, staring at Andrew like he was some sort of time bomb just waiting to explode. He shifted awkwardly on the table, rubbing his arms and trying not to shiver.

A tall man appeared at the door, dressed in flowing black robes and a top hat. Andrew flinched, recognising him instantly. His hair was shoulder length and cobweb white, and his nose pointed into a hook. His dark eyes darted to Andrew, as sharp as bullets, and Andrew felt as if they might pierce through him at any moment.

'Master Vesuvius,' Kritchen said, bowing slightly.

So this is him, Andrew thought. *The one they're so afraid of. The man from my nightmare.* He couldn't help but stare. The old man looked so much like Oran, but without his friendly smile. Vesuvius's face was grey and gaunt, the colour of milky tea. Andrew didn't think he looked very strong. His frail body seemed as if it could snap in two at any moment.

Vesuvius walked towards him, slowly, his footsteps echoing against the stony walls. 'We meet at long last, *in the flesh.*' He spoke in a calm voice. Eerie. Cold. His slender lips creased upwards as he spoke, but it was more of a sneer than a smile.

Kritchen crept forwards. 'They're tagged and implanted, master.'

Vesuvius nodded, not taking his eyes off Andrew. 'Good. Escort them to be fed, ready for the Dark Room.'

'Dark Room? What the hell is the Dark Room?' Andrew said. Poppy grabbed him by the arm, staring deep into his eyes.

'Andrew, don't. Let's just do whatever they say.'

Vesuvius sneered at them and turned to leave.

'No,' said Andrew, anger flaring inside him. 'You're

not just going to walk away. We deserve to know why we've been brought here,' he shouted.

He raced towards Vesuvius, trying to grab him. But as if he had eyes in the back of his head, Vesuvius spun around. He raised his skull cane in the air. The eyes glowed red, and Andrew bashed into something solid between them. He was thrown backwards, landing on the floor with a thud. He was stunned, mind spinning. What had just happened? It was as if Vesuvius had created some sort of invisible barrier. Andrew pressed his finger into the wall of rock-hard air between them. It shimmered slightly, like oil on water.

'I don't know what you're doing but you better let us out of here!' he yelled, scrambling to his feet, ignoring the searing pain in his back. 'You can't keep us locked up here forever. You'll go to jail for this!' He could feel his face turning red with anger. Once more, he tried to force himself through the impenetrable wall between him and Vesuvius, but he was thrust backwards onto the floor again.

Vesuvius stared at him with a face devoid of emotion.

'I'm warning you,' he spat. 'Do not try and defy me. You will not live long enough to regret it.' He brought his cane back down to his side, turned, tossed his cloak over one shoulder and walked away.

Kritchen led them down a long, narrow corridor with an arched ceiling. Everything was built from stone, like some kind of medieval castle, but it was lit with electric lights. There was a smell of mould in the air. Thick green slime covered the walls where dampness had seeped through the brickwork, and this, combined with the darkness, made him think that maybe they were underground. The corridor sloped steeply downwards. Every few metres there were steel doors with numbers engraved on the front. The further they walked, the darker it got, and the dim spotlights blinked on and off, sending flickering shadows over the cave-like passages.

'Where do you think it's taking us?' Poppy whispered. She was pale in the gloom, her usually rosy cheeks drained of their colour.

'The Dark Room…wherever that is,' Andrew said. 'Don't worry, I won't let them hurt you.'

Kritchen was floating inches above the ground. He stopped at a set of metal doors, which looked a bit like a lift. He punched a number into a keypad on the wall and the doors slid open silently. Electronic

technology and old stone? It didn't make sense...
What kind of place was this?

Andrew peered through the doorway. Beyond was
a large hall, filled with rows of tables and chairs.

'Eat,' Kritchen said, pointing a skeletal finger at a
queue of children. Andrew gasped, realising that they
weren't the only ones who had been stolen from their
dreams. He stared at the swarm of kids in horror;
some only looked about six, others as old as sixteen,
and all in their pyjamas. There must have been about
a hundred of them. Most had skinny, malnourished
bodies, some with wild hair. Their skin and clothes
were covered in grubby stains.

'Well this just added a whole new level of weird,' he
said, trying to force a smile.

'More children,' Poppy whispered, frowning. 'But
I don't get it. What do they want with all of us?'

'I don't know,' Andrew said. He took a step forwards.
'Come on, maybe we can find out.'

5

Andrew stared around at the enormous hall as they shuffled forwards. It was made from stone, with a high ceiling supported by thick pillars. There was a kitchen at one end, a bit like a school cafeteria. It would have looked quite grand, if it weren't for the green mould that covered everything like a disease. Gazing up at the domed ceiling, Andrew saw that it was painted with strange dark pictures. It was hard to make out what they were, because the paint had faded and cracked with age, but it looked like the shadowy creatures were drinking some kind of black smoke.

This just gets weirder and weirder, Andrew thought.

He switched his attention to the other end of the hall where there was a large marble fireplace, and two enormous metal cogs, with a handle attached to one of them. Next to it there were lots of white objects lodged into the wall. Andrew swallowed to stop himself from gagging.

He nudged Poppy in the ribs, feeling sick.

'Skulls,' he said, pointing. 'Skulls in the walls.'

She turned and gasped. 'Oh my God.'

Her legs gave way and he quickly grabbed her, scared that she was going to faint.

'They're so small,' she whispered, voice cracking. 'Do you think they belonged to children?'

He gulped, not wanting to think aboout it. He turned to look at the row of children again. A few of them were pointing and whispering. 'Poppy, they're all staring at us.'

'I guess they don't see a lot of new faces here.'

'Come on,' Andrew said. 'Let's go and say hi.'

They crossed the cold, dusty floor on their bare feet and joined the back of the queue. A girl with a sleek black ponytail stood in front of them, talking to a boy with jet-black hair and glasses in what sounded like Chinese. Andrew couldn't understand what they were saying, but he knew they were talking about him and Poppy. Andrew coughed, and the girl looked up, blushing.

'Hi,' Andrew said.

The girl waved shyly. 'Ni Hao.'

'What is this place?' Andrew asked, but the girl looked back at him, face blank. She bit her lip and shrugged.

'I don't think she understands you,' Poppy said. 'Let's try someone else.'

They moved over to the next girl in the queue, who had long orange hair and yellow pyjamas. She wasn't staring at them like all the others, but seemed to be preoccupied with picking a hangnail off her finger.

'Hey,' Andrew said. 'Can you tell us what we're doing here?'

The girl looked up at him with a vacant stare, her green eyes crossed over so that they appeared to be focused on her nose. She spoke in a calm, soft whisper.

'This is the place where the Shadowmares walk, they'll find your fear, they'll make you talk.'

'What do you mean?' Poppy said. 'You're not making any sense.'

The girl moved closer, so that she was inches away from them.

'They'll make you scream until you wish you were dead, and if you try to escape, they'll cut off your head!' She made a fierce slicing action with her hand, and Poppy jumped back.

Andrew sighed – this was going to be harder than he'd thought.

'I wouldn't bother,' came a wry voice from behind them. A tall, skinny boy stood there, smirking. He was wearing pyjamas like all the others, but he had his sleeves rolled up around his shoulders, so that his thin pasty arms were exposed. His black hair was short and uneven, as if he'd attacked it with a pair of scissors, but his green eyes, although set in dark circles, looked bright and full of life. 'That's Rhyming Rita,' he said. 'Trying to make conversation with her is like trying to talk to a stuffed animal. It just ain't gonna happen. She's completely crackers. A lot of them are. My name's Dan, by the way.'

He stuck out his hand, and Andrew noticed that he was wearing a metal bracelet, identical to his own, only the numbers on his read '2742'.

'Hey. I'm Andrew, and this is Poppy.'

Dan shook his hand energetically. 'Soz about everyone staring. We don't see many new kids around here. Once or twice a year maybe, at the most. I suppose you're wondering where you are.'

'Yeah, just a little.'

'This is the Nightmare Factory.'

Andrew blinked. 'What?'

'They make nightmares here, man,' Dan said, pulling his fingers through his greasy hair and grabbing some food trays off the huge pile stacked up against the wall. He handed a couple to Andrew and Poppy.

'Nightmares?' Andrew said. 'How do they *make* nightmares? I thought we just dreamt them up?'

'Nope, that's what I used to think, but it's a lot more complicated than that.'

'But I don't get it,' Poppy said. 'How does that even work?'

Dan leaned in closer, eyes bright. 'Well, kids produce higher rates of fear. So they steal us from our dreams and bring us here, to the Nightmare Factory. They've been doing it for centuries. Stealing a few children here and there so it won't be noticed. Every other day after breakfast they take us to the Dark Room. Then they hook us up to these machines called Fear Pods, which extract our fear.'

'Extract our fear?' Poppy said, shivering. 'I don't like the sound of that.'

'What? No way,' Andrew said. 'You're messing with us.'

Dan shook his head. 'It's true, man. I couldn't believe it myself at first, but it is.'

Andrew thought about it. Dan didn't have any reason to lie to them, so why wouldn't he be telling the truth? He was just having a hard time getting his head around the fact that nightmares were something that were made…in a factory. It was completely mental.

'Why every other day?' asked Andrew. 'Why not all the time?'

'It takes a day to convert the nightmares into fear.'

'Are they the ones that make the nightmares?' Poppy asked. She pointed to the skeletal figures guarding the door.

'Yep, the Shadowmares.' Dan nodded.

Shadowmares, Andrew thought. *So that's what Rita had meant.*

'But what are they?'

'Some kind of dream demon I suppose. They don't eat. They just feed off people's fear. They can shape-shift too. It's well scary.'

Poppy frowned. 'Shape-shift?'

'Yes, but only when they're in the Dark Room. I don't know why but they can't seem to do it anywhere else. Oh yeah, and they can read minds too. That's why they put these things in the back of our heads. We've all got 'em.'

Dan turned around, revealing a metal plug in the back of his head, identical to the ones that Andrew and Poppy had.

'What are they?' Andrew asked.

'They let the Shadowmares read our minds, and once they know what scares us, they shape-shift

48

into whatever our fear is – and collect it to make nightmares for the rest of the world.'

Andrew ran his fingers over the metal object in his head. He flinched. The pain throbbed like it had a heartbeat. He thought about what fears the Shadowmares might find in there. Ever since his dad had died, he'd spent so long worrying about Poppy and Mum and pretending he wasn't afraid of anything, that it had become second nature. But deep down, he knew that there was a fear lurking, so powerful that he didn't want to have to ever face it again. He shook his head, trying to forget about it. Instead, his eyes flickered to the Shadowmares guarding the door, standing as still as ice sculptures, only their chests moving to take long, drawn-out breaths.

'And Vesuvius – what's he? He doesn't look like the others…he looks more human.'

'I'm not sure. Half Shadowmare maybe,' Dan said. He snorted. 'He's definitely not human.'

'And what about these bracelets?' Poppy asked, jangling her's around. 'What are they for?'

'They set off the alarms if we try to escape. There's a sensor above every door. The Shadowmares have to disable them before we can walk through.'

Andrew glanced up at the door and saw a red light

flashing away like the one on his bracelet.

'Great,' he said, grimly. 'Not getting out of here anytime soon then.'

His gaze trailed over Dan's moth-eaten pyjamas, too short for his tall frame and covered in holes. Then to his pale skin, which looked as if it hadn't seen the sun for ages. 'How long have you been here?' he asked.

'Two years.'

Andrew felt his heart drop to the pit of his stomach.

Poppy put a hand over her mouth. 'Two years?' she said. 'But that's – that's ages.'

Dan shrugged. 'Yeah, you kind of lose track of time after a while.'

'Wait,' Andrew said. 'So when do they let us go free then?'

Dan frowned. 'What do you mean, free? Dude, we never get to go free. I thought you'd realised that by now.'

'Never?' Andrew said. He couldn't imagine *never* going home. He wondered what his mother would do once she discovered they were missing. She'd be all on her own. Andrew instantly pushed the thought away. 'I don't understand. You said they'd been taking kids for centuries. There're no adults here. What about all the kids that have grown up, where do they all go?'

'You won't want to know, man,' Dan said, shaking his head.

'We may not *want* to know,' Poppy said. 'But I think we need to.'

'Well, usually when we reach our sixteenth birthday they just get rid of us.'

Andrew felt his stomach tighten into a knot.

'What do you mean?' he said. 'Get rid of us how exactly?'

'Well, we're no use to them any more. An adult's fear isn't powerful enough to make nightmares, so they send us away…' His voice trailed off.

'Dan,' Poppy said firmly. 'Where do they send us?'

Dan glanced down, fiddling with the drawstring of his pyjama bottoms. 'All right… There's a place out there. It's called the Mountain of Doom.' He looked around, as if checking that none of the Shadowmares were listening. 'I've overheard them talking about it before. Apparently it's full of beasts and creatures from our worst nightmares. They say that everyone who enters there winds up dead within a matter of hours.'

Poppy shuffled from one foot to the other.

'So how long have you got left?'

51

There was a long pause as a shadow passed over Dan's face.

'It doesn't matter. Come on, let's go and get some food. I'm well hungry.'

They were almost at the front of the queue, but Andrew wasn't thinking about food right now.

'Dan,' he said, a little louder.

Dan turned slowly.

'What?'

'How long have you got left?'

'One week,' he said, hunching his shoulders. 'Happy now? I have one week until I'm dead meat.'

6

'A week?' Poppy said. 'Aren't you afraid?'

Dan frowned. 'Of course I'm afraid, numbnuts. I'm terrified.' He lowered his voice to a whisper. 'But I'm going to do something about it. I'm going to escape.'

Andrew leaned forwards, heart racing. 'How?'

'I'm not sure yet, but I am.'

'Well, can we come with you?'

Dan shrugged. 'Sure, if you're willing to risk it. There's a high chance we'll get caught though. I've got nothing to lose.' His eyes moved to the skulls in the wall. 'You on the other hand…'

'We're coming,' Poppy said firmly. 'We're going to end up dead in a few years anyway. We might as well try and do something about it.'

Andrew glanced at his twin and saw that her face was fiercely determined. He was glad that she felt the same way.

They reached the front of the queue and Andrew smelt a rancid stench of cabbage wafting its way down

53

to them. He clutched at his grumbling stomach. He must have been really hungry because never, in all his life, had it ever grumbled like that for cabbage.

They made their way up to the serving station, which was manned by a tall, slim lady. She wore a tailored trouser suit and tie tucked into a spotless white shirt. She didn't look like any of the dinner ladies at Andrew's school. Her chocolate brown hair was moulded into a tight bun on the top of her head, with not a single hair out of place. Andrew grinned despite himself – it looked a bit like a large dog poo.

Her dark eyes followed him as he walked up to the counter and put his tray down. She dumped a pile of cabbage, eggs and some sort of brown mush onto it. Andrew pinched his nose, trying not to retch. It smelt rotten, like it'd been left in the rubbish for a month.

He lingered for a second. 'Is there anything else?'

The lady blinked slowly. Then she smiled sweetly and asked in a gentle voice. 'I'm sorry, dear. Do you not like rotten cabbage?'

Andrew shook his head.

'Would you like something else? Like a big roast dinner, fresh from the oven?'

He got the feeling she was joking. 'There's no need to be rude.'

She glared at him, and snarled, exposing her yellow teeth. She slammed her hand down onto the work surface, making the cups and plates rattle in their holders. 'You get what you're given here, got it, kid?'

'I was only asking,' Andrew muttered, and he hurried over to the table that Dan and Poppy had sat down at.

'Who was that?' he asked, taking a seat opposite Dan.

'That's Madam Bray. She's taken a shine to you then?' Dan said, smirking. He spooned some of the brown mush into his mouth, but some escaped.

'Oops, sowwy,' he said, as it dribbled slowly down his chin.

Poppy turned away in disgust.

'Madam Bray?' Andrew said. 'But who is she? And why is she so mean?'

He swirled his spoon around the tray of brown mush, contemplating what would be the best way to eat it. A bit at a time, so that he wouldn't be sick, or as quickly as possible so that he'd hardly taste it.

'She used to be one of us, you know,' Dan said.

'What do you mean?' Poppy asked, frowning. 'Are you saying that she was stolen from her dreams too?'

Dan nodded. 'Yep. Somehow Madam Bray struck up a deal with Vesuvius when she turned fifteen. He said that she could stay and work for him here in return for her life. I don't know why she'd want to though. Evil witch. She's almost as twisted as him.' He shook his head, picking up his spoon and licking it clean.

'Perhaps you could do the same,' Poppy said. 'Just to buy yourself some time.'

Dan shook his head. 'Nah, others kids have tried in the past and it doesn't work. Anyway, Vesuvius has his favourite already.'

Andrew was certain that he could see Dan's eyes beginning to well up, and he felt the sudden need to change the subject.

'Urghh! This food – it's disgusting,' he said. 'I don't know how you eat it.'

He picked up his spoon again, deciding that he'd better give it a try. If he didn't, he'd starve to death, so he tried to pretend that it was a gorgeous roast dinner smothered in thick gravy. He gagged once more; even his imagination wasn't that good.

Dan was watching him with a smile.

'Here, man,' he said, slipping a bottle of brown sauce from under his sleeve and passing it to him. 'Try some of this. It'll make it taste loads nicer.'

Andrew looked down at the glass bottle. It was just like what they had at home. 'Where did you get this from?'

'Shhh,' Dan whispered. 'You're gonna get me caught. I'll tell you later. Just take some and give it back.'

Being careful that nobody could see him, Andrew tipped the sauce all over his food, then passed it back under the table so that Poppy could have some too. Dan was right. It made the brown mush taste almost bearable, and he was able to finish everything on his plate. He looked around at the other kids in the hall. Most were eating on their own, but a few were in small groups, talking quietly.

'What did you mean earlier, when you said a lot of the others were mad?'

Dan looked up. 'Exactly what I said. Most of them can't handle it here. They go gaga. Not all of them of course. A few are alright, but it takes guts to stay sane in this place.' He gestured to a boy with spiky brown hair, sitting at the table opposite them. 'Take Peter Twelve Taps for example. He has to tap everything he touches twelve times or else he believes his family will die.'

Andrew watched Peter, intrigued, as he tapped his spoon exactly twelve times on the table before picking it up to eat with.

'And you see that boy in the green pyjamas?' he nodded to the far end of the hall. 'Looks pretty normal doesn't he?'

Andrew glanced over to where Dan was pointing. He saw a ginger haired boy, braces, a bit spotty.

'Yeah.'

'Well he's not. Believe me. I have to share a room with him. He keeps me awake screaming all night long. He doesn't talk, just wails this horrible deafening cry until it's morning again. Anyway, that's not going to happen to you guys. I can tell. You're like me.'

'And that's a good thing…?' Andrew asked, lifting an eyebrow.

Dan waved a hand. 'Of course. Tough. Not gonna go down without a fight? I grew up in a care home most of my life, so I know what it's like to have it rough. But trust me,' he said, his face becoming serious, 'this place is way worse than that. Worse than anything you could think of.' He put his spoon down. 'So what's the deal with you two then? Are you boyfriend and girlfriend?'

Andrew nearly choked on his food. 'Are you serious?' he said. 'She's my younger sister.'

Poppy punched him from across the table. 'Hey, I'm only younger by three minutes.' She turned to Dan. 'We're actually twins.'

His eyes switched from Poppy's brown hair to Andrew's blond. 'Twins? You don't look much alike.'

'No, and thank God.'

'Yeah,' Poppy said. 'Glad we agree on something.'

Dan laughed. 'So where are you guys from?'

'London,' Poppy said. 'You?'

Dan's eyes brightened a little. 'I'm from London too.' He scratched his head. 'It's strange. They've stolen a few kids from around that area since I was brought here. I reckon it's got something to do with the Releaser.'

There it was again, Andrew thought. *That word. The Releaser.* Tiffany had mentioned it at the market. Now Dan...

He was just about to ask what it meant, when he was interrupted by a loud churning noise, like the slow grinding of a mill. He turned around, and saw Madam Bray standing by the fireplace, cranking the huge cog that was attached to the wall. All of the kids began to panic. Some were whimpering, clinging to each other. Slowly, the fireplace slid away, revealing a pool of darkness. Madam Bray marched towards them, clutching a bamboo cane in her hand. She cracked it down on the table, making the Chinese girl fall off her chair in shock.

'Everybody up and into the Dark Room.'

'Andrew,' Poppy said, with a look of pure terror. 'I don't want to go in there.'

Andrew eyed the gap in the wall apprehensively.

'Neither do I,' he said. 'But I don't think we have a choice. The Shadowmares are still guarding the exit.'

'Now!' Madam Bray screamed again. This time, even Andrew jumped a little.

Poppy grabbed Andrew's arm, and he could feel shakes running through her body. Dan looked a bit green, although that could have been down to the food.

All of the kids rose from their chairs, an eerie silence radiating through the hall. Slowly, they filed through the gap where the fireplace had been, and Andrew stepped into unbelievable darkness...

7

The heavy sound of grinding began again as the door closed behind them. The lights flashed on, sharp and blinding after the pitch black. When Andrew's eyes had adjusted, he could see that they were in a rectangular room, as large as a football stadium. Six platforms ran around the edge of the room, and each one led to the next with a metal ladder. On the platforms were lots of giant glass Pods. Each one had a black seat inside, and some kind of metal helmet contraption. Tubes and wires sprouted from the top, like hundreds of silver snakes.

'What,' Poppy said, 'are *those*?'

'I think they must be the Fear Pods Dan told us about,' Andrew whispered.

Dan nodded. 'Yup, they're the machines that extract our fear.'

'So what is *that*?' Andrew said, pointing to a giant glass cylinder in the centre of the room. It was attached to all of the wires from the Pods and was about seventy feet high.

'I think that's the…' Dan fell still. Madam Bray was striding towards them, tapping the cane on the side of her calf.

'Silence!' she yelled, as she stopped to straighten the collar of her jacket. 'Make your way to your Pods at once. Three-zero-nine-one and Three-zero-nine-two, wait where you are and I will show you to them.' Her voice sounded nasal, like she had a permanent cold, but her harsh tone seemed to make the other children do exactly what she said.

'Does she mean us?' Poppy whispered.

Andrew shrugged, unsure, and watched as the other kids began hurrying off to their stations.

'Well…good luck, I guess,' Dan said, and he climbed up one of the ladders.

Madam Bray turned to Andrew and Poppy. 'This way,' she said, and she led them up several ladders until they reached the fourth platform. 'Three-zero-nine-two, you're here.' She pointed to an empty Pod with the same numbers that were engraved onto Poppy's bangle. Poppy stared at her wrist and let out a weak sigh.

'Hurry up,' Madam Bray snapped. She lifted the cane up threateningly.

Poppy's eyes widened with fear. Andrew had never

seen her move so fast. She climbed into the Pod and the door closed automatically behind her.

'Three-zero-nine-one, you are here.' Madam Bray said, pointing to an identical Pod a few meters down from Poppy's. 'Get a move on. The Shadowmares do not like to be kept waiting.' She turned to walk away, but as she did so Andrew stood up straight, digging his heels into the ground. 'No,' he said. He clenched his fists tightly by his side.

Madam Bray spun around, eyes ablaze.

'What did you say?'

'I said NO,' Andrew repeated, a little louder than before. 'I won't get in.'

Madam Bray stood very still for a moment, her body stiff and her lips pressed tightly together.

'Is that so?' she said, looking him up and down. 'You're trouble. I've seen it before. Little boys like you who think they'll be brave. And do you know what happened to all of them?' She leaned in closer to Andrew, exuding her foul breath over him.

He shook his head.

'You have seen the skulls in the main hall? Heard about the Mountain of Doom?'

Andrew shrugged, trying not to look bothered. 'Yeah, so what?'

'Then do I really need to say more? Three-zero-nine-one, get into your Pod.'

He glared at her. 'My name's not Three-zero-nine-one, it's Andrew.' But there was no point. Madam Bray wasn't even listening. She didn't care. To her, Andrew was just another number. She stood tapping the steel caps of her shoes against the hard floor.

'So, what's it going to be?' she said.

Several kids staring at him from their Pods with a mixture of curiosity and fear. Poppy was one of them. Her face seemed to plead with Andrew just to do as he was told. Reluctantly, he climbed into the Pod and sat down.

'Good choice.' Madam Bray smiled nastily.

As soon as Andrew's feet had touched the other side, the door crashed down behind him. With a sharp click, it attached itself to the clear semicircle that Andrew was sitting in, so that it formed the shape of an egg. He felt the helmet close down over his head, and the wires quickly snaking around his body, as if they were alive, pulling tightly at his wrists and ankles so that he could barely move.

He looked outside for Madam Bray but she had disappeared. The lights in the Dark Room were fading rapidly, until it was filled with darkness again. The

Shadowmares began to float into view, an eerie glow emanating from their frail bodies. There were loads of them, and the temperature seemed to drop to almost freezing point. Every time Andrew breathed, a puff of steam left his lips. He felt like he was sitting in one of the freezer cabinets at the supermarket. He watched, amazed, as each Shadowmare positioned itself by a Pod. He recognised the Shadowmare that came and stood next to him. *Kritchen.*

His cloak of shadows shape-shifted into several dark octopus-like legs, coiling around Andrew's Pod and finding their way inside. Andrew froze, unable to believe what he was seeing. He felt a cold sharp pain shoot through his head where the metal hole was, as if the Shadowmare was searching through his brain using its shadowy tentacles.

Kritchen lifted his bony arms up to his head and closed his eyes. Andrew guessed he was attempting to read his mind to extract his fear, just like Dan had warned him he would. Well, they weren't getting his fear. *No way.*

He tried desperately to blank out every thought in his head. Kritchen stood like that for several seconds and then something totally unbelievable happened – he began to turn into a werewolf. Jagged, bloodstained fangs pierced through his gums. Red eyes flashed to yellow, and brown fur grew out from every angle until it completely masked the Shadowmare from head to toe. Only the shadowy legs remained, coming out from the werewolf's tail, and hooking into Andrew's brain. The coldness in Andrew's head was so intense he had to do everything in his power not to black out.

What was this? Dan had warned him that the Shadowmares could shape-shift but this was totally insane. It was like a real life horror movie, playing out before his very eyes.

The werewolf prowled around Andrew, floating, still connected by the shadowy legs, pushing its paws up against the sides of the Pod and howling. Slowly, it ran its claws along the glass, making thick scratch marks all the way across it. The noise was unbearable. Andrew covered his ears to mask the deafening sound, worried that the glass might smash and cave in at any moment. Then the werewolf stopped suddenly, and stood very still.

'Come on,' Andrew shouted. 'You can do better than that.' He wanted to show the Shadowmare that he wasn't afraid.

It smiled thinly at him. Moments later, Andrew watched dumbfounded as the brown fur slowly turned into thick black hair and eight spindly legs appeared from beneath it, each one at least a metre long.

'*A spider!*' Andrew whispered.

It continued to grow steadily, until it was almost ten times the size of him. This time the shadowy tentacles were connected to the tarantula's legs. Andrew stared up at the creature's many eyes, black and shiny like marbles. He could see his face reflected in every one.

There was a shuffling sound. Smaller spiders began creeping out of the crevices in the ceiling and walls. Some were just tiny house spiders, others giant tarantulas. Andrew couldn't believe it; had the Shadowmare summoned them here somehow? They flurried in like waves, turning the floor into a sea of spiders.

A few began crawling up into Andrew's Pod, filtering through the holes in the glass. He slapped at his legs, but then stopped, realising that it was pointless. More and more were scrambling onto him until his entire body was just a mass of black hairy legs. No amount of scratching in the world could have relieved the horrible itch that spread up his body like fire. But Andrew was calm.

He grinned. 'Ha! Still not scared. I think tarantulas are cool.'

The giant spider stood still and looked at him through its multiple glassy eyes. Within seconds, the smaller spiders scurried away. Then the giant spider began shrinking in size, its black hairs slowly dissolving into pale skin, until the Shadowmare was back to its normal appearance – not that there was anything 'normal' about it.

Andrew felt another sharp pain in his head as the shadowy legs detached themselves and coiled back inside Kritchen's cloak. Andrew sighed with relief, as the cold melted away from his brain.

Kritchen looked at him with fiery eyes, his yellow teeth grinding together with pure loathing. For a second, Andrew thought that the Shadowmare was going to try again, but then he felt the wires loosen their grip on him and the lights in the Dark Room flashed back to life. When his eyes had finally adjusted to the brightness, he saw that all of the Shadowmares had disappeared, including Kritchen. He wiggled his arms free and rolled the stiffness out of his neck. He caught sight of the large cylinder in the middle of the room, now full to the brim with thick black smoke. *What is that stuff?* Andrew wondered. *Was it fear?* He didn't have time to think about it for long. He could hear Madam Bray's screechy voice echoing out into the factory again.

'Out of your Pods immeeeeediately.'

The top half of the Pod sprung open and Andrew climbed out, searching the platform for Poppy. Seconds later he spotted her stumbling towards him. She looked flushed and sweaty.

'Andrew,' she said, grabbing his shoulders. She could barely stand up, shaking all over and teeth chattering like a windup toy.

Andrew realised they didn't have much time. He may have survived the Fear Pods this once, but if they didn't find a way out of here soon, his sister was going to break.

Madame Bray led them along another dark and dingy corridor, full of numbered metal doors, like the ones they had passed on their way to the hall. They finally stopped at a door marked 3091. Madame Bray punched a code into the key pad on the wall, and the door slid slowly open.

Inside was a bare cell with nothing more than a bunk bed with moth-eaten blankets, a dirty looking toilet and a washbasin with two unwashed glasses on it. There was a ventilator set into the wall, and a window, which had been blocked up with planks of wood.

'This is where you shall stay. The Shadowmares will come and check on you in precisely six hours. Get some sleep.' The door closed. Andrew heard the mechanisms fall into place as she locked it behind them.

Poppy slumped on the bed. Her face was still drained of colour.

'Sleep! That's the last thing I feel like doing. That was awful. I-I can't go through with it again.'

'I know,' Andrew said, giving her a hug. 'You won't have to. We're going to find a way out of here... somehow.'

She gave him a strange look. 'You seem fine. Didn't it scare you?'

He hesitated. He hadn't really thought about it. Why hadn't it scared him? Every other kid had looked terrified.

'Not really,' he admitted. 'It was a bit strange, I guess, sort of like watching a horror movie in 4D.' He laughed, and then stopped when he realised Poppy was still shaking.

'I'll get you some water,' he said.

He walked over to the sink and swilled out a glass. The taps were stiff but he managed to get a few drops out of them. He handed her the glass, but she pushed it away.

'I can't believe you only thought it was strange,' she said. 'I was terrified. There were snakes and maggots everywhere.' She tucked her hair behind her ears and leaned forwards. 'So, what did you see in there?'

Andrew hesitated for a second and then shrugged. 'Spiders, werewolves. That kind of thing.' It wasn't exactly a lie; he really had seen all those things in the Dark Room. But somehow, he had managed to block out his greatest fear of all from the Shadowmares. The one fear that made him freeze with terror every time he thought about it…

Fire…

'No,' he told himself, pushing the thought from his mind. If he allowed himself to dwell on his fear, even for one second, it would consume him. Right now, *especially now*, he needed to keep a clear head.

Poppy looked at him oddly. 'Werewolves? Spiders?' she said. 'Strange, I never would have guessed. I mean, the amount of scary movies you watch… I understand though. I don't like spiders much either. You shouldn't trust anything that has eight legs.'

Andrew laughed. A scratching noise started up from close by. He stopped grinning and sat up straight. It was quiet at first, but it was getting louder. They both froze.

'What is that?' Poppy whispered.

Andrew got up. 'It sounds like it's coming from the walls.' Was it a rat? Or something bigger? The sound grew louder. *Closer.*

Thump…thump…thump! That was no rat. Andrew put his ear to the wall and followed the noise. 'It's as if someone's moving around in there,' he said.

Then, from out of nowhere, the ventilator came crashing off the wall onto the floor. Poppy screamed, diving under the blanket, as a deathly grey figure came tumbling out.

8

Despite the fact that his hair was grey with old cobwebs and his pyjama top had accumulated a thick layer of dust, it was obvious who it was: *Dan.* Andrew laughed, hope rising in his stomach. If Dan had found a route around the Factory, then perhaps there was a way out of here after all.

'Bloody hell, it's cramped in there,' Dan said, brushing some of the dust off his pyjama bottoms and stretching out his arms and legs.

Poppy poked her head out from under the blanket.

'You!' she yelled, wagging a finger at him. 'You scared the living daylights out of me.'

Dan grinned. 'Sorry. It's the only way that doesn't set off any alarms.'

'You crawled all the way here through the ventilator?' Andrew said, impressed.

Dad nodded proudly then jumped up, perching himself on the sink.

'Genius,' Andrew breathed. 'Where else does it lead?'

'Everywhere.' Then he hesitated. 'Well, everywhere except out of here. So how did you both find the Dark Room? Horrible, right?'

Poppy groaned. 'There was this massive python. I thought it was going to strangle me to death. I can't do it again.'

'Yeah, I know what you mean. All the more reason to try and escape though, right? Shall we go now?' he said, jumping down. 'We have a few more hours before the Shadowmares come and check on us.'

Andrew and Poppy stared at him.

'Go where?' Andrew said. 'You mean escape? What, now?… This very second? What's the plan?'

'Of course not *now*, numbnuts, but there's something I gotta show you both.'

'But you do have a plan don't you?' Poppy said hopefully.

Dan hesitated. 'I'm working on that, but I need to show you something first. Follow me along the air vent.'

Poppy was gazing nervously at the small space in the wall. 'You want us to go through there? Won't we get caught?'

He waved a hand at her. 'Trust me, I do this all the time. The Shadowmares don't seem to know a thing about it. You have to be quiet though, and if I give you the signal you have to stop until it's safe, got it?'

Andrew nodded. 'Sure. What's the signal?'

Dan paused. 'I don't know, I've never had to use it before. It's only been me.' He thought for a second. 'I know, I'll put my hand up straight, like this. When I give you the thumbs up it means we can start moving again. So, what do you say?'

Andrew glanced at Poppy. 'OK.' She nodded, although her frown suggested that she wasn't sure.

'Lead the way,' Andrew said.

Dan was the first to enter. Poppy crept in after him, and then Andrew followed straight behind her. Even though he was skinny, it was still a tight squeeze. He pulled the grill back over the hole, so that if the Shadowmares did happen to come in, they wouldn't discover straightaway how they had escaped. They crawled on their hands and knees along the metal tube for what seemed like forever, twisting and turning around corners as if it was a maze.

'Where does this even lead?' Poppy asked. 'I'm getting claustrophobic.'

Finally, Dan stopped at a grill. 'Take a look,' he

whispered, moving aside so that they could see through the bars.

Andrew crawled closer. Beyond was a room full of large metal pipes. There was a basin in the middle with a dozen golden taps attached to it and a shelf full of metal goblets.

'Where are we?' he asked.

'The Fearbulator, man.'

'And that would be what exactly?'

Dan rolled his eyes, as if this was the silliest question he'd ever heard. 'It's like an incubator for fear, isn't it? It stores it up until it's ready to be made into nightmares. See all those pipes? They're all attached to the main fear cylinder in the Dark Room.'

'Well, what are we doing here, then?' Poppy said, sounding nervous. 'And how do you know all of this?'

Dan put a finger to his lips. 'Shhh. Just wait.'

A second later, the door burst open and Shadowmare after Shadowmare floated through it. Andrew put a hand to his mouth, and held his breath. Each creature took a goblet from the shelf and crowded around the basin below. Vesuvius was there too, watching over them.

'Good,' he said in a rasping voice. 'You may begin.'

One by one, the Shadowmares turned on the taps.

A black smoky substance flowed out from them, filling the basin with a dark mist. It was the same strange smoke Andrew had seen in the cylinder after their Dark Room session.

The Shadowmares began sniggering hungrily and glowing purple, like they had in the Dark Room, but this time much brighter. They scooped their goblets into the mist, knocking them back. With every cupful, their skeletal bodies took on a more vibrant glow until they were so dazzling Andrew had to shield his eyes.

'What are they doing?' he whispered.

'They're drinking the fear,' Dan muttered. 'It's how they make the nightmares.'

Andrew watched, amazed, as the glowing figures, usually so dark and cast in shadows, began disappearing into thin air, until the entire room was empty again, except for Vesuvius. He slammed his skull cane onto the stone floor. A flash of orange light shot out from the skull's eyes, and then he vanished as well.

'Where'd they go?' Andrew said, not taking his eyes off the room, just in case they reappeared again.

Dan shrugged. 'Dunno. The same thing happens every evening. I reckon they disappear and enter people's dreams, spreading the fear. And every now and again they steal the odd child and bring them back here. That's the only thing I can think of anyway.' He put his hands over the grill, giving it a small nudge. Already unscrewed, it fell to the floor with a crash. 'Come on,' he said, lowering himself into the room below.

Poppy frowned. 'Are you bonkers? What if they come back?'

'They'll probably be gone for at least a few hours. We'll be fine. Come on.'

'Probably?' She raised an eyebrow. 'Not definitely?'

'We need to find a way out of here,' Andrew said, climbing down. 'We should do as Dan says.' It was quite a height, and he felt a sharp pain shoot through his knees when his feet hit the floor. Poppy grunted from above.

'Fine, help me down.'

Andrew took her hand. He shivered. It was even colder in here than the rest of the factory.

'Follow me,' Dan said.

They followed him through the room. It looked creepy, full of pipes and machinery and plumes of black smoke. The metal pipes were shining ominously in the dark, creaking and groaning like a hungry stomach. Curiously, he reached out to touch one of the metal taps, but as his skin fused with the metal, a terrible burning sensation ripped through his hand.

'Ow!' he yelled, pulling it back.

'Sorry,' Dan said, biting his lip. 'I forgot to tell you about that. I think they're protected somehow.'

'Well thanks for the warning,' Andrew muttered, sucking on his fingers.

They came to a pile of broken pipes at the end of the room. Dan moved it out of the way, revealing a large rusty chest underneath. They helped him pull it out, groaning at the weight of it. Inside were a torch, screwdriver, pocketknife, the brown sauce and a few other items of food. There was also a piece of paper covered in line tallies. Dan took out a stub of pencil and added an extra line.

'Don't mind me. I do this to keep track of how long I've been here.'

'What is all this stuff?' Andrew asked. 'And where did you get it?'

'It's supplies for when I escape,' Dan said. 'I've collected it all from Vesuvius's headquarters, taking things bit by bit, so that he won't notice anything going missing.' He grinned. 'Cool ain't it?'

Poppy folded her arms. 'Are you crazy? You could have got yourself killed.'

'I know,' Dan said, as if this was all part of the fun. 'But I might as well take a few risks. I'm going to be killed anyway.'

'But where does Vesuvius get it all from?' Andrew asked.

Dan leaned forwards, green eyes twinkling in the dark. 'That's what I wanted to talk to you about. There's a special door in the Nightmare Factory. I've seen Vesuvius and the other Shadowmares using it before.'

'Where do you think it leads?' Andrew asked, hardly daring to breathe.

Dan smiled. 'I don't think, man…I know,' he said, eyes brightening. 'It leads *outside*.'

9

Andrew and Poppy looked at each other and grinned.

'Outside?' Poppy said. 'What makes you think that?'

'Yeah,' said Andrew. 'What's out there?'

'I have no idea what's out there, but it's not of this world. Sometimes when the Shadowmares come back, they have snow on their cloaks. Not like the stuff we get at home. It's pale pink.'

'Pink snow?' Poppy gasped. 'How do you know that it's snow then?'

'Because it's cold and it melts the same. What else could it be?'

'My God,' Andrew said. It had never occurred to him that they might be somewhere other than Earth. He had no idea how they were going to get home, but right now, all he cared about was finding a way out of the Nightmare Factory.

He jumped up. 'Then what are we waiting for? Let's get out of here!' He sat back down, scratching his head. 'Hang on. How come you've never escaped before?'

'That's the problem. None of the ventilation shafts seems to lead to the door. It's forever locked and I have no idea where they keep the key. I've searched everywhere, but I just can't find it.'

Andrew felt his heart drop. 'Oh,' he said.

'Yeah, I know, *major* bummer right. Listen, I only have a week left. Will you help me look for it?'

Andrew and Poppy nodded in unison.

'Of course we will,' Andrew said. 'Do you have anything else which might help?' He peered into the chest again, and noticed a half-eaten packet of crackers. 'Can I have one of those?'

'Knock yourself out,' Dan said.

Andrew took a handful of crackers and shoved them into his mouth. They were a bit stale, but he didn't care; he was starving, and anything was better than the horrible food they had been given at breakfast. He handed the packet to Poppy and Dan.

'No thanks,' Poppy said, pulling out a large piece of paper, covered in markings from the chest. 'What's this?' she asked, tracing it with her finger.

'I've been trying to map out the ventilation system,' Dan explained. 'I figured there must be a way out of here somehow.' He picked up a cracker and bit into it.

'Dan, when we arrived here, you mentioned the Releaser. What is that?' Andrew asked.

Dan stopped munching and looked up, suddenly interested.

'A Releaser is someone whose fear is so powerful that it can create a whole new breed of nightmare. A nightmare that comes alive.'

Panic filled Andrew's stomach.

'What do you mean, a nightmare that comes alive?'

Dan tipped the remaining crumbs into his mouth and then hid the empty packet in the trunk.

'I've been travelling through the ventilation shaft for almost a year now and I've overheard a lot of conversations. At first, I didn't know what they were talking about. The Master seemed so obsessed with finding him, that I couldn't understand what could be so important about it. Then I discovered why.' He leaned forwards, shaking his head. 'Honestly, this is going to blow your minds.'

There was a sudden groaning sound from behind them, making Andrew jump. He spun around, trying to pinpoint the source.

'What was that?' Poppy hissed. 'Do you think it's the Shadowmares coming back?'

Dan shook his head. 'Nah, it's probably just the pipes. They always make that noise.'

Andrew nodded, relaxing a little. 'So what did you discover?' He didn't think he could wait any longer to find out.

'Vesuvius and the Shadowmares can only enter people's dreams,' Dan said. 'But a Releaser's fear gives them the ability to go beyond. To our world. Not only that, but it also has the power to create the ultimate nightmare. A nightmare that's real. That comes alive. Can you imagine? If that happened, it'd be like hell on Earth.' He gulped. 'And I mean literally.'

Andrew just sat there, too shocked to say anything, but Poppy nodded. 'An abundance of fear at their fingertips,' she said shivering. 'Vesuvius would be like a kid in a sweet shop.'

'Man, you're telling me,' Dan said. 'A Releaser has one great fear, and it's the most powerful thing in existence. And that's not all. I heard them talking about the last time they found a Releaser, back in the eighteen hundreds. It was a girl. Once they'd extracted her fear there were three thousand deaths in England alone. Vampire bites, people becoming possessed, ghostly sightings all over the world of demons and beasts with two heads. Don't you see? Vesuvius feeds off that kind of destruction. The Shadowmares gain power through other people's fear.'

What if I'm the new Releaser? Andrew wondered, swallowing hard, throat dry. All of the strange things that had been happening recently, his unexplainable strength at the market, the nightmares, Oran and Tiffany giving him the dreamcatchers. The way he was afraid of nothing but fire… It all seemed to make sense now.

'But how come we've never heard about any of this?' Poppy said. 'I think if dangerous beasts had been roaming the Earth, we would have heard about it.'

'You have!' Dan said, sounding exasperated. 'It's just been changed so many times that all the truth's been taken out of it. Like Chinese whispers. Now all that's left is ghost stories and legends. Don't tell me you've never heard of Dracula?'

Poppy laughed nervously. 'Dracula's definitely not real.'

'Really?' Dan said. 'I wouldn't be so sure.'

With a slight moan Andrew sank down on the old chest, letting his weight go before him, so that it squeaked in protest.

'Cheer up,' Dan said. 'It hasn't happened yet. They've been searching for years to find a new Releaser. Chances are they'll be searching for many more.'

Andrew glanced guiltily at Poppy. He wanted to tell Dan what they had overheard that morning, about him being the one, but Dan was their only way out of here and he didn't want to freak him out. Plus he didn't know for certain... There was still time to find out for sure.

'What happened to all the creatures from the nightmares? Where did they all go?' Poppy asked.

Dan put his chin in his hands thoughtfully. 'I suppose when the old Releaser either died or got too old, the fear ran out and they couldn't remain on Earth any longer. Now they just roam the Mountain of Doom, waiting for the next Releaser to send them back again. And that's where I'm heading for in a week's time. We have to escape by then else I'm dead meat.'

Andrew stared blankly at Dan. He couldn't – didn't – want to believe any part of what he was hearing. It was completely insane, but even so, Andrew could feel his heart beating faster, and a sickly feeling rising up in his stomach. Was it really possible that he could be the next Releaser? If so, then a week was too far away. They had to get out of here *now*. After all, if Dan was right, then it wasn't just their lives that were in danger any more, but the entire world...

10

Another noise shook the building, making the contents of the chest dance. It wasn't a grumbling sound this time, but much louder, like thunder.

Dan jumped up and pushed the chest back into the pile of broken piping.

'Come on, move it. I think the Shadowmares are coming back.'

They hauled themselves into the air vent, just as the bright purple glow filled the room again.

'Phew, that was close,' Andrew said, watching the Shadowmares below, as they appeared out of thin air. He crawled on his hands and knees along the stuffy ventilator, mind racing with everything that Dan had just told them.

'Stop kicking up so much dust,' Poppy hissed. 'I can barely breathe.'

Dan turned round awkwardly. 'Shh! Be quiet, will you? We're right above Vesuvius's headquarters…'

'What?' Poppy whispered, sounding scared.

Andrew tried to be as light-footed as he could,

but it was hard crawling on the thin metal, and with the three of them moving all at once, it sounded like someone repeatedly drumming on a cymbal. Andrew tensed. *A voice*, coming from below. Dan didn't even need to give them the signal. They all froze as soon as they heard it.

'Kritchen, get in here!' It was low and powerful, drenched in anger.

Andrew shuffled forwards. He could see Vesuvius through the ventilator grill, dressed in his black cloak and top hat, his white hair cascading over his shoulders. Kritchen hurried into the room, floating inches above the ground.

'Master? What can I do for you?'

'The boy. The one we stole last night. I want to know what happened in the Dark Room.'

Kritchen hunched his shoulders, cowering. 'He didn't produce any fear master,' he said weakly.

'What do you mean, *he didn't produce any fear*?'

'He's different from all the rest. He was too powerful for the Fear Pods. I couldn't read his mind as easily as the others.' He lowered his voice. 'It is as we suspected, sire. I believe he is…the next Releaser.'

Andrew felt his chest tighten and he suddenly felt very faint. *So it was true.* He could sense Dan staring

89

at him but he didn't dare meet his eyes.

Vesuvius let out a nasty cackle. 'Are you certain?'

Kritchen nodded. 'Yes, Master.'

'Good,' Vesuvius said, stroking his chin. 'At last. You have three days to find me his fear.'

'But Master, three days, that's almost impossible. His mind is strong. It may take longer —'

'Three days!' Vesuvius bellowed. 'Kritchen, you are my most trusted servant but…if you fail me you shall pay the consequences. If he is too powerful, then weaken the boy. Do whatever it takes, but bring me his fear. Do you understand?'

There was a short pause.

'Yes, Master.'

Kritchen mopped the beads of sweat from his milky forehead and floated out of the room without another word. Vesuvius got up, stopped to brush a speck of dirt off his shoulder, and then left as well. Andrew realised he had been holding his breath the entire time. He let it all out in one almighty burst.

Poppy and Dan were both looking at him with panic in their eyes, but they didn't say a word. Andrew was in a state of shock. He couldn't believe it. He felt sick. He even felt a little afraid. They continued crawling through the shaft in silence. It was only when they reached their cell that anyone spoke.

'This is bad. This is really, really bad,' Dan said, walking up and down the room.

'I thought you said you were just afraid of spiders and werewolves,' Poppy said. 'I knew that didn't make any sense, not with all the horror movies you watch.'

'No, you asked me what I saw in there, and I told you. But I'm not afraid of them. I'm not afraid of anything.'

'That's not true,' Dan said, shaking his head. 'Everyone's afraid of something. And a Releaser's fear is more powerful than any other.'

Andrew swallowed, his throat dry and tight as if it was closing up. His mind flashed back to the night his father had died. He didn't remember much; he had blanked most of it out, but he knew that every time he smelt smoke his heart flooded with fear. How could he admit to them that he was so afraid? He was supposed to be the tough guy. The one that looked after everybody else… He wasn't allowed to be afraid of anything.

'Andrew, stop worrying about what we'll think of you and tell us what it is,' Poppy snapped, as if reading his mind.

He looked up. 'I can't,' he said, slumping against the wall. 'I just…can't.'

Poppy came and perched opposite him. 'Andrew, we won't think any less of you. I promise. Everyone has fears. It's completely normal.'

'Yeah,' Dan said. 'I'm afraid of clowns for God's sake. You think that's not embarrassing?'

Andrew grinned.

'OK,' he said. 'I'll tell you. But it's not easy.' He took a deep breath. He hadn't spoken about this to anyone. 'I'm afraid of fire.'

Poppy put her hand to her mouth. 'Of course,' she said, gently. 'I should have known.'

'Fire's not bad at all,' Dan said. 'I was expecting it to be something girly like worms or something.'

Andrew let out a sigh of relief. It felt strangely comforting to talk about his fear. He'd kept it inside for so long, like a horrible parasite gnawing away at him. 'We were only little at the time. We still don't know what caused the fire, but it ripped through the house while we were sleeping. Poppy got out with our mum, but I was trapped in my bedroom and got some nasty burns.' He lifted up his T-shirt and showed Dan the scars on his back. 'But my dad…' he said, trying hard not to cry. 'He didn't get out at all.'

'Oh,' Dan said, taken aback. 'I'm sorry.' And for the first time all day, he fell completely silent.

Andrew paused. 'It's OK. What does this mean for us now then?'

'It means we can't let Vesuvius discover your fear. It's going to be tough though, they're going to be keeping a closer eye on you now than ever, and trying even harder to find your fear. Which means we don't have long to get out of here. We need a plan.'

'But we don't have a plan,' Poppy said, her face a picture of worry.

'Well *durr*!' Dan said. 'That's why we're going to have to come up with one pretty damn fast.' He glanced at the door. 'Look, the Shadowmares will be doing their nightly checks any second now. I'd better get back to my cell, but take this.' He reached into his underpants and pulled out the map of the ventilation system. 'Here,' he said, passing it to Poppy. She looked at it in disgust.

'Come to the Fearbulator tomorrow, straight after lunch,' Dan said. 'That way we'll have a few hours of undisturbed peace to plan our escape.' He climbed into the ventilator opening. 'And make sure you bring some ideas…' His voice faded as he disappeared down the shaft.

As soon as he'd gone, Poppy turned to Andrew.

'I'm really scared now. What if we don't manage to get out in time? What if they find your fear?'

Andrew was just about to reply when he heard the lock on the door turn from the other side. His eyes darted to the ventilator grill still lying on the floor and his heart skipped a beat. They couldn't let the Shadowmares discover their exit.

Luckily, Poppy saw it too and dived for the grill, trying to slot it back onto the wall. Andrew raced over to help her, praying that the door would stay shut. It rattled against its metal frame, threatening to crash open at any moment. Andrew felt sick with panic. If Vesuvius found out how they'd been using the ventilator to move around the factory, he'd block it up. There'd be no way out after that, and Dan would be killed.

'It won't go on. I think it's broken,' Poppy said, as the grill fell off the wall again. 'What are we going to do?'

Please, Andrew thought, willing the grill to slot back into place. *Just go back on!* He had barely finished thinking these words when the ventilator grill sprang up from the floor and floated in mid-air. Andrew and Poppy stared at each other, too shocked to move.

The grill fitted itself perfectly onto the wall, as if an invisible hand had put it there.

The door rattled violently again.

'Quickly,' Andrew said, snapping back to life. 'Get into bed.'

Poppy jumped into the lower bunk, pulling the blanket all the way up to her neck, while Andrew raced up the ladder to the top bed. He shut his eyes.

The door burst open. The Shadowmares exploded into the room. Andrew felt the temperature drop to below freezing point.

'What happened, Kritchen? Why couldn't we get in?' one of them asked in a dry voice.

'I'm not sure. I think the door was jammed,' Kritchen replied.

'Hmm,' the other one growled. 'We had better wait here and keep an eye on them. Make sure everything is how it should be.'

Andrew felt the Shadowmare's icy breath on his skin for what seemed like forever. He counted the seconds in his head, concentrating hard, so that he didn't pass out from the cold. He couldn't stop thinking about the ventilator grill, and how it had moved on its own. It wasn't his imagination. Poppy had seen it too. And then there was the door... Why hadn't it opened? It was as if some unknown force was trying to protect them.

But who? Oran…?

He felt the temperature rise as the Shadowmares left, and the door clicked into place.

He sighed with relief.

'Poppy,' he said. 'Are you awake?'

He was desperate to talk to her about what had just happened. He listened for a reply, but all he got was silence. He hurried down the ladder.

'Poppy!' he said again, but she was fast asleep. He guessed the cold must have knocked her out.

He climbed back into bed and tried to relax, but he couldn't stop tossing and turning. Two days ago he'd been blissfully unaware that the Nightmare Factory even existed. Now, he had discovered he was the new Releaser – that he might become responsible for the destruction of Earth, where ghosts, vampires and two headed beasts would walk the planet, and where demons from your worst nightmares would become real. But Andrew knew one thing for certain – he couldn't let the Shadowmares find his fear…

He drifted off to sleep, into a dream. He was in his bedroom, surrounded by fire, but it wasn't the bedroom that he had now. It was different, much bigger. In fact, everything was much bigger. As he stared down at his tiny arms and legs, he realised that he was a toddler again. Overhead, the fire alarm was blaring. He could hardly see anything through all the smoke and flames. His head was pounding with the heat, his body dripping with sweat. There was no way out of the bedroom; he was too small to reach the door handle. He just sat in the middle of the bed, crying, feeling the tears burning his face.

Suddenly, everything went dark. When the light returned, Andrew was in an empty white room. There was no more fire. No more smoke. A figure was standing before him.

Andrew sighed with relief. '*Oran…?*'

The man from the market was wearing the same green suit and purple hat with yellow stars that he'd had on before. He was carrying a pearly white walking stick, which had a spiral effect running up it. It seemed to be glowing.

'Andrew,' he said. 'Heed my warning. You must escape from the Nightmare Factory. You are in great danger. You do not have much time.'

Andrew gazed into the man's pale blue eyes. 'But

how?' he heard himself ask. 'I'm trapped here. There's no way out.'

'I can guide you, but I do not have the power to enter the Nightmare Factory. You need to get out on your own. Vesuvius carries a key around his neck. Retrieve this key and come to the final door of the passageway. From there I will show you the way.' He pointed his stick towards one of the white walls and the image of a door appeared. It was made from thick metal, like all the doors in the factory, but this one had a huge padlock chained to it. Andrew felt a rush of excitement. Was this the door that Dan had told them about?

'The key,' Oran repeated. 'Retrieve the key from around his neck.'

'From Vesuvius's neck?' Andrew said. 'How am I supposed to do that? He'll catch me!'

'You must get out,' Oran said.

'I know that, but there must be another way!'

'You must get out,' Oran repeated.

Oran was beginning to break up, as if he were a bad transmission on a television.

'Wait,' Andrew said. 'You haven't told me how I'm going to get the key.'

But Oran's image continued to fade, until it was no

98

more than a hazy blur, still repeating the same words. 'You must get out…' Then it vanished.

Andrew woke with a start. The room was freezing cold, but he was sweating. Sticky tears stung his cheeks like acid. He laid there for what felt like hours, thinking about his father, the fire…Oran. He knew he couldn't ignore the old man's warnings for a second time. The whole reason he'd ended up here was because he hadn't taken the man's advice seriously. This time, he had to do as he was told. He had to steal the key and escape. No matter how dangerous it was, he was determined to do it.

11

Andrew was still awake when he heard the latch on the door slide open. Kritchen entered, studying him and his sister with glowing red eyes.

'Follow me,' he said with a snarl.

They were escorted down the dark passageway, the artificial lights above their heads waning and flickering as they passed.

'Andrew,' Poppy whispered, pulling him closer. 'What the hell happened last night? It wasn't just my imagination was it? That grill moved on its own.'

Andrew nodded. 'Yeah, but I have no idea how. I think it might have been Oran. I dreamt about him last night…' His voice trailed off as they reached the hall. 'I'll tell you about it later.'

Kritchen stopped and typed a number into the keypad on the wall. The small red light above the door blinked out, disabling the alarms, and the door slid open.

Most of the children were already sitting at a table eating, including Dan, who looked up and waved when he saw them. Poppy and Andrew quickly collected their food from Madam Bray. She watched them with beady eyes as she slapped a dollop of brown mush onto their trays, but Andrew did his best to ignore her. They went and pulled up two chairs opposite Dan.

'Tell me about the dream you had,' Poppy said, as soon as she'd sat down.

Andrew flashed her a razor-sharp glare.

'Not now,' he told her. 'It's not safe.'

Just as these words had left his mouth, the door to the Nightmare Factory burst open and a rush of cold air hit them like an ice storm. Vesuvius entered with a pair of Shadowmares by his side. One of them was Kritchen. A shocked murmur passed through the room. Vesuvius was holding his black stick with its skull head on top. He strode past them to the far end of the hall, his dark cloak billowing behind him, and sat down on a throne that had been positioned by the wall of skulls. Andrew had never seen it there before. It was huge, and made from dark wood, with intricate carvings of snakes twisting around the arms. Vesuvius's lips curled inwards into a menacing smirk.

'What's he doing here?' Andrew whispered.

Nobody answered. An eerie silence had descended over them.

There was something hanging on a thick metal chain around Vesuvius's neck, but Andrew couldn't make out what it was. He leaned forwards, hoping to see better. It looked like a small gold triangle. Perhaps that was the reason Dan had never managed to find the key. *Perhaps the key didn't look like a key at all.*

Vesuvius snarled, and Andrew quickly turned away. He didn't want him getting suspicious.

He watched from the corner of his eye as Madam Bray hurried over to Vesuvius carrying a large tray of food. He couldn't see what was on it, but he would have bet his life that it wasn't the brown mush that they had all been given. Madam Bray watched anxiously as Vesuvius took his first bite. He didn't say a word, but instead shooed her away with a flick of his wrist. A gentle hum of conversation returned to the room.

Andrew chewed a fingernail, puzzled. 'That's odd. Does he often come and eat here?'

'Nope,' Dan whispered. 'It's well weird. He's never done this before.'

'Maybe he got lonely,' Poppy suggested.

'Yeah right,' Dan said. He picked up his spoon and began eating. 'Nah, he's come to keep an eye on

Andrew. I told you he'd do that, didn't I?'

'Perhaps they're going to take us to the Dark Room again,' Andrew said, turning to Dan with a frown.

Dan looked thoughtful. 'Nope. Not possible. They did that yesterday. It's every other day, remember?'

Poppy breathed a sigh of relief. 'Well that's something to be thankful for.'

She stopped talking as Kritchen swept past them, making all three of them shiver uncontrollably. Andrew lifted his eyes up from the table. He watched in silence as the Shadowmare floated over to Vesuvius and whispered something in his ear. Vesuvius nodded and ordered Madam Bray to his side.

'What do you think they're saying? Do you think Kritchen overheard us talking? Do you think he knows about my fear?'

'No idea.' Dan frowned.

Madam Bray marched towards their table and Andrew felt his chest tighten with panic. His breath quickened as he wondered what she was about to do.

'Give me your tray,' she hissed, spraying saliva onto Andrew's face.

'What?'

'I said give me your tray,' she repeated. 'Are you deaf?'

Andrew glared at her, and wiped the spit off his forehead. 'No. I just choose to ignore evil witches like you,' he mumbled under his breath.

Her eyes sharpened. 'What?'

'Nothing.' He smiled. 'I said I sometimes struggle to hear certain pitches.'

She tilted her head back contemptuously. 'Watch it,' she spat. 'You wouldn't want to end up in the Mountain of Doom.'

She strode up the hall where she emptied the contents of his tray into the bin, her cruel eyes fixed on his. Andrew turned away, putting his hand to his grumbling stomach as the other children in the hall began hurrying their food down as fast as they could.

'They're trying to make you weak,' said Dan, darkly. 'So it's easier to read your mind.' Andrew hadn't thought of this, but remembering the conversation they'd overheard yesterday, he realised that it made perfect sense. Andrew had barely eaten anything since they had arrived at the Nightmare Factory and now he was really feeling it.

'Here, have some of mine,' Dan said, nudging the tray closer to Andrew.

Andrew reached for the spoon but before he could bring it to his lips, it flew out of his hand and across the room. Vesuvius had his cruel black eyes fixed on Andrew.

He did that, thought Andrew. *But how?*

'You can't beat me, Andrew,' Vesuvius hissed. He turned to Madam Bray. 'Deal with him.'

Madam Bray marched back over to their table and slammed the cane down hard. They all jumped backwards. She picked up Dan's tray and cleared her throat, coughing up a huge ball of phlegm into the middle of it.

'Eat it,' she said, placing the tray back down in front of Andrew.

He eyeballed the glob of green slime, feeling as if he was about to throw up. All of the kids in the hall were staring at him, wondering if he was going to do it or not. He shook his head and turned away.

'I can't.'

Madam Bray's eyes narrowed. 'Then I suggest you do not try that again.' She turned to Dan. 'The same goes for you. Give him your food, and your skull will become a permanent decoration in our wall.'

Dan peered over at the wall of skulls and gulped nervously.

The hall fell silent as the other children finished their food. Andrew could feel the Master's dark eyes burning deep into him, like two bottomless pits. He saw a disturbing sneer flash across his face, and Andrew shuddered. *What was he planning?* When everyone had finished, Kritchen lead them back to their cells.

As soon as the door had closed, he grabbed Andrew by the arms and opened his mouth, exhaling a long breath of cold air over him. Andrew felt his body freeze. His head pounded like he'd bitten into an ice cube. His legs crumbled, and he collapsed to the floor, shivering uncontrollably.

Kritchen sneered nastily, and floated out of the room again, the sound of the door locking behind him.

'Are you OK?' Poppy said, rushing over to him. Tears were streaming down her face.

'They're trying to weaken me,' Andrew said, putting a hand to his spinning head. 'And it's working.'

'No,' Poppy said, helping him up. 'You have to stay strong.' She rubbed the tears from her eyes. 'We both do. We've got to escape, remember?'

'About that,' Andrew said. 'The dream I had last night...'

Poppy put a finger to his mouth. 'Not now. We have to go and meet Dan. You can tell us all about it in the Fearbulator.'

Andrew nodded. He pulled the grill away slowly from the wall, expecting it to jump out of his hands. But nothing happened. They crawled into the ventilator and travelled along the metal shaft. When they reached the grill leading to the Fearbulator, Andrew and Poppy carefully lowered themselves down. Dan was already waiting for them on the chest when they arrived. He gave Andrew an appraising glance.

'It's weird. I always expected the Releaser to be tough looking with loads of muscles and, well, don't take this the wrong way mate, but you're just so...so ordinary.'

Andrew scoffed. 'Well thanks very much.' It was true though. He was just a normal kid. There was nothing special about him.

'So, you guys got any ideas of how we're going to find the key?'

'I know where it is,' Andrew said.

Poppy and Dan looked at him with stunned faces.

'You do?' Dan said.

Poppy crossed her arms. 'You never said anything to me.'

'I was trying to tell you earlier. I saw it all in my dream.'

'What…like a premonition?' Dan said sceptically.

'Sort of. I'm not sure. It was weird. Oran, the guy that came to see us at the market, he visited me in my dream.'

'And what happened?' Poppy asked, leaning forward on the trunk.

Andrew sat down next to her, and told them all about the dream. When he had finished, Dan jumped up.

'Of course!' he said, clicking his fingers excitedly. 'No wonder I could never find the key. This is brilliant.' All the hope drained from his face and he sat back down. 'Wait. Around his neck? That doesn't make it very easy for us, does it?'

'No, but did you expect it to be?'

Dan sighed. 'I guess not. So this man… Oran was it? He's the same guy that gave you the dreamcatchers?'

Andrew nodded.

'But who is he?'

Andrew shrugged. 'No idea. All I know is that he's trying to help us. He tried to help us at the market. Now, somehow, he's contacted me through my dreams and he's trying to help us again. He told me where the key would be. He said he'd meet us outside the door and take us home.'

Dan smiled. His eyes glazed over. 'Home. That would be amazing.'

'But why can't he just come and open the door himself?' Poppy asked, with a puzzled expression.

Andrew shrugged. 'He said he couldn't.'

'That makes sense,' Dan said. 'It must be magically protected so that only certain people can open it. Like the fear taps.'

'Then how are we supposed to open it?' Poppy asked.

Dan rolled his eyes. 'We'll have the key then won't we, numbnuts? Honestly, am I the only one with a brain around here?' He spread the ventilation map across the floor. 'Right, so what's the plan then, Batman?'

'That's the thing,' Andrew said, biting his bottom lip. 'I don't actually have one. Oran told me what to do in the dream, not how to do it.'

'Brilliant,' Poppy said. 'So what do you propose we do, just go and steal the key from Vesuvius while he's sleeping? We'll all be killed.'

'Actually,' Andrew said, allowing a smile to creep over his lips. 'That's not such a bad idea.'

12

'You can't be serious? I thought *I* was daft for stealing stuff from Vesuvius, but you're one brain cell short of crazy.'

Poppy sighed. 'He's right, Andrew. It's just too dangerous. He's bound to wake up.'

Andrew smiled. 'Not necessarily. Remember on our first night here, we awoke in that strange room with all the hospital equipment in it?'

Poppy looked at him. 'Yeah, so?'

'Well, when we heard the Shadowmares talking, they said they'd given us some kind of sleep-inducing drug to knock us out. If we could just get back into that room, then we could find whatever it was, give it to Vesuvius and steal the key.'

Poppy's eyes sparkled and she laughed. 'That's brilliant, Andrew.'

'Brilliant? It's pure genius!' Dan said, jumping up and punching the air. He cleared his throat and sat back down. 'I mean it's OK, I suppose. We don't have any better ideas.'

Andrew grinned. 'Coming from you, Dan, I'll take that as a compliment.'

'There's just one thing I don't get,' Poppy said. She lifted her wrist up. 'Aren't you forgetting about these?'

Andrew felt his heart sink as he stared at the metal alarm triggers. She was right, he hadn't thought about those.

'It's OK,' Dan said. 'That's what I created the map for, remember? As long as we travel above the doors, we'll be fine. And by the time we make it into the corridor, we'll have the key and it'll be hasta la vista, Vesuvius!'

'Well that's sorted then,' Andrew said, grinning. 'So are we all agreed? We do it tonight?'

'Tonight?' Dan said. 'Don't you want to plan it a little better first? We still have a few more days before they kill me. If we take some time to work it out —'

Andrew shook his head. 'We don't have any more time. There's a Dark Room session tomorrow, remember? What if they discover my fear?'

'I agree,' Poppy said. 'It's now or never.'

Dan folded his arms, grinning. 'Well I'm not going to be shown up by a girl. Count me in. I just hope it works…'

'It's going to be OK,' Andrew reassured them,

smiling. Hearing his own voice, he couldn't help but notice how confident it sounded. If only he could have felt that way on the inside…

That night, the three of them were sitting in Andrew and Poppy's cell, waiting for the factory to fall silent. A crippling sensation of nerves had invaded Andrew's stomach like a terrible sickness. Was his plan going to work? What would happen if it didn't? It wasn't worth thinking about.

All three of them sat staring at the wall, not uttering a word. There was a sound of a key turning on the other side of the door, and breathtaking cold engulfed them. Dan quickly dived under the bed, just as the door crashed open.

It was Madam Bray, with two Shadowmares on either side of her. She didn't seem to notice the ventilator grill lying on the floor, or Dan's foot poking out from under the bed. She just stared at Andrew, her brown eyes cold and unblinking.

'Three-zero-nine-one,' she said. 'Come with me.'

Andrew sat on the bed, his head swimming with panic. The Shadowmares darted forwards and he felt their icy grip around his arms. They breathed a gush of cold air over him. Andrew blinked, trying to stay conscious. But he felt so weak…

His eyes closed.

The next thing he knew, he was being dragged towards the door and off down the corridor.

'Andrew, be careful,' he heard Poppy shout. 'Don't let them read your mind. Don't let them get inside your head.' Then the door slammed shut and he couldn't hear her any more. He was being taken down the narrow passages towards the main hall. It was empty, with only a few lights turned on. Madam Bray led him over to the fireplace, and when she started turning the cog on the wall, Andrew knew what was coming.

Why was this happening? It wasn't supposed to be until tomorrow. A familiar grinding noise echoed through the air, and Andrew watched the fireplace roll behind the wall. They were taking him into the Dark Room again. They were going to discover his fear…

Andrew stared into the darkness.

'Hello, Andrew,' Vesuvius said, in his soft hiss of a voice. Andrew heard the sound of a match striking up, as Vesuvius lit a candle. In the flickering light, he could see every crease and line in his skin, like a streetlamp shining over the cracks of a pavement.

'Interesting,' Vesuvius mused, his white hair hanging loosely over his scarred face. One side of his mouth tilted up into a crooked grin. It was a strange, twisted smile, as if his lips weren't used to parting in that way.

Andrew scowled up at him. 'What do you want with me?'

Vesuvius looked at Andrew for what seemed like an eternity, tapping his skull cane against the floor. 'Tell me, Andrew, what are you afraid of?'

'Oh sure, like I'm just going to tell you.' Andrew was trying to sound brave, but he could hear his voice cracking as he spoke. 'I know you want my fear, Vesuvius. But why did you have to steal my sister too? Couldn't you have just left her alone?'

Vesuvius was still smiling crookedly. He bent down next to Andrew so that their eyes were level.

He shrugged, his black eyes glistening in the light of the candle. 'Two for the price of one, I guess.' And then he laughed. 'Perhaps if you tell me your fear, we can come to some sort of arrangement.'

He took a step backwards. 'What kind of arrangement?' Andrew could smell his foul breath.

'If you tell me what your fear is, then I shall let your

sister go. Your friend too, if you like.'

Andrew looked at him uncertainly. 'You'll let them go?' he said. 'What, just like that?'

'Just like that,' Vesuvius replied, and he clicked his bony fingers together. A sharp snapping sound echoed around the room.

Andrew shivered.

'You're lying,' he said. 'And anyway, I wouldn't tell you if my life depended on it.'

Vesuvius stood up tall again, his face twitching irritably. 'Well maybe your life does depend on it,' he snapped, wielding the skull cane at Andrew. He had a sudden menace in his voice now, as if something had snapped inside of him. It was like…it was like he was barely human one minute and the next he was turning into something worse, something monstrous.

Andrew stared at the skull cane, his heart beating rapidly against his chest. He knew what it was capable of…but somehow, he remained calm. The moment he showed fear was the moment he became weak.

'Go ahead,' Andrew said boldly. 'Kill me. You're going to do it anyway. You might as well save yourself some time.'

Vesuvius glared at Andrew, eyes burning with fury.

For a moment Andrew thought he was going to do something awful, but he lowered his skull cane and smiled his crooked grin again.

'Fine,' he said softly. 'Have it your way.' He turned to Madam Bray. 'Take him to the Pod. Do not let him out until you have his fear.'

With that, Vesuvius turned and left the room. Madam Bray dragged Andrew to the Pod by the scruff of his pyjama top, muttering as she went.

'I warned you. I told you not to be cheeky, but what did you go and do? If you ask me, it's your own fault…'

'Well I didn't ask you, did I?' Andrew growled back. She was really starting to get on his nerves.

Madam Bray fell silent, but scowled at Andrew as she forced him into the Pod. Andrew tried to escape but the wires twisted around him, slamming him straight back down again. They were so tight, he could barely breathe. His head was swimming with dizziness, but he could see Kritchen drifting over to him from the distance. Other Shadowmares joined him until there was a whole swarm of them, perhaps one hundred in total. Andrew wasn't sure if he would be able to withstand their interrogation for long. It was so cold; he could feel the blanket of icy air slipping over his skin. He wiggled his toes. They were completely numb.

'Don't try and block us out this time,' Kritchen warned him, his red eyes glowing in the darkness. 'It'll all be over much sooner if you don't.'

Andrew grunted. 'That's what worries me.'

Kritchen opened his mouth again, and a rush of icy air blew out over Andrew, cold filling his veins. He knew that it was to weaken him. *It was working...* For a moment he felt completely paralysed, and he could feel his body turning to jelly. With the last of his strength, he tried again to wriggle out of his constraints, but the wires holding him down were too tight, and every time he tried to move, he could have sworn they got even tighter.

The glass lid of the Pod descended. Kritchen shut his veiny eyelids. The shadowy tentacles grew out from under his cloak and twisted around Andrew until they found their way into his head. Cold shot through him. The other Shadowmares did the same. Andrew could barely take the pain. It was as if his whole head was being frozen from the inside. Andrew concentrated hard on thinking about nothing, but it was too difficult. It had been easy before, when it was just Kritchen, but now every Shadowmare in the factory was searching through his head, scrambling around in there with icy tentacles. Kritchen began to shape-shift into a scarecrow from one of his favourite horror films, and soon all of the others followed him, wearing brown potato sacks for clothing and hair made from straw. Their arms were thin and gangly, and ended in sharp metal hooks.

Andrew felt the sweat bead on his forehead.

If the Shadowmares had managed to pluck that from his head, what else would they discover? He could *feel* them all rooting around in his mind, causing a strange sensation that felt like a migraine.

His legs were growing heavy as if he'd just run a marathon.

He blinked in disbelief as Kritchen turned into the bully who had been harassing Poppy all those days ago in the market. Narrow green eyes and bulging muscles. It wasn't his fear, but it was still a memory. At this rate, they'd have his real fear in no time. He had to stay calm and focused, but his head pounded.

Don't think about the fire. Don't think about the fire.

Kritchen transformed back and peered at Andrew with a crooked grin. 'Fire, eh? What fire?'

Andrew's heart sunk. *Oh God. What have I done?* The pain was becoming more intense by the second, as if his brain was being ripped to shreds.

A few seconds passed and then Kritchen nodded. 'Oh yes, here it is.'

The pain stopped.

It was all over; they had discovered his fear.

'Vesuvius will be so pleased.' The other Shadowmares began nodding and smiling, their eyes a bright fiery red.

Andrew felt the temperature in the room soar, along with his heart rate. The Shadowmares had disappeared but smoke filled the Dark Room and angry flames licked the sides of the Pod like giant orange tongues. He stared down at his arms and legs, which were being swallowed by the smoke. He tried to scream but he couldn't – the black air was choking his lungs.

'No, God, make it stop,' he rasped.

He was about to pass out. Then, a ripping pain flashed through his head. The room melted into a blur around him. There was the sound of smashing glass. The wires keeping him down loosened, hissing and wheezing as they coiled away.

He stared down at his arms, which were completely unburnt. The fire had vanished, but the Dark Room was a mess, full of glass and broken piping. Apart from the chair that he sat in, Andrew's Pod was completely destroyed. He couldn't understand it. Had the heat of the fire caused it to smash? No, it couldn't have. The fire was just a hallucination. It wasn't real. He wasn't hurt, wasn't burnt. Then how? He surveyed the Dark Room again. Nobody else was there. Could it have been the same mysterious force that had caused the grill to move?

He noticed the smoke curling up the walls of the cylinder. It was a strange bright green colour, not black like all the other kids' fear. *My fear*, thought Andrew. There was no time to worry about that now though. He had to get out of here. He set off racing for the door, but Kritchen appeared from nowhere, blocking his path.

'You,' he said. 'Don't move.' Andrew considered running again but there was no point. After all, he had *nowhere* to run to; it would take forever to wind open the door. In one quick movement, the Shadowmare dashed towards Andrew and grabbed him by the collar. He felt a sudden rush of cold shoot through his veins, as if his blood was being turned to ice. A needle pricked into his side. Andrew tried to stay awake but he couldn't fight it; his eyelids were drooping. Within seconds, he was unconscious.

*

Andrew awoke in a room he'd never seen before. He sat up and rubbed his eyes. It was completely bare – no bed, no sink, no toilet, *although it smelt like one*, and he realised he was lying on a stone floor. He thought of Poppy and Dan and a pang of guilt stung him hard. He hoped they'd still try and escape without him.

Someone cleared their throat. Andrew looked up. Kritchen was standing over him, his hot eyes boring deep into his.

'Vesuvius is furious. What happened? You've completely destroyed the Dark Room. Glass everywhere, and your Pod is a mess.'

Andrew rubbed his head wearily. What did Kritchen mean? It wasn't Andrew's fault the Pod had smashed.

'You shall remain here until we've cleaned it up,' continued Kritchen. 'Then you shall return to your Pod. We will extract every last drop of fear until you die.'

'Well, I've got news for you,' Andrew said, scowling. 'I'd rather die before giving you another drop of my fear.'

'We'll see about that,' Kritchen said. He left the room and bolted the door from the outside.

Andrew got up and paced around the room in frustration. He looked up. There was an air vent in the corner of the ceiling. Yes! He could get out of here, he could escape! But his heart sank when he realised there was no possible way of reaching it. He jumped up, scrabbling to get a foothold, but he slipped and fell on his back. He got to his feet again, searching the walls for a nook that he could use to hoist himself up with. The air vent was almost seven feet above him, and the walls were flat and smooth.

He slumped back down against them. 'It's no use!' he said out loud.

'Guess you won't be wanting my help then?' A familiar voice spoke from above.

Andrew looked up in surprise, bashing his head against the wall. Dan was hanging out of the ventilator, grinning.

'Dan! I was beginning to think I'd never get out of here.'

'Really?' He grinned. 'Well it was quite funny watching you try. Only joking, I only just got here. Grab hold of this,' he said, throwing down a rope. 'I've attached it to the grill in the next room, so it should hold your weight.'

Andrew grabbed the other end and heaved himself up. Every muscle and tendon in his body ached as he kept climbing.

'Nearly there,' Andrew said, but as he grabbed the sides of the ventilator, pain ripped through his biceps.

'I can't do it,' he said. 'I can't lift myself through the hole. I'm too weak.'

'Yes you can,' Dan said. 'Here, take my hand. I'll pull you up.'

He grabbed Dan's wrist, pulling himself up into the ventilator.

'Cor,' Dan said. 'You weigh a ton.'

'Shut up.' Andrew smiled. 'Where's Poppy?'

'She's waiting in the Fearbulator. We're going there now.'

They shuffled along the cramped passageway until they came to the Fearbulator grill. They lowered themselves down and made their way over to the trunk, where Poppy was walking up and down anxiously.

'Oh, Andrew!' she said, running up to him and giving him a hug. 'Are you all right? What did they do to you in there?'

'I'm fine,' he said. Then he sighed, dropping his head. There was no point lying to them. 'Actually I'm not. They found my fear.'

Silence descended on the room. It seemed to last forever.

Finally Dan spoke. 'Are you sure?'

'Yes,' Andrew said, hanging his head. 'I saw it in the cylinder. It was bright green. I'm sorry. I guess I'm not as strong as you thought I was.'

'What do we do now?' Poppy asked.

'There's nothing we can do, man. The whole world is in trouble now they have Andrew's fear.'

Andrew slumped down against the chest, guilt flooding through him.

'Come on,' Poppy said, dragging him up. She opened the chest and grabbed the map, a pocketknife, torch and a small screwdriver. 'We're not giving up yet. Vesuvius may have your fear, but we still need to get out of here. Maybe then we can fight.'

Andrew looked up.

'She's right you know,' Dan said. 'We can't let him win. We need to go and find the sleep-inducer, and get the key off Vesuvius. Then we need to get the hell out of here.'

They crawled through the ventilator at a snail's pace, making sure that every step was as quiet as possible. Suddenly a loud banging noise broke the silence, echoing around them like a drum.

'What was that?' Andrew said.

'Sorry,' Poppy whispered. 'I banged the side with my foot.'

'Well be more careful,' he hissed.

They carried on moving in silence, but Andrew couldn't shake the feeling that they had been heard. He forced himself to breathe calmly. This wasn't the time to panic. They soon found themselves staring down into the room they had woken up in when they had arrived at the Nightmare Factory.

'Which one of us is going down there?' Dan asked.

'I will,' Andrew said firmly. He was the reason they were here, so it was his responsibility to get them out. 'Where's the screwdriver?'

Poppy fumbled around in her pyjama pockets. She pulled out a blue and red screwdriver.

Very carefully, Andrew began to loosen the screws on the grill. When all six had come free, he gave it a little jiggle, removed it and lowered himself down onto a table directly under his feet. The room was smaller and much darker than he remembered. He moved the torch around, tracing it over the trolleys and their contents. He saw a few scalpels and knives, but nothing that looked like sleep-inducer.

'Any sign?' Poppy whispered from above.

'Not yet,' Andrew replied. 'I'm going to keep looking.'

'Try the cupboards,' Dan suggested.

Andrew padded quietly over to the cabinets that ran along the bottom of the walls. He opened the first one and peered into it. The pungent smell of antiseptic rushed out at him. The cupboard was full of different creams and ointments, but no syringes. He tried the next one. A few bandages. He felt sure the sleep-inducer had to be in here somewhere. He was trying to be as quiet as possible, but he was making an awful racket in his haste to find it.

'Andrew!' Poppy hissed from above. 'I think a Shadowmare's coming. You have to get out of there.'

She was right. He could *feel* the room getting colder. Andrew glanced at the ventilator. He didn't have time to get up there, and he didn't want to risk Poppy and Dan getting caught as well. He had seconds to act. He leaped into one of the cupboards and pulled the door shut.

A small crack in the door was just big enough for him to make out the shape of a Shadowmare entering the room. As it came closer, Andrew saw the big angry scar on the side of its face and he knew who it was. *Kritchen.*

He floated towards Andrew, slowly, teasingly…
and Andrew wasn't sure if the Shadowmare could
see him or not. Then he noticed something that
made his stomach feel as if it was turning inside out.
Kritchen was carrying the most horrifying weapon
Andrew had ever seen. A long metal bar, with one end
sharpened into a deadly point and the other a ball of
raging fire…

13

Andrew felt sweat trickling down his face, but he didn't dare try and wipe it away. His heart was pounding and he could hear blood rushing through his ears. He began to carefully feel around for something he could use to defend himself, but there was nothing, just cotton swabs and bandages – not even a glass bottle or something sharp. He peered out of the crack in the door again. The Shadowmare was almost upon him. Andrew held his breath and shut his eyes as Kritchen moved his bony hand towards the cupboard door, holding the spear of flaming fire in the other. *This is it*, Andrew thought. *The last few moments of my life. They have my fear now. This is how I am going to die.*

Then, just as Andrew was preparing himself for the final blow, there was a loud banging noise somewhere in the distance. Kritchen paused and turned around. The banging started again, and the Shadowmare glided out of the room.

Andrew felt a surge of relief. But there was no time

to waste. He got out of the cupboard, and as quietly as possible, carried on searching.

'What are you doing?' Poppy whispered urgently from above. 'He might come back. Get back up here!'

'I can't. I have to find the sleep-inducer.'

'Andrew… Dan went to another room to distract Kritchen, but when he realises that nobody's there he's going to —'

Andrew looked up. 'That was Dan making all the noise?'

'Yes. So will you just hurry up? Kritchen'll be on his way back by now.'

'Hang on, there's still a cupboard I haven't checked.'

Andrew drew a breath and opened the last cupboard door.

'Jackpot!' he whispered, staring at hundreds of syringes.

But which one was the sleep-inducer? Each one was slightly different, and there was no time to check the labels. He could already hear Kritchen hissing and grunting as he made his way back down the corridor. Andrew grabbed a handful of syringes and raced over to the table. He hoisted himself back into the ventilator and managed to replace the grill just as Kritchen entered the room. The Shadowmare took long, rasping breaths, holding the flaming spear in the air, ready to bring it down at any moment. His eyes burned furiously inside his skull.

'Andrew, where are you?' he hissed.

Andrew, Poppy and Dan remained silent in the darkness of the air vent, watching the Shadowmare searching every inch of the room. He looked in the cupboards and behind the door. He upturned the tables, hurling them across the room in a fit of rage. Eventually, with an angry flick of his hand he tossed his shadowy cloak over his shoulder and floated off.

Andrew allowed himself to breathe again.

'You were so lucky. If it hadn't been for Dan's quick thinking...' Poppy said.

'I know, I know, I'd be either dead right now or back in the Dark Room.' Andrew shivered at the thought. 'Thanks, Dan.'

Dan waved his hand dismissively.

'No problem, man. Actually, I almost got caught myself. I climbed into some room, I think it was an empty cell. I made a bit of noise and then I leapt back into the ventilator again, just as Kritchen hurried inside. You should have seen the look on his face. He was furious. Couldn't work out what was going on.'

'Serves him right,' Andrew said. He pulled out

a handful of the syringes he'd stolen. 'This one has the initials "S.I." on it,' he said, studying a bright blue one.

'Great,' Poppy said. 'That's got to be it.'

Andrew tucked it between the elastic of his pyjama bottoms and tossed the others to one side.

'Come on, if this plan has any chance of working, we have to get a move on,' Dan said, beginning to crawl along the ventilator. Andrew and Poppy followed him. Retrieving the sleep-inducer had taken longer than any of them had anticipated and it was only the first step. They had to get to Vesuvius, and fast.

Dan led them quickly to Vesuvius's headquarters. Andrew peered down through the air vent and saw a few candles scattered about, giving the room a flickering glow. A damp smell of sewage lingered in the air. It had the same grotty stone walls that fashioned the rest of the factory, yet the carpet was plush red. In the middle of the room there was a grand mahogany bed, and a chandelier festooned with cobwebs. Vesuvius was asleep on the bed, although every few seconds he would let out a loud snore, his lips vibrating like jelly. His mouth was wide open and saliva leaked from the sides.

Poppy giggled nervously.

'Shhh! You might wake him,' Andrew said.

Dan began to carefully pull the grill off the ceiling.

'Wait,' Poppy whispered. 'We can't just jump down there. The bed's right underneath us. He'll wake up.'

Dan stopped, looking confused. 'So what do we do then, clever clogs?'

Poppy didn't answer. Instead, in one quick movement, she snapped the button off Dan's pyjama top.

'What are you doing?' Dan hissed.

'Stop moaning and hand me the pocketknife.'

'Here…' Dan replied. They watched curiously as Poppy began cutting into the waistband of her pyjama bottoms.

'What are you doing?' Dan asked again.

'I'll explain in a minute.' She pulled a long piece of elastic out of the material and started threading it through the button. She carefully took the ventilator grill off and lowered herself out of the hole.

'Hold onto my legs,' she whispered. Andrew grabbed hold of her ankles, as she positioned herself directly above Vesuvius. Slowly, she lowered the elastic down bit by bit until it was dangling just above his lips. 'Now pass me the syringe.'

Andrew and Dan looked at each other.

'Hurry!' she whispered. Andrew quickly handed

his twin the syringe, still unsure about what she was doing. He watched curiously as she squeezed the end of the syringe and the clear liquid began trickling all the way down the strand of elastic. One drop fell into Vesuvius's mouth, and then another, and another.

'Genius!' Andrew muttered.

She smiled, looking pleased with herself. 'I read about it once.'

Just as these words had left her tongue, the elastic in her hand started swaying and a drop of sleep-inducer splashed onto Vesuvius's cheek. The muscles around his chin began twitching and he snorted like a pig. They all kept very still, ready to make a dash back up the ventilator at any second, but then Vesuvius groaned and turned over, falling completely still.

'Did it work?' Andrew said, barely whispering.

Poppy wiped the beads of sweat from her forehead. 'Let's hope so.'

The three of them lowered themselves one by one onto Vesuvius's bed. His breathing was slow and heavy, more of a growl than a snore. Was he just pretending to be asleep? Andrew swallowed hard, and poked him tentatively on the arm, but Vesuvius lay there like a waxwork model.

Andrew breathed a sigh of relief. He could see the

tarnished triangular key around his neck, attached to a thick metal chain.

'Poppy,' Andrew whispered. 'On the count of three Dan and I will lift his head up. As soon as we do, you can grab the necklace from around his neck.'

She nodded.

'OK. One…two…' He paused for a second, taking a deep breath. 'Three.'

They tugged at Vesuvius's shoulders with all their strength. He was deadweight, and Andrew wasn't sure how long they could hold him up. Poppy moved swiftly and pulled the necklace out from around his neck. They let Vesuvius collapse onto the bed again. He groaned, eyelids fluttering.

'He's waking up. Quick! Air vent!' Andrew said, heart racing.

'We don't have time.' Dan took the necklace off Poppy and slung it around his own neck. 'We're going to have to make a run for it.'

The three of them raced for the door. As soon as they had crossed the threshold, the deafening sound of the alarm split the air. They sprinted along the corridor as fast as they could. Andrew could see the door at the end of it. Just a few more seconds and they'd be there.

The door looked exactly like it had in his dream – thick and wide with a huge padlock chained to the wall. Dan was ahead of Andrew by a few feet. He was fumbling around with the key, struggling to get it into the lock, but then suddenly the big metal door swung open and Andrew saw him disappear inside. He was just about to do the same, when he realised Poppy wasn't in front of him. He spun around. The corridor was empty. Where was she?

'Poppy!' he yelled. 'Poppy, where are you?'

It was no use. His voice was drowned out by the noise of the alarm, like an entire orchestra playing the same deafening note.

Vesuvius appeared from around the corner. Poppy was in his grasp. He had his cane held up to her throat, the skull pressed tightly against her jugular vein. He laughed icily. He could see the fear in Poppy's eyes.

'You should run,' she croaked.

Andrew stood frozen, the escape door open.

'No,' he said, firmly. 'Not without you.' He looked into Vesuvius's eyes. It was like staring into two black holes, and again he felt cold filling his veins. 'Let her go and take me. I'm the one you want, aren't I?'

The master's eyes glistened madly and his smile widened.

'Very well,' he said. 'Just step away from the door and walk towards me.'

'I will,' Andrew said. 'But let go of her first.'

Vesuvius shook his head. 'It doesn't work that way. I'll let her go when you're safely in my reach. And bring the key.' His expression froze for a moment. 'You do still have the key?'

'Yes,' Andrew lied. He let out a deep breath and began to walk towards Vesuvius.

'No, Andrew! He'll kill you,' Poppy cried, thrashing about.

Andrew wasn't listening. He didn't care what Vesuvius did to him, didn't care if he died, as long as Poppy went free. He had only moved two steps towards her when he felt a pair of strong hands grabbing his shoulders and pulling him backwards.

'Nooo!' Vesuvius screamed as Andrew was dragged through the doorway.

'Let go of me,' Andrew shrieked, jerking his body to try to free himself, but it was hopeless. Whoever or whatever had seized him was stronger than he was.

Vesuvius pointed his skull cane at Andrew, still gripping tightly onto Poppy. A blast of light shot out from the skull's eyes, but before it could reach Andrew, the door slammed shut.

Andrew rattled the handle, twisted and pulled, but it wouldn't budge. He was in here, wherever 'here' was, and Poppy was still in the Nightmare Factory, about to be murdered by Vesuvius. And there was nothing he could do to save her.

14

Andrew crouched, panting, bent over on the floor. He took a deep breath and stood up. There were two staircases leading up. They were long and steep, and appeared to go on forever. The staircase to the left of him was dark and narrow. It had metal steps and stone walls covered in green slime. The staircase to the right was made from frosted glass and had several glistening chandeliers hanging above it, which reflected off the glass steps like iridescent crystals.

He jumped when he felt a tap on the back.

'I'm sorry, Andrew,' Dan said. He was standing in the darkness, his face masked by shadows.

'Why did you pull me through the door?' Andrew snapped. 'Poppy's still in there. We need to go back.'

'It wasn't me,' Dan said. 'I tried to help her but this horrible creature stopped me.' He stepped forwards out of the darkness, and Andrew realised that behind him was a man with a shiny bald head and pink skin, as if he had spent too long in the sun. He was holding Dan by the scruff of his pyjama top. He had a thick, fish-like mouth and wide blue eyes and was dressed in white overalls. Andrew wondered how he had managed to pull him with such strength. He was only short with a big round belly that made him look pregnant.

'Are you going to let go of me now?' Dan growled at him.

The man looked at Dan as if he had completely forgotten what he was doing, and released him at once. Dan pulled away, straightening up. Andrew noticed he still had the key around his neck.

'Try and open the door again,' Andrew said.

Dan moved forwards and slotted the key back into the lock, but he flinched, grabbing his arm.

'*Ahh!* It burned me! It won't seem to open from this side.'

'You!' Andrew said, and he grabbed the strange person by his overalls, forcing him to look up. 'Why won't it open?'

The man blinked but didn't speak. He just pointed to the glass staircase and made a strange gurgling sound.

'What's he doing?' Andrew asked. He ran his fingers through his hair. His head felt hot. His sister was in danger, and this strange creature didn't seem to care.

'I reckon he's trying to tell us something. Perhaps he wants us to follow him,' Dan said.

Andrew pulled the man closer. 'Listen, I don't care what you want. That's my twin out there. Open this door at once so we can get her back.'

The little man shook his head and pointed to the glass staircase again, making the same odd gurgling sounds as before.

Andrew could feel himself getting more and more agitated. He stretched his hands out, allowing the tension to run through his fingers.

'Open this door, or else…or else I'm going to do something I'll probably regret.'

The little man didn't seem to be listening. He began trotting up the stairs, which were too big for his stumpy legs. He turned around and beckoned for them to follow. Andrew stormed up the stairs after him.

'Fine,' he snapped. 'Have it your way, but you better be taking us to see Oran. Maybe he can help us get out of this mess.'

The muscles in his legs were still aching and weak, but he barely noticed as he climbed the giant staircase. He couldn't stop thinking about Poppy. It should be him in there. What if Vesuvius killed her in revenge?

They finally reached the top, where they stopped at a frosted glass door. The man pulled a ring of keys from his pocket and put one of them into the lock. With a small turn the door creaked open.

Andrew gasped. The interior looked strangely futuristic. Everything was white and gold. There was a disk-shaped table, which reminded Andrew of a flying saucer. It had four tall, egg-like chairs placed around it. The fluffy carpet was soft between his toes. Every time he put his foot down, he seemed to bounce back up again as if he was on a trampoline. It was such a contrast to the stone floors in the Nightmare Factory.

There were pictures on the plain white walls of purple skies and rocky mountains. Except they didn't look like pictures at all. They looked like stills of real life, as if they were windows hanging in frames. There was also a picture of an elderly man and woman, both smiling, but Andrew had no idea who they were. A large grandfather clock stood in the corner. It was made from glass, so that you could see the mechanism inside it.

'Look over there,' Dan said, pointing. 'What do you think that is?'

In the corner, by the table, was what looked like an oven, except it had some sort of satellite dish pointing down at it. Underneath the satellite dish was a pot of bubbling liquid. There was a wonderful smell of herbs and cooking in the air. Andrew rubbed his stomach hungrily. He remembered his sister. *Stop being so selfish!* he thought.

'Where's Oran?' he asked. 'We need to see him. It's urgent.'

The little man pointed to the golden chairs around the table, gesturing for them to sit, then he waddled out of the room.

Dan turned to Andrew. 'Don't worry, mate. Poppy's going to be OK.'

Andrew nodded. He couldn't speak. His stomach was churning with sickness.

'Look,' Dan said, pointing to a door with a welcome mat and shoes by the bottom of it. 'Do you think it leads outside? Where do you think we are?'

Andrew glanced at the frosted glass door. It was pitch black outside. He shook his head hopelessly. 'I dunno. All I care about is getting my sister back.'

At that moment, Oran rushed through another door looking flustered. He had the little man by his side. This time Oran was wearing a suit to match his purple top hat with yellow stars. He looked a bit like a wizard, with his long grey hair tumbling over his shoulders. He was holding the pearly walking stick he'd had in Andrew's dream. Dan gasped and stumbled backwards.

'It's Vesuvius,' he said in a squeaky voice. 'It's —'

'It's not him. They just look alike,' Andrew said, cutting him short. 'Where were you, Oran? You said you'd be here.'

Oran shook his head, looking dismayed. 'I told you before that I can't enter the Factory. Tarker informed me that something went wrong. The girl – she was captured?'

'But —' Dan started up again. 'Why does he look so much like him?'

Andrew ignored him. 'Yes, my sister was taken, probably killed and it's all *Tarker's* fault. He stopped me from saving her,' he said bitterly. He shot a hateful glare in the little man's direction, who stood there nervously pulling on his stumpy thumbs.

Oran sat down on one of the egg-shaped chairs. Andrew expected him to look shocked, guilty even, but he wasn't…he was unusually calm. He loosened the collar of his shirt and sighed.

'He was only following my orders, Andrew. I told him to make sure you arrived here safely, no matter what.'

'Well that "no matter" was what got my sister killed,' Andrew hissed. 'And anyway, how come you couldn't come yourself? Have something more important to do?'

'No,' Oran said firmly. 'If you would allow me to explain.'

'I hate Vesuvius,' Andrew said, clenching his fists. 'I really *hate* him.' He was so furious he didn't know what to do with himself. It was as if he'd ingested a whole heap of caffeine and now he just couldn't stand still. Suddenly, the grandfather clock in the corner started chiming, the hands whizzed around crazily, and the pictures on the wall began rattling violently in their frames. The saucepan came hurling towards them, spilling boiling soup all over the carpet. Dan spun around in panic.

'What's happening?' he shouted, as several cups and saucers flew off the shelves at them. He ducked and hid under the table. 'Is it an earthquake?'

Oran exhaled a sharp breath. 'I'm afraid it's Andrew.'

Dan peered out from under the table. 'Say that again?'

'I said it's Andrew. His emotions are wreaking havoc with his abilities...not to mention my dining

144

room. Do try and get him to calm down.'

Andrew was pacing the room as Oran's words came filtering through. He glanced around at the chaos that had wiped out the tidy room like a tsunami. He stopped, and took a deep breath.

'What do you mean, *my abilities*?'

The clock stopped chiming, the pictures stopped rattling. Everything was calm again. For a moment, nobody said a word.

Oran arched his eyebrows. 'I think you had better sit down.'

This time, Andrew did as he was told, and Dan came and sat in the chair next to him. He was still staring at Oran like he was from Mars, but was now glancing at Andrew with equal uncertainty.

'Andrew,' Oran said softly. 'As you are already aware, you are the new Releaser. Your one and only fear is so strong that it can provide Vesuvius with the power to enter your world, and create a living nightmare. He's been searching for you for years, but as he's grown closer to finding you, some of his power has leached into your body.'

'Huh?' Andrew said. He thought he knew what Oran was saying, but he had to make sure. It seemed impossible.

'In all his efforts to find you, thinking about you one hundred per cent of the time, concentrating on you and nothing else, an accidental connection has occurred between the two of you. Part of his spirit has bonded to yours, and in turn, some of his abilities have transferred to you.'

'What kind of abilities?' Andrew asked. He felt numb. He didn't want this. He didn't want to be connected to that evil creature in any way.

'Surely you must have noticed them?'

Andrew shook his head. He wasn't sure what Oran was getting at.

'At the market, the first time we met,' Oran said, 'Tiffany Grey was searching for you. We hoped to get to you first, to protect you from Vesuvius. We already had a notion that the Releaser might be living in London, but when Tiffany saw you pushing that bully all the way across the street, she knew you were the one. She contacted me immediately.'

'Wow,' Dan said, taking a deep breath.

Andrew put his head in his hands, feeling as if his brain might explode. He stood up, and then sat back down. He didn't know what to do.

'In the Nightmare Factory, when the grill moved —' Andrew began.

'All you,' Oran said. 'Your abilities will tend to manifest when you have a huge rush of emotion. Soon you will learn to control them, but until then, they may come and go erratically.'

Andrew's mind span. *Power? Abilities?* This was crazy. He was a normal boy. Well, he had been until the other day... All this time, he had assumed it was Oran who had been making all the weird stuff happen.

'What about when the Fear Pods smashed?' he asked.

Oran nodded. 'You again.'

Andrew got up and paced around the room. None of it made any sense. But it was all real. It was happening. And he was just going to have to deal with it. He had so many questions, but there was something else that needed answering first.

'Where are we?' he asked. 'Why are you trying to help me? And what has Vesuvius done to my twin?'

'Calm down,' Oran smiled. 'I will explain everything in good time. Right now, it is vital we start planning for when we go and save Poppy.'

Andrew glanced at Dan, whose expression mirrored his own disbelief.

'What? You mean she's alive?' Andrew whispered, scarcely able to believe it.

'It is not definite,' Oran corrected him. 'But there is a chance. After all, Vesuvius has no reason to kill her. It is you that he wants, and…if he thinks that you might go after her, then…'

'Then he'll use her as bait,' Andrew finished. 'Why didn't you say so before?'

'I was trying. You seemed rather intent on not listening to me.'

Andrew looked at the floor, letting his blond hair fall over his face. 'I'm sorry. So what happens now?'

'If your sister's alive, she will have been expelled to the Mountain of Doom. We'll set off as soon as it is light.'

'Why not now?' Andrew asked impatiently. 'I want to go now.'

'*You* won't be going at all, Andrew. If Vesuvius finds you again…' He shook his head. 'The Mountain of Doom is very dangerous. It's too much of a risk. Dan and I will be leaving in the morning. The journey there is long and difficult, over treacherous ground. To attempt it in the dark would be a suicide mission, and we will be of no use to your sister if we are all dead.'

'I want to come,' Andrew said. 'I *need* to come. She's my sister, Oran. Can't you understand that?'

'Yeah,' Dan said. 'It should be up to him. Unless you're going to keep him locked up here like Vesuvius did…'

Oran stroked his beard. 'I suppose you're right.' He sighed. 'Alright, you can come, Andrew, but we go in the morning, after a rest.'

'But I can't rest, not when I know my sister's trapped in some terrible mountain somewhere. I really think that we should leave now and —'

'NO!' Oran snapped, slamming his hand down on the table. He cleared his throat, straightening his top hat. 'We go tomorrow, or not at all.'

'Fine,' Andrew said, slumping back down in the chair again. After all, they needed Oran's help. There was no way that they could do this alone. He thought about what Oran had said, about it being dangerous.

'Where are we?' he asked.

'We are in the Dream Factory,' Oran said. 'I make dreams here. Pleasant, fun-filled dreams.'

Dan took a step back and Andrew gasped. He hadn't been expecting that.

'Don't worry, I don't steal children to make

149

dreams,' Oran said, and then he frowned. 'Why do you look so shocked? You have already encountered the Nightmare Factory. Is it so unbelievable that there would be an opposite?'

Andrew scratched his head. 'I guess not...' He suddenly remembered Dan telling them that they were in another world. 'So, this is the Dream Factory, but what's outside?'

'It's called Nusquam. It's a parallel universe to Earth. It exists at the same time, but on a different plane.'

Dan's mouth fell open. 'So what kind of place is it? Who lives here?'

'Nusquarium people of course. We are very similar to humans in appearance, but we live a great deal longer. I will be three hundred and seventy six next year.'

'Wow, and I thought *my mum* was old,' Andrew muttered. He felt a rush of sadness. He wished with all his heart that he could go home and see her.

'But if there are people here, how come Vesuvius doesn't steal them from their dreams? What's so special about our world?' Dan asked.

Oran stroked his stubbly beard, looking thoughtful. 'For starters, Nusquarium people don't dream. They also have a very different kind of fear. It's hard to explain, but it doesn't taste very pleasant to the Shadowmares.'

'Huh?' Andrew and Dan said simultaneously.

'Try to think of it this way. The Shadowmares feed off fear, correct? Well, a human's fear is like a rich chocolate pudding, and a Nusquarium person's fear is like mouldy brussel sprouts. Which one would you rather have?'

'OK, but that still doesn't explain why you and Vesuvius look so much alike,' Dan said, eyes narrowing suspiciously. 'It's a little strange, don't you think?'

'Dan, shut up! You're being rude,' Andrew hissed, but even he was curious.

Oran put his finger in the air. 'No, Andrew, it's quite all right. There is something that I need to explain to the pair of you.' He took a sip of water and licked his lips. Andrew and Dan sat in silence, waiting. Oran pressed a finger over the golden locket around his neck, and with a small click, it sprang open. On the left side of the locket was a photograph of a man and a woman. Andrew recognised them from the pictures on Oran's wall. The man had his arms around the woman and was smiling brightly. On the right side of the locket was a picture of Vesuvius and Oran. Andrew felt his stomach crumble with dread, suddenly wondering if this had all been one big trap.

15

'Vesuvius is my twin brother,' Oran said, 'of sorts.'

'Of sorts?' Andrew repeated. His lips were trembling, his head swimming.

'My family used to run the Nightmare Factory and the Dream Factory together. After all, for something to exist there must be an opposite to balance it out. It is only natural.'

'You used to run the Nightmare Factory? That's awful!' Andrew said. He couldn't imagine Oran stealing children from their dreams. The thought made him feel physically sick.

'Please, it is not as horrendous as you may think. It was different in those days. We didn't use children to create the fear. We had discovered a way of making it artificially. The fear wasn't as powerful as it is today, and the nightmares could actually help a person *overcome* their fears.'

Andrew shifted in his chair a little. He wasn't convinced.

'Then…I don't get it. Where do the Shadowmares fit into all this?'

'The Shadowmares are a type of Letchian.'

'OK, and that would be what, exactly?' Dan said.

'Letchians are a bit like parasites, except they feed off emotions,' Oran said. 'There are many types of Letchians in Nusquam. Some feed off happiness, others feed off anger. The Shadowmares feed off fear. They showed up at the factory one day and asked for a job.'

'What, and you trusted them?' Andrew said dryly.

Oran sighed. 'We had no reason not to. Nusquam is densely populated with many strange creatures. The Shadowmares were no different. They told us that their previous source of fear had run out and we didn't really question it. We needed help making the nightmares. It seemed like the perfect arrangement.'

'So let me get this straight,' Dan said. 'A group of half skeletal creatures show up at your door and you don't even think to question their motives?'

'It's hard to explain, but Nusquam is a mysterious land. We help your world function. We don't just create dreams and nightmares – we provide more than you could possibly imagine.'

'Like what?'

'We have idea planters. People who plant ideas and inspirations in people. Edison didn't come up with the light bulb all on his own, you know.' He chuckled. 'And we have mischief-makers. They're Nusquarium creatures who balance the order of good and bad luck in life. Haven't you ever wondered why some people are incredibly lucky and others always seem to lose their keys or receive parking tickets? It's no coincidence.'

Andrew felt a rush of anger.

'So we have no actual control over our lives? It's all planned out for us?'

'You have plenty of control over your lives,' Oran said. 'We just interfere when we need to. We simply make sure the forces of the universe remain balanced.' He coughed. 'Anyway, we're getting off track here. I was trying to explain to you about the Shadowmares. They were working for us. Helping to make the nightmares. They convinced us that we could trust them.'

'So what happened?' Dan asked, staring at Oran in fascination. 'What went wrong?'

A heavy frown creased Oran's forehead.

'The Shadowmares were not happy merely creating nightmares. That was never their plan.' He shivered angrily. 'One day, they turned on my twin, Burtrum, while he was working down in the Factory and killed him. Vesuvius took over my twin's body, allowing him to take on the form of a human. And since that day, his powers have increased immensely.'

Andrew found himself leaning in closer, eyes and mouth wide open. 'And then what?'

Oran turned, staring at the wall, although his mind seemed to be somewhere a lot further away. Andrew thought he could see a tear forming in one of his eyes.

'And then he murdered my parents.'

Andrew and Dan gasped.

'He took over the Nightmare Factory, stealing children from their dreams and using their fear to create the nightmares. All the while, searching for a child that would provide the Shadowmares with the ultimate power they so desperately desired.'

'What power?' Andrew asked, even though he already thought he knew the answer.

'The power of the Releaser,' Oran said breathing heavily. 'The one fear so powerful that it will allow the Shadowmares to enter your world and turn people's fear into reality. Into one big living nightmare. If it was to happen again, I fear it would be even worse than the last time. Earth would become a terrible place to live, full of demons and beasts. Once the Shadowmares start releasing your fear, whatever phobia a person has, whatever nightmares they dream, would instantly become real, giving the Shadowmares all the fear that they desire. So you see, Vesuvius may look like my brother on the surface, but I can assure you he is no relative of mine.'

Andrew took a deep breath. Now that Vesuvius had his fear, was this what was going to happen to the world? So much chaos and destruction? And it would all be his fault… But he still couldn't bring himself to tell Oran the truth. What if Oran wanted to go after Vesuvius instead of saving his sister? No. He had to keep it a secret for now.

Andrew glanced at the photograph in the locket again. Oran's twin had brown eyes, full of warmth, not the cold black eyes of Vesuvius.

'The only thing I don't get, is why didn't Vesuvius kill you too?'

Oran shrugged. 'I suspect it was down to the spell.'

'Spell?' Dan said.

'The last thing my father did before he died was to cast a spell between the two Factory walls. Vesuvius was forbidden from entering mine, and I was forbidden from entering his. My father did it to protect me, as a

157

final act of love. I'm afraid that's why I couldn't help you earlier. I hope you understand.'

Andrew nodded.

'I'm not sure if that's what's kept me alive for so long or not. I think if Vesuvius really wanted me dead, he'd have found a way by now. The truth is, he probably doesn't think I'm worth bothering with.' Oran jumped up suddenly. 'Anyway, at least you'll be out of harm's way here. I'm just thankful that Vesuvius didn't have you long enough to find your fear. If he had, he'd be so powerful by now that it doesn't even bear thinking about.'

Andrew licked his lips nervously.

'I just need to go and fetch something. I'll be right back,' Oran said. He hurried out of the room, leaving Dan and Andrew alone.

Dan turned to face him, eyes serious. 'You need to tell him, Andrew. You need to tell him the truth about your fear.' It was as if Dan was reading his mind.

Andrew shook his head. 'I can't tell him until we've rescued Poppy. If I do, he might say it's too risky, or that we have to go after Vesuvius instead, and we can't let that happen. You heard him, he didn't even want me to come in the first place.'

There was a moment of silence, and Andrew wasn't

sure what Dan was thinking. His forehead creased into a frown. 'Alright,' he said. 'I'll keep your secret, but you better tell him as soon as we find her, deal?'

Andrew smiled with relief. 'Deal. I promise, Dan.'

The door creaked open and they jumped as Oran returned to the room carrying a pair of sharp tweezers and something that looked a bit like a pen.

He grinned. 'What are you two looking so guilty for?'

Dan bit his lip. 'Nothing.'

Oran stared at them, eyebrows raised. Then he shook his head. 'I never will understand humans,' he said with a chuckle. 'Right, we must get rid of the alarm sensors. Hold out your wrists.'

Andrew held out his wrist. A sharp red light burst out from the tip of the pen, hot and bright like a laser.

'Whoa!' Andrew gasped, flinching backwards. 'What is that thing?'

'It's a laser pen, to melt off your bracelet. Keep still and you'll be fine.'

Andrew held his arm back out, and Oran began burning the clasp of his bracelet, cutting clean through the metal as if it was paper.

'Cool,' Andrew said, as the bracelet fell to the floor, and the red light on it blinked out. Andrew wiggled his hand about freely, while Oran went to remove Dan's.

'Now to get rid of the fear plugs. Turn around and hold still, this might sting a bit.'

'Only a bit?' Andrew said, turning around.

Oran raised a hand to Andrew's head. 'Actually, that was a lie,' he said, holding him down. 'It's going to sting a lot.'

A fierce pain shot all the way through Andrew's head, and he collapsed to the floor. When he came to a few minutes later, he was dizzy and his head throbbed like someone had hit it with a club. He got up, the room spinning. Dan was lying on the floor, out cold. Andrew felt around the back of his head, slipping his hand over a thick bandage. He could see two metal plugs lying on the table.

'Geez,' Andrew said, rubbing his head. 'At least in the Nightmare Factory they knocked us out first.'

Oran smiled, looking a little guilty. 'Sorry,' he said. 'But we have a lot to do. I don't have time to muck around with sleep-inducer. I thought it would be better just to rip them out, short and sweet.'

Dan groaned.

'Well it didn't feel very sweet,' he said, sitting up.

Oran smiled. 'Ah, good. Now that you're both

conscious, you can take these painkillers.' He handed them two red pills each. Andrew took the tablets, studying them carefully. They were big and round, and had the letters 'NP' on them.

'It stands for No Pain,' Oran said. 'Take them and you'll see what I mean.'

Andrew shoved them in his mouth, feeling the pain melt quickly away.

'How do you feel?' Oran asked.

'I feel great,' Andrew said.

Oran smiled, and picked up a tall pearly stick.

Where have I seen that thing before? Andrew wondered. Then he remembered. He'd seen Oran carrying it in his dream. It had been glowing.

'What is that thing?' Dan asked, before Andrew had the chance.

'It's a unicorn horn,' Oran said casually.

'Of course it is,' Andrew said, dripping sarcasm. All this weirdness was beginning to seem almost normal.

Oran took out a notebook and pen from his pocket. 'We must go and send a message to your sister. What do you want to tell her?'

Andrew drew back, confused. 'What?'

'Yeah, man, what do you mean?' Dan asked

Oran rolled his eyes. 'Come on, it's not hard. What

will you say to her? Will you tell her that everything is going to be all right? Will you let her know that we are coming to her rescue?'

Andrew hesitated. 'Yeah…I suppose so, but…' he faltered, watching uncertainly as Oran scribbled it all down.

'I suggest we tell her to hide and stay put until we find her, too,' Oran suggested, sucking on the end of the pen. 'That's important. We don't want her stumbling around in the Mountain of Doom.' He began writing again, and Andrew stared at him, wondering if he had gone completely mad.

'I don't get it. What are you going to do, post it to her?' Dan said sarcastically.

Oran let out a chuckle. 'Not exactly.'

'Then how…?' Andrew began, but Oran put a finger to his lips.

'Too many questions. Just come with me,' he said, and left the room, leaving Andrew and Dan with no choice but to follow.

16

The little man with pink skin was waiting for them in the hallway. He hobbled along a few feet, opening various doors for them on the way. The interior was much more inviting here than in the Nightmare Factory. Big chandeliers hung from the ceiling, drenching the place in a warm yellow light. The walls were painted metallic gold and there were plenty of windows, but because it was dark outside all Andrew could see was his own reflection. He screwed up his nose in disgust. It was the first time he'd seen himself since arriving at the Nightmare Factory and it wasn't a pretty sight. His blond hair was greasy, his pyjamas grubby, and he had dark circles under his eyes.

The little man stopped at a final steel door and opened it using one of the keys. 'Thank you, Tarker,' Oran said and they walked inside, leaving the man behind.

'What kind of creature is he?' Dan asked.

'Tarker is one of my many workers here. The

Luguarna people are a species native to Nusquam and have existed here for many centuries. They are amazing creatures, and extremely strong. Did you know it only takes two of them to move something the size of a truck?'

'Really?' Dan said. 'Why's it so fat then?'

'Tarker is not fat. He is pregnant.' He took out a key and began to unlock another door. 'Luguarna people are not like humans. They can reproduce on their own. And in their case, it is usually the male who goes through the process.'

Andrew and Dan didn't have time to react to Oran's strange explanation, because he pushed open the door and they were faced with something even more peculiar.

'What *is* this place?' Andrew asked.

Oran stepped in front of them, spinning his unicorn stick in the air. 'This is where the dreams are made,' he replied proudly.

Andrew gasped, staring around at a large, spotlessly white factory with lots of machinery running through the centre. It was as if someone had swept a white paintbrush over every single thing in the room. Several of the Luguarna people were rushing around. They were also dressed in white overalls, and would have blended into the background completely if not for their hot pink skin and rosy cheeks. The male Luguarna people had bald, shiny heads, while the females all had thick blue hair, like wool, which they wore in two plaits.

A strange whistling noise travelled through the air and Andrew's eyes flitted back to the machinery. A man and a woman were cranking a lever attached to a large cylinder. Every time they pushed the lever down, a puff of pink vapour would fill the cylinder then travel along a glass tube to the next piece of machinery.

'Amazia,' Oran called. The female working the lever stopped what she was doing and came to see what he wanted. With her small frame, big green eyes and pink cheeks, she reminded Andrew of a rag doll.

'Amazia, we need a dream created. It is of the upmost importance.'

Amazia simply nodded to show that she understood. Oran handed her the piece of paper and she clutched it between her stubby fingers, reading it carefully.

'Follow me,' Oran told them.

Further along, the Luguarna people were wearing white masks over their faces, so that only their eyes showed. They were busy bottling the pink smoke up into tiny flasks that were now being carried along on a large conveyor belt.

They passed several more machines, each one adding something new to the pink smoke, so that it became an array of different colours. The various Luguarna people were checking each of the flasks, stirring them, and adding other bits of ingredients to them.

'Each flask contains a dream,' Oran told them. 'And each dream is unique. The Luguarna people must add exactly the right ingredients. A bit like baking a cake.'

Andrew watched curiously as one of the Luguarna men stuffed what looked like old fingernails into one of the vials, and feathers into another.

'If that's *anything* like baking a cake, then I wouldn't trust his cookbook,' Andrew muttered.

At the end of the room, the conveyor belt passed into a small hole in the wall.

'Where are the dreams going now?'

'You'll see,' Oran replied, as one of the Luguarna men opened up another door for them and a stuffy heat billowed out. Andrew found himself entering a sort of greenhouse, filled with all kinds of lush, vibrant plants. It was hard to see where they were walking because of all the vegetation. A high pitched tweeting noise echoed through the place, just as something small and pink flashed past Andrew's face. At first he thought it must have been a bird but when a trail of glitter followed it, he wasn't so sure.

'What was that?' Andrew asked, trying to see where it had gone.

'A fairy of course,' Oran replied, as if it was obvious.

'A...*fairy*?' Dan said, sceptically. 'As in, the little creatures that take teeth from under your pillow?'

Oran rolled his eyes. 'Teeth fairies are a whole different species.'

One of them whizzed past Andrew and Dan again. It was so fast, it was just a gold blur, but when Andrew put his hand out, the fairy came back and rested on it like a butterfly. It was tiny, about three inches tall, and had pointed ears and a slender figure. Its hair was blonde and it was wearing a dress made from leaves. It chattered happily on Andrew's hand, staring curiously up at him. Andrew reached out to stroke the fairy, but before he had the chance, the fairy leaned forwards and nipped his finger, causing blood to spring to the surface.

'Ouch!' Andrew yelled. 'It bit me.'

The fairy danced from one foot to the other, making a quiet twittering noise, as if it found this quite hilarious. Andrew tried to grab hold of it but it flew off into the distance.

'Damn critter,' Andrew hissed.

Dan clutched his belly, laughing. 'Ha! You got bitten by a fairy!'

'That's right,' Oran said. 'They're mischievous little creatures with terrible mood swings, but they do serve a great purpose here. See the dust on your hand?'

Andrew looked down to where a trail of gold dust glistened over his palm. He nodded. 'Well those are fairy droppings...otherwise known as fairy dust. It's the final and most important ingredient in making the dreams.'

'Eww!' Andrew said, wiping his hand down his top.

They wandered through more plants until they reached the end of the room, where three Luguarna people were sorting through flasks on the conveyor belt, putting stoppers in them and marking them up with labels. One of the females turned and handed Oran a flask.

'Thank you,' Oran said, and they walked through another steel door into a room where the walls and the floor were so shiny and sparkly, it was as if there were a million tiny diamonds trapped inside them. Andrew's eyes focused on the rows of wooden shelves in front of him, spaced out like library shelves, but seeming to go on forever, upwards and outwards, as if unending. Each shelf was made up of thousands of square cubbyholes.

Andrew strolled up to the nearest shelf and peered into it.

'Careful,' Oran said. 'Don't touch anything.' His voice echoed deeply around the enormous space.

The cubbyholes were only about a foot in width, but each one contained a mass of blackness, as if Andrew was looking through a window into space. A whirlpool of purple and blue swirled around inside of them.

'Wow,' Andrew whispered.

'What are these things?' Dan asked.

'If you look closely you will see that each slot has a name above it,' Oran said.

Andrew studied the hole nearest to him. There was a tiny silver plaque with the name '234 – Aadi Sharma, Age 43' inscribed on it. The plaque next to that said '235 Sarah Moass, Age 25' and the one next to that '236 Luke Schneider, Age 31'.

'They're called Dream Drops. Each one belongs to a different person. It's where we deposit the dreams. There's one for every single person on Earth in here.'

'But how do you fit them all in?' Dan said. 'There must be millions.'

'Nusquam magic,' Oran said, with a glint in his eyes. 'The room expands and shrinks to whatever size it needs to be. Every time someone dies, their Dream Drop disappears. And when a human is born, one is created.'

Andrew gazed up at the Dream Drops, and just as he was watching one that said 'Toshio Toyama, Age 89', it vanished before his eyes and was replaced a few seconds later with a new plaque saying 'James Knee, Age 1 minute'.

'What about Nusquarium people?' Andrew said. 'Do you make dreams for them too?'

Oran shook his head. 'Nusquarium people cannot dream. On the rare occasion that one of our kind does have a dream, it is considered to be a prophecy. Shall we go and find Poppy's Dream Drop?' Oran asked.

Andrew and Dan nodded, and followed him over to a Luguarna person, who was standing next to a long bookcase full of tatty looking leather books. The Luguarna man was wearing thin metal glasses and looked a bit grouchy.

'This is Aster,' Oran said. 'He's the oldest Luguarna person in the Factory. Aster, will you find me the depository number for Poppy Barns of London, please?' The little man stared curiously at Andrew and Dan.

'Aster,' Oran repeated. 'The number for Poppy Barns, please.'

Aster nodded, and waddled quickly along the bookcase, mumbling to himself as he went.

'Sorry about that,' Oran whispered to them. 'The Luguarna people aren't used to seeing humans around here. I suppose you must look quite strange to them.'

'*We* look strange?' Dan replied. 'They're the ones who'd need a ladder just to reach a toilet seat.'

'Remember,' Oran said, 'it is better to exist a short man than not to exist a tall,' and he smiled, leaving Dan bemused.

They hurried over to Aster, who pulled out a very large, heavy looking book and held it out between his hands.

Oran bent down, so that his face was just above the book.

'Poppy Barns,' he said, in a loud voice.

The cover snapped open, and the pages began moving as if an invisible hand was flicking through them. They stopped about halfway through the book.

Then a pair of eyes popped out from the page. And a nose. And then a mouth.

'Poppy Barns. Eighty-six-thousand-and-seventy three,' the book said in a booming voice that filled the room.

'Man alive!' Dan said, jumping backwards.

Andrew stood stunned. 'The book…it just *spoke*.'

Oran chuckled. 'Ah yes. Enchanted with Nusquarium magic and extremely rare. Thank you, Aster.'

Aster placed the book back on the shelf and glanced up at Oran through his half-moon spectacles.

'Will there be anything else?' he asked.

Andrew gasped. It was the first time he'd heard a Luguarna person speak.

'No, thank you, Aster, that'll be all,' Oran said.

Aster took one last curious look at Andrew and Dan and then waddled off.

'How come it spoke?' Andrew asked. 'The Luguarna person I mean. Tarker never speaks. He only gurgles.'

Dan snorted. 'Never mind Aster! I still can't get over the fact that a book spoke. I mean…it's a *book*.'

Oran smiled. 'The Luguarna people can all speak when they choose to. It's just that most of the time they prefer to communicate in their own language.'

Andrew felt a stab of anger.

'*What?* So when I'd wanted Tarker to open the door and save Poppy, he'd been able to understand every word that I'd been saying? That cheeky little —'

'Come on,' Oran interrupted him. 'We must deposit the dream to Poppy.'

Andrew nodded. There was no point focusing on the past; especially when he was running out of time to save his sister.

They followed Oran along a row of Dream Drops. After what seemed like forever they came to a ladder. It was on two wheels, like the kind you would find at a library. Oran dragged it along the shelf a few metres and then paused, turning to them.

'Poppy's is the third from the top. Andrew, do you want to deposit the dream?' Oran smiled and handed him the glass flask. Andrew cupped it tightly in the palm of his hand, careful not to drop it as he climbed up the ladder. When he had reached the third hole from the top, he paused, heart suddenly caught in his throat.

The Dream Drop had disappeared.

17

'It's not there,' Andrew said, heart pounding, sickness churning through his stomach. It couldn't be true...he didn't want to believe it. His mind whirled with panic as he climbed shakily down the ladder. 'She – she must be dead.'

Oran scratched his chin, confused. He turned around. 'Oh, sorry,' he said, looking guilty. 'I got the wrong shelf. It's on this one. Eighty-six-thousand-and-seventy-three. Look, here it is.'

Andrew spun around and spotted the plaque. Relief washed through him. Tears fell down his cheeks as he read it.

86,073 Poppy Barns, Age 13.

'So she's definitely alive? Thank God! Oran, don't scare me like that again,' he said, climbing up the ladder. He squeezed the stopper off the flask and poured the contents into the Dream Drop. There was a fizzling noise and a thick vapour puffed out at him, making him cough and splutter. The purple and blue whirlpool inside the hole began spinning faster and faster until the multicoloured liquid had completely disappeared. *Cool,* thought Andrew, although he wondered where it had gone.

'What now?' he asked, turning around.

'That is all we can do for the moment.' Oran smiled. 'We must hope she listens to the dream and finds somewhere safe to hide. Come. We must go and plan our attack on the Mountain of Doom.'

They walked back along the golden corridors until they reached the dining room again. Andrew sat at the spaceship-like table and watched as Oran fiddled about with the satellite dish that was placed above the oven.

'What is that thing?' he asked. But Oran didn't answer. He simply took out a large leather book from a drawer and placed it flat on the table. Andrew wondered if this book could talk too. Cautiously, he opened it. It was a photo album, but instead of photos it was full of vibrant pictures of all kinds of food. There were pictures of spaghetti bolognese, chicken nuggets, giant choc-chip cookies and bowls of ice cream. He leaned forwards, looking at the pictures longingly, and his stomach growled with hunger.

'Oran, why are you showing us this?'

'What do you fancy?' Oran asked.

'What do you mean?' Andrew said, starting to feel annoyed. 'I thought we were planning our attack on the Mountain of Doom?'

'We are.' Oran smiled. 'But we can't do it on an empty stomach, can we? Now come on, what would you like?'

Dan's eyes lit up like two light bulbs, and he grabbed the book. 'You mean you've got all this stuff here?' he said, peering around the room.

Oran shook his head. 'No, the pictures are good enough.'

'Pictures?' Dan slammed the book back down. 'I've been living off brown mush that tastes like garbage for two whole years. What good are pictures?'

'You don't understand,' Oran said, chuckling. 'Watch.' He took out a picture of a big chocolate cake and placed it under the satellite dish. He turned the knob on the oven and a strange buzzing sound started up. Andrew wondered what Oran could possibly be doing, then there was a zap and a flash of light and the biggest chocolate cake that he had ever seen appeared. Andrew stared at it in amazement. It looked just like in the picture, with thick creamy icing and a glazed cherry on top.

'Wow,' Dan said, jaw dropping.

Oran smiled. 'It's called a Satebite oven. It produces human food. I thought you might like it.'

'Like it? I gotta get me one of these babies,' Dan said, staring at the contraption in wonder.

Oran took a knife out from a drawer and began slicing the cake into pieces. He handed them each a huge chunk. It tasted wonderful, and Andrew wolfed his down within seconds.

'Can it make fish and chips?' Dan asked, eyes gleaming. 'You know, the kind you get from a chippie?'

'Yeah, and pizza,' Andrew added, licking his lips. He hadn't realised how hungry he was until now.

'Of course it can,' Oran said. He began putting different pictures under the Satebite oven and Andrew watched as a banquet of food magically appeared before his eyes. He washed it all down with a can of cold coke, relishing the feeling of the liquid wetting his parched throat.

'Right,' Oran said. 'Now you are fed and watered, we must plan our route to the Mountain of Doom. Obviously Vesuvius and his army of Shadowmares will be expecting us, so we need to be ready for them.'

Dan gulped. 'You think they'll be waiting?'

'Most definitely.' Oran nodded.

'But how do you kill a Shadowmare?' Andrew asked.

'They can't be killed,' Oran said. 'They're Letchians. But we can trap their soul inside one of these.' He lifted up an object that looked like a simple glass bottle. 'It's called a soul-catcher. When the stopper is removed it acts as a vacuum for their spirit. Of course, they'll fight all they can to avoid it. So it's best to use when they are already injured.'

'Awesome,' Dan said, studying the bottle. 'But how do we injure them?'

'I'll come to that part in a moment,' Oran said.

Andrew felt hope rise in his stomach. 'Will it work on Vesuvius too?'

'Unfortunately not,' Oran said gravely.

'Then what will work?' he asked, but Oran coughed and glanced away, suddenly awkward. Andrew feared he knew what that meant – perhaps there was nothing that could stop Vesuvius. Or perhaps Oran didn't know how.

'I have my own plan of how we're going to get past Vesuvius, which I'll explain before we leave.'

'But —'

He pressed on loudly, before Andrew could

interrupt. 'Now, when we get inside the mountain, we'll have plenty of beasts to fight. The Mountain of Doom is full of creatures and some are pretty terrifying. I suggest on our journey we rely mainly on these.' He emptied a bag onto the table and a pile of items tumbled out. A few of them were bottles containing colourful liquids. There was an object shaped like a dagger, except it was glowing bright blue.

'What are —'

'Weapons,' Oran said, anticipating the question. 'I inherited most of them from my parents. I also have some potions that Tiffany made for me. They're extremely dangerous, so no touching unless I say so, OK?'

They nodded.

'Andrew, I feel I must warn you. You may find your abilities becoming stronger the more Vesuvius searches for you. Unfortunately, there isn't time to train you to control them, so it may come unexpectedly. It could be dangerous for all of us, so try and keep your emotions in check. We don't want any accidents.'

Andrew didn't like the sound of that. He hated the thought of not being in control. 'Why?' he said, noticing the fear in his own voice. 'What do you think

I'm capable of?' He didn't want to hurt anyone, but what if he couldn't help it?

'I am not certain at this point. The important thing is to remain level-headed.'

Oran glanced at the grandfather clock. It was almost 2 am. 'Come, you had better get a few hours' sleep whilst you still can. Tomorrow is going to be extremely dangerous. You will need all the rest you can get.'

They followed Oran out of the dining room and along the brightly lit corridor until they reached a winding staircase made entirely of glass. It looked so fragile, as if it was made from ice. Andrew was afraid to walk on it at first, thinking its delicate structure might break under his weight, but to his surprise it remained intact.

They reached the corridor at the top of the stairs, where everything was white and gold, like the rest of the Factory. There were glass statues of unicorns and elves, and other imaginary creatures that Andrew had only ever thought existed in fairy tales, lined up against the walls. Although after seeing the fairies earlier that day, he suspected that the word 'imaginary' probably didn't have much meaning in a place that created dreams.

'Unicorns are the ultimate dream creature,' Oran

said fondly. A unicorn hair makes the perfect dream. The other creatures are all important as well of course, in their own individual ways.'

Andrew stared up in wonder at the glittering chandeliers that hung from the ceiling, illuminating the glass statues with an iridescent glow. They continued along the corridor until they came to a fountain spraying golden water. Intrigued, Andrew stopped and dipped his finger in the cool liquid. It smelt sweet and delicious, so he tried some.

'Ummm, honey,' he said.

Dan tasted some too.

'That isn't honey. It's chocolate, you numbnut.'

'Chocolate hey? That's funny, I always taste peanut butter,' Oran said, smiling.

Andrew and Dan looked at him.

'Huh?'

'It's whatever you want it to be.' Oran laughed. 'This is the Dream Factory after all.'

He stopped outside two frosted glass doors. 'These are your rooms. There's a bathroom inside each where you can have a wash. I'll see you in the dining room bright and early tomorrow morning,' Oran said, and then disappeared back along the corridor and down the snaking staircase.

Andrew turned to Dan.

'If only Poppy could see this place. She'd love it.'

'She will, mate,' Dan said with a smile. 'Once we've saved her.'

'Strange day we've had. I feel like everything that I thought I knew was completely wrong.'

'I know what you mean. If someone had tried telling me yesterday that talking books, biting fairies and strange satellite ovens existed, I would have told them to go see a doctor. Now, Oran could tell me that the laws of gravity were wrong and I'd probably believe him.'

Andrew sighed. 'Thanks for not letting Oran know about my fear. I owe you one.'

Dan shrugged. 'That's alright, mate. I still reckon you should tell him, but if it wasn't for you, I don't think I'd even be here right now, so I guess we're even-Stephen.'

'I wouldn't say that. We haven't got back home yet.'

Dan nodded, frowning. 'Which is why we need to rescue Poppy as fast as we can. Who knows, maybe then we can work out a way to stop Vesuvius from releasing your fear.' He fiddled with the triangular key around his neck. It glinted in the light.

'How come you're still wearing that thing?' Andrew asked.

'I dunno. I guess I forgot to take it off. I'll give it to Oran tomorrow.' He opened the door to the bedroom. 'G'night, man.' He grinned. 'Don't let the fairy bugs bite.'

'Night, Dan.' Andrew laughed, opening the door to his own room.

Inside, there was a cloud-like mattress hovering inches above the carpet. He prodded it cautiously with his finger. It felt like cotton wool. It had several pillows at one end and a large dreamcatcher hanging from the ceiling above it. *Was this his bed?* At the other end of the room was an en-suite bathroom.

Finally, he thought. *I can have a wash.* He pulled off his dirty pyjamas and took a shower, scrubbing the layers of grime off his skin. Afterwards, he climbed into bed, sinking into the warmth of the clean, fluffy mattress. He thought about his sister all alone in the Mountain of Doom. *What trials would the day ahead bring?* he wondered. But he could hardly keep his eyes open. The pillows were big and soft, and within minutes of his head touching down on them, he drifted into a deep, dream-filled sleep.

18

Andrew woke to a stream of light filtering through the shutters over the window. His body ached with exhaustion. All he wanted was more sleep, but then he remembered Poppy, and he jumped out of bed. He walked apprehensively over to the window, and ripped open the shutters.

The breath caught in his throat as he stared at the unfamiliar setting. The sky was a blanket of violet, shards of lilac breaking through it like the fragmented glow of a spotlight. The trees and shrubbery were mostly blue. All Andrew could see for miles were black rocky mountains, positioned like giant pieces of charcoal against the horizon, and covered in a thick covering of pink snow. He ran straight next door and shook Dan awake, who grunted like a pig.

'Ughhh! What time is it?'

'Time to get up,' Andrew said, pulling open the shutters on his window and letting purple light flood in. Dan's bedroom looked exactly the same as Andrew's, with a cloud-like bed and golden walls, reflecting the eerie light.

'Wow,' Dan said, coming up behind Andrew and peering out of the window. 'It looks so strange. As if a child's coloured in the landscape with all the wrong crayons.'

'It's a whole new world out there, with completely different rules. I bet we haven't even heard of half the creatures we're going to have to face today,' Andrew said gravely.

Dan hesitated, biting his nail. 'Andrew, will you do me a favour?'

'Of course. Anything.'

'If I die today…will you let my foster parents know that I love them?'

'You're not going to die,' Andrew said firmly. 'We're in this together. Oran too. He's not going to let anything happen to you.'

'But just in case? Please, I've never told them. I want them to know.' He was looking at Andrew with such serious eyes, full of desperation. Andrew swallowed hard. The reality was starting to sink in; they might not make it back alive.

He nodded, and placed a hand on Dan's shoulder.

'Yeah, mate, I'll tell them. Come on, let's go.'

They made their way downstairs to the kitchen

where Oran was busy putting pictures of eggs and beans under the Satebite oven. He'd made a pot of strong tea, which Andrew sat sipping gradually, turning his nose up at the taste.

'Drink it all up,' Oran said. 'It's made from a special plant in Nusquam which is very rare. It'll give you extra strength for the journey.'

Andrew wasn't sure if this was true or not. It could have been one of those things that adults sometimes told kids to make them eat stuff. His mother had once told Poppy that if she ate all her crusts her hair would turn curly like a princess. Andrew had never finished another sandwich again. He felt sad just thinking about this memory. He hoped his mum was OK. The thought of her worrying, wondering where they both were, was almost too much to bear.

He sat at the table and tried his best to force down some breakfast. He wasn't feeling particularly hungry, but he didn't know when they'd next get a chance to eat again.

The grandfather clock chimed, pulling him from his thoughts.

Andrew looked up. 'Hadn't we better get going? It's seven o'clock already.'

'Not like that,' Oran said, pointing at Andrew's bare

feet. 'You'll cut them to shreds.'

'But we haven't got any shoes,' Dan said.

Oran hurried out of the room. When he returned, he brought with him a strong smell of leather.

'I had the Luguarna people make you these in the night.' He handed Andrew and Dan a pair of leather shoes and a Poncho each, as they were still dressed in their pyjamas. 'I wasn't sure of your exact measurements, so I'm sorry if they don't fit perfectly.'

'Thanks,' Andrew said, putting on the shoes. They were brown, with black laces, but they were comfortable enough. The poncho was just a cream coloured blanket with arms and neck holes cut out of it.

'It's incredibly cold in Nusquam,' Oran said. 'So I suggest you slip them on now.'

Andrew pulled the poncho over his head, but as he was doing so, he caught sight of a green leather book on the table, which was faded and tattered around the edges. On the front was the title, *Beasts of Nusquam and How To Defeat Them*.

He glanced over at Oran, who was busy sorting through the weapons and potions, and opened the book up on a random page. There was a picture of a beast with wings and a long red tongue. It looked like a dragon except it had a row of sharp spikes running along its spine and a horn sticking out of its head. The text underneath was written in neat, blue handwriting.

The prickled Draghorn. Can be killed with a Glow Knife or a Fire Gun.

'A fire gun?' Andrew murmured. *What was that?*

He turned the page and saw another creature with three snake-like heads and a thick, scaly body with two legs. Dan was looking over his shoulder at it.

'Woooow!' he said.

'Stop that,' Oran yelled, grabbing the book from them and slamming it shut. His face turned red with fury.

'Why?' Andrew asked. 'Surely if we're going to be fighting these creatures we need to know how to do it.'

Oran nodded. 'And you will, because I will tell you exactly what to do when the time comes. But this book is mine, do you understand? You must not touch it.'

He slipped it quickly inside his bag, looking agitated. Andrew didn't understand. Why was Oran being so protective over a stupid book? It didn't add up. But he didn't push it any further. Oran was already in a bad mood, and Andrew needed him to be calm. He would just have to sneak a look when Oran wasn't looking.

'Sorry,' Oran said. 'I'm tired. I've been up most of the night preparing supplies for you two. Here,' he said, handing them both a rucksack. Inside there was a torch, blanket, pocketknife, food and a few bottles of water. Andrew slung it over his back, feeling the weight of it digging into his shoulders.

Oran passed them a soul-catcher each. 'You might also need these. The Shadowmares could be waiting outside the Factory for us.'

'What about Vesuvius?' Andrew asked. 'Won't he be waiting there too? You said you had a plan to —'

'I do,' Oran said. 'I was just about to get to that part, although I'm not sure you'll like it.'

'Why? What is it?' Andrew asked, still holding the soul-catcher tightly in his hands.

Oran's eyes flickered to the unicorn horn by his side. 'Andrew, there's not enough power in this to fully transform you, but if you combined your abilities with mine then maybe it would work.'

Andrew stared up at him. 'Maybe what would work, Oran?'

'Transforming you…into someone different. Only physically of course, so that Vesuvius doesn't recognise you.'

'Can you do that?' Dan said, eyes widening.

Oran scratched his head, frowning. 'I'm not sure. It's very difficult. It takes a lot of power. In fact, I've only ever known one other person able to do it.'

'Vesuvius?' Andrew whispered, throat dry.

Oran nodded.

'Well what makes you think that I can pull it off?' Andrew said, voice suddenly high. 'I can't control whatever this power is that Vesuvius has leaked into me.'

'Because I believe in you,' Oran said. 'More than you believe in yourself. If Vesuvius can do it, then chances are you can too. You just have to focus.'

'OK,' Andrew said. 'I'll have a go.'

Oran looked at him, his eyes narrowing with concern. 'You're sure you're OK with this? If it goes wrong, you could end up with three heads. I don't want to force you into anything.'

Andrew paused, then laughed nervously. 'If that happens, I could always get a part in a horror movie.'

Dan laughed. 'Ha, you could do that anyway. So who are you going to turn into? Someone cool like Arnold Schwarzenegger?'

'No,' Oran said firmly. 'It has to be someone that wouldn't look out of place in this world. Someone who's not likely to raise suspicion.' He chewed thoughtfully on a nail, and then put a finger in the air. 'I've got it. One of my workers, a Luguarna person. It makes perfect sense that I would bring one with me.'

Dan roared with laughter. 'Ha, Andrew, you're going to look like a right freak!'

Andrew thought of the little men with bright pink skin and fish-like mouths, and he wondered what would happen to him if it didn't work…or even worse, if it did, and he had to spend the rest of his life as a Luguarna person…

19

Andrew bit his lip. 'How long will it last?'

'Oh not long…if all goes to plan. A few days at the most. I think it'll wear off quite quick. You're not as powerful as Vesuvius.'

'And if it doesn't go to plan?'

Oran shrugged. 'A little longer. Perhaps a year or ten.'

'*Ten?*' Andrew said. Then he thought about the alternative and what would happen to his twin if he didn't do it. 'Alright, let's get on with it.'

Oran picked up his unicorn stick. 'Very well. Now it's all up to you, Andrew. I'll do my best to transfer my powers, but you'll have to do the majority of the work yourself. Concentrate on becoming a Luguarna person. As hard as you can, do you understand? That's all you have to do.'

Andrew nodded. He wasn't sure he really understood, but all he wanted was to get to Poppy. He looked on nervously as Oran lifted up the unicorn stick and the pearly white spirals began glowing and shimmering, filling the room with a brilliant light. Dan watched avidly from behind.

OK, Andrew thought. *I can do this.* He shut his eyes and imagined his skin turning red, his mouth forming into fish lips, his nose flattening into a squashed gooseberry, and his body shrinking to three feet tall. He wasn't sure anything was happening at first. He could feel his skin tingling all over, but when he heard Dan gasp in amazement, he opened his eyes, holding his breath.

'Did it work?'

Dan put a hand over his mouth, laughing. 'Did it? You look like a monk who's forgotten his suntan lotion.'

Oran put down his unicorn stick and reached out his giant hand to touch Andrew's bald head.

'Andrew, it's amazing,' he said. 'Your powers are more incredible than I ever imagined.'

'Thanks,' Andrew said, pride sweeping through him. He gazed down at his pinkish skin and tiny legs in amazement. He could hardly believe it had worked. *Had he really done this? Or had Oran's unicorn horn done most of the work for him?* He rolled up his pyjama bottoms, which were now way too long for his stumpy legs.

'Come on,' Oran said, as he moved towards the front door. 'We need to get going. Ready?'

Andrew and Dan looked at each other and nodded.

'Good. You'll need to be.'

They stepped outside into a sudden blast of icy wind. It buffeted against Andrew's body as he fought to stay on two feet. He turned to protect his face from the cold sting, and gasped as he caught sight of the huge Factory, which towered into the sky like something out of a fairy tale. It had hundreds of windows; some of them stained glass, and golden turrets and spires that pierced the purple clouds. He thought of the Nightmare Factory deep underground and shivered. He was glad to be out of that place. *But what about the others?* He had been so busy worrying about his sister that he hadn't stopped to think about all the kids who were still trapped down there.

'Oran, what'll happen to the other kids in the Nightmare Factory?' he asked. 'Peter Twelve Taps and Rhyming Rita and all the rest. We can't just leave them there.'

Oran frowned. 'I'll think of something. But let's just deal with one thing at a time, shall we? Keep your eyes peeled for Shadowmares.' He pulled out a map and buried his nose in it.

As he did so, a black shape darted between the trees. It was a flash of blackness, gone before Andrew could really get a proper look at it, but there was no mistaking the creature's cruel red eyes.

'Oran,' Andrew gulped. 'There's one in the trees.'

Oran nodded, and slowly raised his unicorn stick. Andrew scanned the trees again, careful not to make any sudden movements.

'Over there,' he whispered, pointing at two sets of glowing blood-red eyes from within the branches.

Two Shadowmares came floating out of a small grove of blue trees and then raced towards them through the air.

'Stay back,' Oran warned, as he brandished his unicorn horn at them, which was now emitting a bright pearly glow. The Shadowmares continued floating forwards. Andrew felt the coldness engulfing his body, weakening his muscles. He could barely stand up.

Suddenly, a ray of purple light shot out from the tip of Oran's Unicorn horn. The Shadowmares wailed in pain as the light hit them, sending them flying backwards onto the ground. Andrew stared in amazement.

'Boys! Open the soul-catchers,' Oran yelled.

Snapping back to life, they quickly pulled the stoppers out of the soul-catchers.

A high-pitched wailing noise filled the air as the Shadowmares were sucked into the bottles in two thin ribbons of black smoke. When the soul-catchers were completely full, all that remained were two skeletons lying on the floor. Andrew shoved the stopper back on the bottle, and then collapsed onto the ground.

'Mate, that was unreal!' Dan said, clutching the soul-catcher in his hands as if it was a grenade. 'What should I do with this thing?'

'Give them here,' Oran said, taking them and putting them inside his bag. 'I'll dig a hole and bury them later. We don't want Vesuvius finding them.' He took the map back out. 'We need to press on. If we head north we should be able to go up and over the mountains and arrive straight at the Mountain of Doom.'

Andrew gazed over the long stretch of colourful vegetation. The rocky skyscrapers ahead of them were so tall that they sent a long shadow over everything in sight. There was a wide lake at the foot of the mountains, reflecting the trees like a mirror, but from here it looked like a tiny dot. He swallowed as he realised how far away they were.

'How long will it take to get there?' he asked. He was worried about his new Luguarna legs. They were so short and stumpy, and it was hard to balance on them.

'How long is a piece of string?' Oran replied.

Andrew rolled his eyes. 'Well haven't you ever been there?'

'I rescued some children from the Mountain of Doom once before, but it was a long time ago.'

Andrew nodded. He felt better knowing that Oran had saved children before. It gave him some hope.

'Listen, the faster we walk, the sooner we'll get there,' Oran said. 'There's a short cut of course, which leads around Nusquam Town, but this is a game of wits and that is exactly what Vesuvius expects us to do. It'll be packed full of Shadowmares by now. You may be disguised as a Luguarna person, but we're not. Believe me, it'll be safer to take the longer route around.' He hurried forwards, and Andrew and Dan struggled to keep up with him.

They walked across the hilly ground, populated with fiery orange shrubs, and bright blue and pink flowers. The colours were so vibrant, that they looked as if they belonged in a cartoon. Andrew sniffed the air. It smelt like candy. He reached out his hand to touch a pretty red flower, as if in a trance.

'Don't!' Oran warned him. 'Some of the plants here are extremely dangerous. They give off an alluring scent to trap their enemies, and then ensnarl them with their teeth.'

'*Teeth?*' Dan echoed, backing away. Andrew looked at the flower again, and realised that the edges of its petals were actually shaped like razorblades. He sidestepped another row of sweet smelling plants, careful not to get too close.

Eventually they came to a path leading up to the mountains, which was cut with tall trees, their bright blue leaves masking the daylight like an enormous umbrella. The mountain was extremely steep, and pink snow was falling over everything like a thick layer of frosted icing.

'How much further?' Dan moaned. 'I've been locked in a cell for two years. I'm not used to exercising.'

'No, but your mouth is,' Andrew laughed.

'Hard to tell,' Oran said, gravely. 'But I'd say at least another day of walking. We need to up the pace if we're going to get to Poppy before she —' his voice trailed off, but Andrew knew what he was about to say.

'Before she dies?' he said, swallowing the lump in his throat. He marched forwards.

They reached the foot of the first mountain, and began hiking up the slope, cutting through paths and tunnels where they could. Andrew noticed some bright vines, which twisted and coiled as the three of them crept past. They were glowing like lava lamps against the black terrain, as if they were made from some sort of radioactive material.

Andrew stepped back, accidently treading on one. It hissed at him like a snake, spitting venom from its stem. The venom hit the ground, narrowly missing Andrew's chubby Luguarna ankle, and burnt away a small patch of mountain beside it.

'What is that stuff, *acid*?' Andrew said, moving his foot away.

'Similar,' Oran said with a smile. 'Just be careful.'

Dan let out a tiny shriek as a giant bird flew above them and dived down, beak open wide like a pair of garden shears.

'Help!' Dan screamed, grabbing Andrew's arm. 'It's going to attack me.'

The bird had its eyes fixed on a bug next to Dan's foot and within seconds it had scooped the huge grub into its mouth and was off again into the dusky sky.

Dan let out a nervous laugh.

'What?' he said, unlatching himself from Andrew. His cheeks had turned a bright shade of red. 'I was just testing your reactions.'

'Sure,' Andrew said, raising his eyebrows and grinning. They carried on. Andrew could feel his whole body aching. The soles of his feet were sore and blistered. He glanced down at his makeshift shoes, which were coming apart at the seams.

'Oran, I think your Luguarna people should stick to making dreams from now on. These shoes are falling apart.'

Oran laughed. 'You may be right.'

'How much longer?' Dan asked in a whiney voice. 'My legs feel as if they're about to drop off.'

Andrew coughed loudly. 'Excuse me, but my legs are *half* the size of yours. How do you think I'm coping?'

Oran laughed. 'It's not far now. In fact it's getting dark. I think we should stop, wait until it's light again.'

'About time, I think I have trench foot,' Dan said, perching on a rock. He took off his shoes and began examining his feet.

'Do you even know what trench foot is?' Andrew said, shaking his head. 'Oran, we can't stop now. You said yourself we're almost there. Why don't we just carry on? We have our torches.'

'Because it is far too dangerous,' Oran said. 'We could slip or fall to our deaths. Not to mention freezing to death.'

It was true. The continuous snowfall was blanketing everything, making it impossible to keep a steady footing.

'I don't care,' Andrew said. 'Think about my sister. Think about what *she's* having to face right now.'

'If she's got any sense she will have listened to our dream and found a safe hiding place,' Oran said, taking a swig of water. There was a fierce howling noise from somewhere in the distance. 'And we should probably do the same.'

'No, we have to —'

'Please, Andrew,' Dan interrupted him. 'I can't carry on. My feet are killing me.'

Andrew could tell he wasn't just being melodramatic. Huge marble-sized blisters had formed on his feet, turning yellow, and ready to pop.

He sighed.

'Oh, all right. So where do we hole up for the night?'

'I know of a small burrow in the mountain not far from here. It'll offer us protection from any passing predators,' Oran said, moving off again.

Dan jumped up. 'What predators?' he said, just as another howl blasted through the night air.

Andrew spun around, but he couldn't see anything in the dark.

'Claw Rippers, Mountain Growlers, Two Bellied Bears, Snort-munches. All sorts of terrifying beasts native to Nusquam.'

Dan frowned. 'But if those sorts of creatures exist here, then what sort of things will we find *inside* the Mountain of Doom?'

Oran opened his mouth in reply, but Dan quickly put a hand up to stop him. 'Actually, don't answer that. I'm not sure I want to know.'

They stumbled slowly along until they came to a small cave in the mountainside. It could have been naturally formed, but it looked as if someone had purposely dug it out years before. Inside, the hollow was extremely low. Oran had to crouch to avoid hitting his head. He pulled a blanket from his bag and laid it on the ground. Andrew and Dan did the same with theirs.

'I'll keep watch while you two get some sleep,' Oran said.

Andrew's mouth was dry and sticky. He grabbed

a bottle of water and gulped it down thirstily. Then he lay down on the hard floor next to Dan, the muscles in his legs twitching and throbbing. He just couldn't seem to drift off. The wind was whistling and howling outside, bringing ice-cold waves of air into the cave.

Dan shivered. 'Brrrr! It's freezing in here.'

'Exactly what I was thinking,' Oran said, stroking his beard. 'I'll go and fetch us something we can burn.' He got up to leave, but must have forgotten how tall he was because he bashed his head on the ceiling.

'Fender's feather!' he yelped, clutching his head. Andrew noticed that Oran often liked to use this phrase when he got upset.

'Are you OK?' he asked, trying not to smile.

'Fine,' Oran replied, face pink with embarrassment. 'Just a little…dizzy, that's all.' He got onto all fours and began crawling out of the cave.

'Oran, stay there, I'll go,' Andrew said.

Oran looked at Andrew with his hand to his head, soothing the bump. 'Are you sure?'

'Yeah, just tell me what I'm looking for.'

'Look for the big orange plants that grow up the sides of the mountain. They'll burn slowly and will last us the night.' He paused. 'You will be careful, won't you?'

'Yeah, yeah,' Andrew said, grabbing his torch. 'I will be.'

'I'll go with him,' Dan said, jumping up.

'Thanks,' Andrew said. He was glad that he wouldn't be alone.

They left the cave together, out into the darkness of the night. Their torches provided little light in the storm of thick snow.

'Look, what about these?' Andrew said, moving towards some orange plants that were growing nearby the cave entrance. 'They're what Oran was talking about, right?'

'Yeah, I think so.'

He started slashing at them with a knife, while Dan carried what he could back to the cave. Suddenly one of the plants started hissing and growling at him. He went to take another swing but it pushed him back forcefully with its leaves, as if it was alive. Andrew had not realised how close he was to the mountain ledge and he stumbled backwards, losing balance. Then he was falling, the air rushing past his ears. Mountain, sky, trees all blurring into one. Falling to an almost certain death. And then…

THUD!

He hit the ground.

He opened his eyes. Unbelievably, he was still alive. He tried to get back up but a searing pain shot through his ankle. 'Ow!' he yelled, collapsing to the ground again.

'Andrew,' he heard Dan's faint voice yell from above. 'You alright?'

'Yes,' Andrew replied. 'But I've hurt my ankle. I can't walk.'

'Stay there,' Dan said. 'I'm going to get Oran.'

Andrew snorted. *Stay there? What else am I supposed to do with a twisted ankle?*

In the process of falling, Andrew had dropped the torch. If he could just find it, then maybe he could see how bad his ankle was. He felt around the ground with his hands. There was something round and hard to the side of him… *Got it!* But there was something else there too – something soft and hairy underneath the torch. Underneath him.

A loud grumbling sound rumbled from above him. Andrew panicked and flicked the switch on the torch, a stream of yellow light flooding out from it. He pointed it at the ground and then reeled in shock.

Andrew was lying on an enormous brown and hairy foot, with great big claws the size of his legs. Slowly, Andrew moved the torch further up the creature's body, past the hands and more claws, until he reached a chest, where the hair seemed to taper off into pasty grey flesh from there upwards. A thick, bristly neck sat on muscular shoulders almost three meters in width – and then there was the head.

Andrew felt his lips tremble as he focused on the beast's blue eyes, set into crumpled flesh, which was pulled around the nose like papier mâché. Some skin sagged around the right eye, making it appear half shut. There were no lips around the creature's mouth, which made the huge set of teeth appear more pronounced. The creature roared an almighty, gut-wrenching howl and Andrew shuffled off its foot and onto the ground, edging back as far as his ankle would allow him. He sat staring up at the beast, which growled fiercely again. Then, as Andrew began to move further away, the creature roared and lunged forwards, opening its gaping mouth like a great big pit. Andrew froze and shut his eyes, waiting for the huge fangs to come crashing down on him…

20

He waited. Nothing happened. No pain, no huge teeth ripping him to pieces. Andrew opened one eye. The beast was still there, inches away from him, but it was swaying from side to side, as if in some sort of a trance. He opened the other eye and turned around, pointing the torch. Dan and Oran were stood behind him – they must have found another way down to him. Andrew stared in disbelief. Oran's unicorn horn was glowing like a red-hot poker, somehow enchanting the beast, which was rocking back and forth, cooing and dribbling like a baby. Andrew looked up just as a lump of green goo dribbled out of its nostril and came crashing down towards him. He rolled out of the way, but not before some of it splashed onto his face.

'Eww! Gross,' he said, wiping the sticky liquid off with his poncho. It left a slimy film on his skin. Andrew didn't care though; he was too busy staring at Oran, hypnotising the beast with his glowing unicorn horn.

'Andrew, this spell isn't going to hold forever. Can you walk at all?' he said, sweat pouring down his face. Andrew tried to stand up and felt another burning pain tear through his ankle.

'Not easily,' he admitted.

'Then Dan will have to help you.'

'Say what?' Dan glanced uncertainly at the huge beast and then back at Andrew, who was sitting underneath it clutching his ankle.

'No way. I'm not going near that thing.'

'Please, Dan!' Andrew said. 'I can't move.'

Dan sighed. 'Fine, but if I get eaten alive I want it on your conscience,' he said, pointing a finger at Andrew.

Andrew nodded quickly, putting his arm around Dan's shoulders and letting him carry most of his weight. Together they climbed the path back up to the cave, getting as far away from the beast as possible.

'Thanks, Dan,' Andrew panted. 'I owe you big time.'

Dan grinned. 'Yeah, you do. You're even heavier as a Luguarna person. So is this the second time I've helped save your life, or the third?'

'Don't push it,' Andrew said. He smiled and wiped some of the beast's snot onto Dan's face. Dan groaned and pulled away.

'What'd you go and do that for?' he said, and Andrew began laughing.

With Dan's help, they made it back up to the hollow unharmed. Oran appeared minutes later, looking sweaty and exhausted.

'You do realise how stupid that was?' he said, propping his unicorn stick up against the cave and wiping his face with his hands.

Andrew turned to look at Oran. 'What?'

'Cutting a Glowing Growler. You know? The bright orange plants, which grow in between the mountain bushes? They have tentacles for leaves. Everybody knows not to cut them down!' He bit his lip. 'I told you all of this, didn't I?'

Andrew and Dan shook their heads. 'No,' Andrew said, bluntly. 'You definitely didn't.'

Oran looked embarrassed for a second. 'Oh, well I meant to,' he said. 'Anyway, no harm done. You didn't hurt yourself too badly, did you? And the Flesh-gobbler didn't eat you either. Quite a result really.'

'Flesh-gobbler?' Dan said, looking worried.

'Yes, they love to feast on the flesh of humans. It was lucky that you were disguised as a Luguarna person, Andrew. It could obviously smell you, but your appearance probably confused it. They'll usually rip a person to shreds within seconds.'

'Nice,' mumbled Dan. 'Can you say something else to make us feel at ease? I don't feel quite afraid enough.'

Oran pulled a lighter from the bag of supplies and lit the small pile of plants that Andrew and Dan had collected. They erupted into an energetic blaze, and burned quickly, filling the place with a thick smoke. Andrew found himself coughing and moved as near to the back of the cave as possible, afraid of getting too close.

'What's wrong with him?' Oran asked.

'He's afraid of fire.'

'I was thinking,' Andrew said, pulling the poncho tightly around himself.

'Oh no,' Dan said. 'We all know what happens when you do that.'

Andrew scowled at him. 'Shut up. I mean, apart from the Shadowmares, surely there's going to be something at the entrance to the mountain stopping us from just strolling in?'

Oran nodded. 'There is. There's a big iron gate.'

'A gate? To the mountain?' Dan said. 'Why would there be a gate?'

'Vesuvius put it there years ago to stop me from saving the children.'

'Then how are we supposed to get past it?' Andrew asked.

Oran stopped throwing twigs into the fire and looked up.

'I have a plan.'

'Oh…? Care to share it?' Dan said.

Oran smiled. 'The Flesh-gobbler. We'll take it with us. They're incredibly powerful creatures. It can knock down the gate for us.'

'Right,' Dan said. 'That's reassuring to hear. 'Cos I thought you were going to say something daft.'

Andrew felt his insides sink. 'Oran, are you sure you didn't hit your head a bit too hard? How exactly do you suggest we capture a beast that size? And why do you think it's going to just stroll into the mountain and knock down a gate for us?'

Oran looked at them, his mouth twitching at the sides. 'I didn't say capture.'

'Then…?'

'Flesh-gobblers have a very strong sense of smell,' he explained. 'They're hunters. They sniff out their prey just like dogs do. Human blood is rare around here, so when they sniff some out, they'll do anything to have it.'

Dan looked anxious. 'Then shouldn't we be getting as far away from here as possible?'

'Don't worry,' Oran said. 'A Flesh-gobbler would never fit inside a cave this small. Anyway, we can use it to our advantage. If we leave a trail of blood from here to the mountain, then we can hide and wait for the Flesh-gobbler to turn up, which it surely will, and hopefully it'll knock down the gate in order to get to the blood.'

'That's stupid,' Andrew said, tossing a stone against the wall. 'I mean, no offence, Oran, but it seems like a bit of a long shot to me. Why can't you just use your magic stick again?'

'It's not a magic stick,' he growled. 'It's an ancient unicorn horn, and I can't just use it whenever I feel like it. Once power has been drawn, it takes time to restore itself again. And thanks to you two, it's all used up for now.'

Andrew bit his lip. 'Oh,' he said. 'The Flesh-gobbler idea sounds like an awesome plan then.'

'I reckon so too,' Dan said.

'You do?' Oran beamed, cheering up a bit.

'Yes, but we're not using my blood.'

'Well we can't use mine either,' Oran said.

Andrew sighed. 'Let me guess. Nusquarium blood tastes like mouldy brussel sprouts?'

'That's right.' Oran nodded. 'How did you know?'

Andrew sighed. 'Just a lucky guess.' He was starting to think Nusquarium people had all the luck. 'It's fine anyway – we can use mine. It's my fault that we're having to do this in the first place.'

Dan seemed to relax a little. 'That's what I thought. I mean, it's not because I'm scared or anything.'

Andrew smirked. 'No, of course it isn't.'

Oran chucked the last of the broken twigs into the fire, making it spark upwards. 'That's settled then. Now, let's get some sleep. Tomorrow's going to be a long, hard day, and take it from me, the Flesh-gobbler will be the least of our worries.' He pulled a small dreamcatcher out from the bag of supplies.

'Mustn't forget this,' he said, smiling as he attached it to the ceiling of the cave. He lay down, clutching the green leather book tightly between his arms. Andrew watched him, still wondering what could possibly be so important about it. His plan was to stay awake and prise it out of Oran's hands when he was sleeping, but he was so exhausted from their journey, that he found himself falling asleep within minutes of lying down.

21

As morning approached, light bled through the darkened sky in purple veins of sunlight, filling the cave with an eerie glow. Andrew opened his eyes – wondering where he was. Dan was beside him, fast asleep. Oran was nowhere to be seen.

He glanced at his bright red skin and short, stumpy legs, and jerked backwards.

What the…?

Then he remembered. He was still disguised as a Luguarna person. He thought about his sister, alone in the Mountain of Doom, and Dan's words came ringing back at him. *'Full of beasts and creatures from our worst nightmares. Everyone who enters there winds up dead within a matter of hours.'* Poppy had been there two whole days now. What if she was already dead?

'Get up! We've got to leave,' he said, shaking Dan awake.

Dan groaned, and sat up, rubbing his eyes.

'Where's Oran?' Andrew said, walking towards the

cave entrance. He was surprised to find that his ankle was no longer hurting. The swelling had subsided and the bruising was completely gone. He jumped up and down on the spot, testing it out.

No pain. Nothing.

Strange – he'd hurt it pretty badly, but now it felt almost *stronger* than before, like nothing could break it. He turned to Dan.

'It healed itself overnight, while I was sleeping.'

'That's weird. Perhaps it was the herbal tea that Oran gave us before we left,' Dan suggested. 'He said it would make us stronger.'

'I guess,' Andrew said. He bounced up and down a few more times.

'Marvellous,' Oran said, making Andrew jump. He turned around to find Oran holding a pile of firewood. 'Your abilities are starting to show more, and you're subconsciously starting to control them. You've obviously developed Vesuvius's talent to heal yourself.'

Andrew felt himself blush.

'Really?' Dan said. 'Cool.'

Oran lit a match to the pile of firewood, and orange flames rose high into the air. Andrew shuffled back hesitantly. He'd rather freeze than sit by a fire. He watched from the back of the cave as Oran sat down and began rifling through his bag of supplies.

'What are you doing?' Andrew asked. 'We've already spent enough time in this stupid cave. We need to leave and save Poppy.'

'Wait,' Oran said.

He pulled out his pocketknife and began sterilising it in the fire. Andrew wondered what he was doing, before he remembered their plan to lure the Flesh-gobbler to the mountain.

'Do you want to do it or shall I?' Oran asked, walking over to him.

'You can,' Andrew said, holding out his arm for Oran to cut with the knife. 'Wait. What are we going to do with the blood?'

Dan stopped staring and started rummaging through his own bag of supplies. He pulled out an empty water bottle and handed it to Oran.

'Here, you can use this if you like.'

Andrew shut his eyes expecting it to hurt like hell, but was surprised when Oran only made a small prick in his finger. Nonetheless, blood oozed from it like juice from an orange and trickled onto the floor. Slowly, Oran drained some blood from Andrew's finger into the bottle.

'Are you all right? You don't feel faint or anything do you?'

'Nope,' Andrew said. He'd seen enough blood in horror movies not to be fazed by it. It was Dan who looked as if he was about to pass out.

When Oran had finished, Andrew sucked on the tip of his finger. The blood had a strange metallic taste to it. He couldn't understand why the Flesh-gobbler would find it so appealing. The tiny slice in his stumpy finger was barely visible now, and when Andrew looked closer, he could see the wound sealing up before his eyes.

'That's so unfair,' Dan said, watching him enviously. 'Why couldn't I have been born a Releaser?'

'Sure,' Andrew grunted. 'If you want a mad man like Vesuvius after you.'

Dan nodded. 'You make a good point, mate.'

Oran put the knife back in his bag and got up to leave. 'Come on.' He tapped his unicorn horn on the floor impatiently. 'We have things to do and a child to save. It's not too much further.'

They left the cave and set out on foot again. Andrew was dismayed to find that Oran's definition of 'not far' turned into six long hours. He was aching all over and he wasn't sure how much more walking he could take. He still hadn't got used to his new Luguarna legs. Dan was limping beside him, red raw blisters covering every inch of his feet. The weather didn't help either, with cold icy winds whipping against their skin unrepentantly.

Oran stopped every few metres and placed a drop of Andrew's blood on the ground, but there was no sign of the Flesh-gobbler behind them.

They made it over the first mountain, and approached a mountain that towered above the rest. Andrew stopped and gazed up at its black jagged shape, silhouetted against the violet sky. It could have been just his imagination but he was sure there were faces in the rock. They reminded him of the ones on Mount Rushmore, except these faces weren't of famous presidents. Instead they were sad, scared looking faces, crying out in pain.

He shuddered; this *had* to be the Mountain of Doom. The land around it was barren and black. Only the withered skeletons of plants and trees remained. There was a lake surrounding the foot of the mountain, but it looked more like a swamp, with coal black water and grey mist rising up off the surface.

The hole in the side of the mountain was like

a huge black mouth, ready to swallow up anyone who dared enter.

'Woooh,' Dan said, staring up at it.

An old and battered iron gate stretched from one side of the opening to the other, and Andrew wasn't sure if it was there to keep Oran out, or to keep the poor souls of the Mountain of Doom *in*.

'Quickly,' Oran whispered. 'Go and hide over there.' He pointed to a large rock near to the mountain opening, and Andrew and Dan hurried over, trying to be as light-footed as possible.

They watched nervously as Oran scattered the rest of the blood in a trail leading up to the gate, leaning in to sprinkle some inside.

'I didn't see any Shadowmares at the gate,' Oran said, as he tiptoed back over to them. 'Perhaps Vesuvius didn't think we'd come after all.'

'Perhaps,' Andrew said, trying to be positive, but deep down he knew this was just wishful thinking.

They began a long and tedious wait. *What's taking so long?* It had been three whole hours, and still no sign of the Flesh-gobbler.

'I don't think it's work—' Andrew said, but his voice dried mid-sentence, as an explosive sound of pounding feet started up. Everything began to shake.

Small pieces of rock flew off the mountainside and tumbled to the ground below. The Flesh-gobbler came into view along the path. Andrew stared up at its gigantic head, sagging skin swaying from side to side, teeth like sharp spikes. It stopped, bent down and sniffed the ground like a dog. Then it continued towards the mountain. The Flesh-gobbler was taking the bait. Their plan was working.

'Yes!' Andrew whispered, clenching his fists, but froze when he saw the Flesh-gobbler stop and sniff the air some more. Then, slowly, it turned in their direction.

'What's it doing?' Andrew whispered, as it clambered hungrily towards them.

'I don't know,' Oran said, honestly. 'But I think we've just become its lunch.'

22

Oran had begun to sweat. He dabbed at his brow with his sleeve. Andrew felt the colour drain from his cheeks.

'Oran, your poncho, it's got blood on it.'

There was only a tiny splash, but it was enough to confuse the Flesh-gobbler. Oran quickly tugged off his poncho and screwed it up into a tight ball. Then, he hurled it towards the mountain. It landed right next to the creature. It stopped and picked it up, sniffed for a while, and then threw it away again. The Flesh-gobbler roared, as if frustrated about which direction to carry on in. Luckily, it turned and continued towards the Mountain of Doom. Andrew allowed himself to breathe more easily, but not for long. As the Flesh-gobbler approached the entrance, roaring and beating at its chest, several pale figures in black cloaks appeared from within the darkness.

'Shadowmares,' Andrew whispered, heart pounding against his chest.

They glided towards the beast, eyes a furious shade

of red, but the Flesh-gobbler didn't seem to be taking any notice, as it fought to get to the blood. It grabbed the gate with both hands and began rattling it like a cage. When this didn't work, it stood back and took one almighty swing with its fist. The hinges on the gate started to bend, and with the second swing, it came crashing down with an enormous bang, crushing the Shadowmares beneath it. The Flesh-gobbler disappeared into the mountain.

Andrew stared, mouth open, unable to believe his eyes.

'Wow.'

'Did that just actually happen?' Dan asked, blinking rapidly.

Oran grinned. 'I think it did. I told you that Flesh-gobblers will do anything for human blood.'

Andrew shook his head in disbelief. 'That couldn't have gone any better if we'd tried. If I ever say a plan of yours is stupid again, Oran, you officially have permission to slap me.'

Oran chuckled. 'I'll bear that in mind.' They crept out from behind the rock and tiptoed closer to the mountain. Oran took the soul-catcher from his backpack and removed the stopper. He aimed it at the Shadowmares trapped under the gate. Their red eyes glowed amber like fiery embers, and then slowly began to fade. A strange black substance drifted up out of the Shadowmares' mouths and into the soul-catcher. All that remained were their skeletons.

'There,' Oran smiled, replacing the cork so that the black smoke was trapped inside. 'That was easy.'

Yes, Andrew thought with a nervous fluttering in his stomach, *a little too easy...*

Together, they ventured into the darkness of the mountain. It was pitch black, and Andrew couldn't see anything even with his torch. A damp, rotten smell lingered in the stale air, and Andrew could hear the slow drip of water.

'Be quiet,' Oran reminded them. 'The Flesh-gobbler may still be nearby.'

Oran walked in front of them, holding his unicorn stick up in defence. The glow from it was faint, and Andrew doubted if it had any power left in it at all. He could hear the Flesh-gobbler's growls getting more and more distant. And then a scratchy voice from within the darkness.

'I thought you would come.'

Andrew spun around, his torch producing a weak sliver of light. Vesuvius stepped into it, snarling. A group of Shadowmares hovered by his side. His shiny black eyes glistened with wickedness and Andrew felt his heart drop. *He should have expected this.*

'Where's the boy?' Vesuvius growled.

For a moment, Andrew forgot that he was disguised as a Luguarna person. As Vesuvius's eyes trailed over him, panic surged through Andrew.

Oran raised his stick defensively. 'He is at home, Vesuvius, where he is safe from *you*,' he said, eyes narrowing. 'You didn't really expect me to bring him here, did you?'

Andrew watched Vesuvius, and for a split second, thought he saw genuine surprise on his old, haggard face. Then his mouth twitched and he let out a dry laugh.

'He is safe nowhere, Oran. Are you forgetting something? I have his fear now.' He turned to the remaining Shadowmares. 'Come,' he ordered. 'We must find the boy. The beasts in the mountain will take care of these three.' He let out a deep cackle as he turned and glided out of the mountain, his cloak billowing after him. The Shadowmares followed, red eyes glaring as they swept past them in a rush of icy wind.

There was an uncomfortable silence. Oran's eyes fixed on Andrew's.

'Why didn't you tell me Vesuvius had your fear?' he said, angrily.

'I-I…' Andrew began. 'I wanted to. I was afraid you wouldn't help us save Poppy. I mean, you didn't want me to come here with you in the first place.'

'Yes, to protect you,' Oran said, frowning. 'But I wouldn't have let any harm come to Poppy. I know how important family is. After all, Vesuvius killed mine. Do you really think I would have let him do the same to yours?'

Andrew felt a pang of guilt sweep through him. He had underestimated Oran.

'I-I-I'm sorry,' he said, but Oran was silent, his face a terrible mixture of anger and hurt.

A howling noise echoed through the mountain.

They spun around to find three fierce looking beasts snarling back at them. They were like dogs, except four times the size, with long black bodies ending in not one, but two fierce heads. *And two more mouths to bite us with*, Andrew thought darkly, edging backwards as they snarled and growled at him, saliva dripping off their tongues.

'Oran, what the hell are those things?' Dan asked, moving away.

Oran charged forwards with his unicorn stick and

a shard of red light flew out from the end, hitting one of the creatures in the belly. It roared in agony and retreated a few steps.

'Sheefs,' Oran said, regaining his balance. 'A type of two-headed dog. But I can't remember how to kill them.' He reached and pulled the book from his bag, urgently flicking through the pages as best as he could with one hand. Andrew spotted a fourth Sheef prowling up behind Oran. He opened his mouth to shout out and warn him, but the dog launched itself onto Oran's back, ripping into his flesh like he was a piece of meat. The others, not missing their chance, also pounced and he struggled to fend them off.

'What do we do now?' Dan shouted, grabbing at Andrew's sleeve.

Andrew's mind whirled. Oran was fighting a losing battle. If they didn't do something soon, he'd be ripped to shreds. His gaze fell on his bag, contents spilled all over the floor. He ran to grab the book, flicking through the pages, trying to find anything about Sheefs that he could. He spotted a picture of the two-headed beast. He skimmed the text, until he found the sentence, 'Can be killed using a Glow Knife.'

'Look for a blue knife,' Andrew said, quickly remembering the bright blue knife he'd seen on

Oran's table. He began searching around the floor but it was pitch black, and he could hardly see a thing.

'Is this it?' Dan yelled, holding up something blue and faintly glowing.

'Yes,' Andrew said, feeling his heart rise. 'Chuck it here.'

Dan threw him the knife, and Andrew removed it from its leather case, pulling it out to reveal an even brighter glow. It filled the entire mountain with an eerie blue light. He rushed forwards, stabbing the knife into one of the Sheef's backs. Its two mouths yelped out in pain, and its body crashed to the floor with an almighty thud. The remaining three Sheefs paused, and looked up at Andrew, eyes fierce with vengeance. They let out an ear-piercing cry and then pounced on him. Andrew had to use all his strength to stay on his feet. He gripped the knife firmly in his hand, as the Sheefs opened their mouths, pink gums sliding back to reveal pointed fangs. As all six mouths snapped to reach him, Andrew ducked and plunged the knife deep into their stomachs, and one by one, they collapsed on their sides, groaning weakly.

Dan ran over to check if Oran was all right and Andrew slumped to the ground, exhausted. He lifted his head when he saw the extent of Oran's injuries. He had big red gashes all over his skin.

Andrew could hear footsteps pounding towards them. He knew exactly who was causing them: *the Flesh-gobbler.*

'The healing potion,' Oran said, in a weak, barely audible whisper. 'Bring it to me. Quickly, before the Flesh-gobbler gets here.'

'But I thought Flesh-gobblers didn't like Nusquarium blood?' Dan said.

'They don't, but if it's hungry, it might not care.'

They began scrabbling around the floor.

'Which one is it?' Andrew asked. He stared at all the bottles in desperation. He could barely see in the dim light of his torch.

'Gold,' Oran said, gasping for breath. 'Hurry!'

Andrew spotted a small bottle full to the brim with gold liquid. He rushed over to Oran, undid the lid, and handed it to him. Oran grabbed it, downing the contents.

Nothing happened for a moment, but then the bloody gashes on Oran's body began to disappear, and new pink skin formed in their place. After a while, he looked completely normal again.

'Thank you.' Oran smiled, staring into Andrew's eyes. 'I see you're back to your usual self again too.'

'Am I?' Andrew said, peering down at his human arms and legs. He put his hand to his head, and felt his familiar mop of hair. 'Hey, so I am.' He grinned. He crouched down next to Oran. 'I'm sorry I didn't tell you about the fear.'

Oran put a hand up.

'Please, consider it forgotten.' His eyes travelled to the book lying on the floor. 'When we get out of here, there is something that I must show you. It is hugely important.'

'Is it to do with the book?' Andrew asked.

Oran nodded.

'I didn't want you to see it before, but now, I know that you're ready.' He got up and collected the book and weapons, placing them back in the bag. 'But there is no time now. We must press on. If Vesuvius has your fear, he will be releasing it on the world soon. We must hurry and find your sister so that we can stop him.'

'Yeah,' Dan said. 'And before that Flesh-gobbler catches up with us.'

As much as Andrew wanted to see what was inside the book right now, he didn't argue. Saving his sister was much more important.

They hurried deeper into the mountain.

'Keep close to the sides,' Oran told them, holding his unicorn horn out in front of him. A thin sliver of light illuminated the mountain walls, which were covered in a thick green slime. Andrew gulped, taking a step back – there were human bones scattered around the floor. He took a deep breath and carried on walking, trying not to look at them. He dreaded to think who they belonged to, and how they had been killed.

Oran took out a chalk from his bag, and handed it to Dan.

'Mark our steps so that we don't get lost,' he said.

Andrew turned his head, and jumped as he saw a vampire with huge fangs and a tall collar, glaring back at him. He was hidden within a recess in the wall, so that his face was partially masked in shadows. Oran's unicorn stick glowed bright purple, and the vampire began swaying from side to side, as if caught in some sort of a trance.

'What are you doing?' Andrew asked.

'Putting it into a hypnotic state,' Oran told them. 'But my unicorn horn has very little power left. We'll have to be quick.'

They crept past the vampire, hurrying down another passage. The walls veered inwards, making it impossible to walk side by side. They reached a section where the tunnel opened up. Andrew stopped, taking a sip from his water bottle. His throat stung from the dry, stale air.

'Errm, Andrew,' Dan said, tapping him on the shoulder. 'You might not want to stop here, mate.'

Andrew looked around, lighting up the cavern with his torch.

They were surrounded by a pack of tall gangly creatures, with curling horns, and fierce red eyes, which bulged out of their elongated heads.

'What are they?' Andrew whispered.

'Cave demons,' Oran replied, holding his stick out closer towards them. 'Chances are they won't hurt us if we move slowly past.'

Andrew's eyes trailed down their thin bodies, with ribs that jutted out of their lumpy, peeling flesh, and hands that ended in long, yellow claws. He swallowed, thinking about what would happen when his fear was released and creatures like this were set free upon the world.

He edged past them until the tunnel thinned out again, too narrow for the demons to fit down.

'Where do you think Poppy is?' Andrew asked, but Oran didn't have time to answer because a storm of bats flew out at them. Andrew waved his hands above his head, trying to scare them away, but these were no normal bats. They were persistent, and unafraid, their long pointed teeth completely disproportionate to their small bodies.

'Cover yourself as much as you can,' Oran shouted. 'Trust me, you don't want to get bitten by vampire bats.'

'*Vampire bats?*' Dan said, scrabbling to pull the poncho over his head as quickly as he could. Andrew did the same, tucking his arms inside so no skin was left visible. Oran's unicorn horn didn't seem to be having any effect. He could feel the bats biting at him through the woollen material. Andrew tried to fight them off, but it was no use. They clawed through his poncho, hungry for his blood.

23

'Why isn't your unicorn stick working?' Andrew yelled.

Oran growled. 'Horn,' he corrected him. 'Unicorn *horn*. And bats are blind. They can't see the glow so it doesn't affect them in the same way that it does the other beasts.'

Andrew could just make out Oran through the material of his poncho. He was frantically searching through his bag of supplies. Finally, he pulled out a small bottle of clear liquid, opened it up and threw it at the bats. They squawked and flapped around madly, and Andrew felt their wings beating against his head as they tried to dry themselves off, finally disappearing inside the crevices of the mountain.

'What was that stuff?' Dan asked, sticking his head out from the poncho. 'Holy water?'

Oran chuckled. 'That only works in the movies. This bottle contains pollen from a mixture of Nusquarium flowers. Vampire bats can't stand the stuff, it irritates their skin.' He frowned. 'You didn't get bitten did you?'

Andrew studied the length of his arms. Even through the thick knit of the poncho, the bats had managed to draw blood. Both he and Dan had shallow red gashes all over their skin.

'Only tiny cuts,' Andrew said. 'We'll survive.'

Oran looked relieved. 'OK. Their venom is located at the back of their fangs. They need to get a good chunk out of you before…' He let his voice trail off. 'Well, you know the way the story goes.'

'What, we'd turn into vampires?' Andrew said, biting down hard on his lip. He knew the stories, but he didn't want to think about it, didn't want to think about any of the nasty creatures inside this mountain. He just wanted to find Poppy and get out of here.

They trekked deeper into the mountain.

'Poppy, where are you?' Andrew yelled, listening to his voice bounce against the stony walls.

A deep growling noise echoed in reply, and Andrew felt his whole body freeze.

'What is that?' Dan whispered.

Oran shrugged, looking worried. 'I'm not sure. Perhaps we should search in silence for a bit.'

The passage started to get wider and smaller passages forked off from the main one.

Andrew shook his head. 'It's like a maze in here. We're never going to find her at this rate. I think we should try down one of these tunnels. After all, we told her to hide, didn't we?'

'Yes,' Dan said, face brightening. 'That sounds like a good plan.' He paused, stiffening at the noise of another growl. 'Plus I don't want to hang around here and get eaten.'

Andrew turned and headed down the nearest tunnel, the others following close behind. The passage was long and narrow, and they had to move through it in single file, breaking through the thick cobwebs that draped from the ceiling. Andrew could feel them brushing against his face like strings of cotton. He paused, thinking that he saw something stirring in the shadows. He directed the beam ahead. It hadn't just been his imagination, the wall was moving! Andrew looked more closely and saw that it was completely covered in tiny spiders. Within seconds, they were all over his face. He wasn't scared, but he knew someone that would be.

'I don't think Poppy would have come down here,' Andrew said, brushing the spiders off. 'She hates creepy crawlies. We should try another tunnel.'

'Phew! I think you're right, mate,' Dan said, as they

backtracked into the main passage again. 'So which one now?'

Andrew looked hopelessly at the many tunnels on each side.

'I don't know,' he replied irritably. He was beginning to think they'd never find his sister and get out of here.

'Concentrate,' Oran told him. 'Try and think where she'd hide.'

'OK,' Andrew said, standing still for a moment and closing his eyes.

Then, from out of nowhere, he felt an overwhelming urge to turn down one of the tunnels. He couldn't explain it, but he just knew that he had to listen to his instinct. He'd never been surer of anything in his life.

'She's down here,' he said, stepping into the passage.

'How do you know?' Dan asked.

'I can't explain it. You're just going to have to trust me. Call it a twin thing.'

Without another word, Oran and Dan followed Andrew into the darkness of the tunnel. It was wider than all the others, and had plenty of cracks in the walls, perfect for someone small like Poppy to hide in. It sloped upwards in a steep incline then flattened out again after a while. There were no cobwebs to push through and better still, no sign of hellish creatures.

'This is a good tunnel,' Dan said, striding forwards. 'I like this tunnel.'

'I wouldn't speak too soon,' Oran said, as a heavy breathing sound came from up ahead.

'Oh, wow, bad tunnel. Bad tunnel! Turn back guys,' he said, rushing back past them.

'Wait a second,' Andrew said, grabbing him by the arm. He paused to listen and then walked forwards, flashing the torch around the mountain walls.

'Andrew, what are you doing? Trying to get us killed? Come on, let's get out of here. We'll try another tunnel.'

'Wait,' Andrew replied. 'I'm sure she's down here somewhere.' He moved the torch over the wall again, this time more slowly. It flashed over something pink. Andrew stared into the light, feeling his heart beating quickly against his chest. 'Poppy?' he whispered.

He stepped closer.

'Poppy!' he yelled, grinning. She was hunched into a tight ball, rocking back and forth. Andrew put a hand on her shoulder and she let out a terrified scream.

'Poppy, it's alright, it's me.'

She looked up, eyes full of terror and confusion.

'Andrew?' she said, squinting in the light of the torch.

237

'Yes.'

The creases in her forehead vanished. Her voice cracked with relief. 'I…I thought you'd never come.' She clambered out from the crack in the wall and Andrew felt her cold arms wrap around him.

'I'm sorry we took so long. Are you all right? Are you hurt?'

'I'm OK. Just tired and hungry.'

'You must have been so scared.' He took out a bottle of water from his bag and some biscuits. 'Here,' he said, handing them to her. 'Remember Oran? He helped us find you.' He moved the torch in Oran's direction.

Oran stepped into the light and gave a small wave.

'You were in my dream,' Poppy said, staring at him. 'It was so vivid. You told me to hide somewhere and not to come out. It felt so real…it was as if you were actually speaking to me.' She hesitated. 'How did you do that?'

'We'll explain later,' Andrew said. Of course, Poppy had no idea about the Dream Factory.

'Let's get out of here,' she said, glancing nervously around the tunnel.

Dan snorted. 'Believe me, we didn't plan to stay

here and have a dinner party.'

'How did you manage to avoid all the beasts for so long?' Andrew asked her.

'I don't know,' Poppy said, biting down on her lip. 'It was as if they couldn't see me. They just…seemed to ignore me.'

They started walking again.

'What? But that doesn't make any sense,' Dan said.

Poppy shrugged. 'I didn't say it made sense.' She shivered. 'This place is huge. How did you know where to find me?'

'We didn't at first,' Oran admitted. 'Then Andrew had a feeling that you'd be down this tunnel. Twins can have strange connections. You must have been sending each other unconscious signals. I suspect that's why you managed to avoid the creatures for so long. Andrew must have been unconsciously using his abilities to place a protective barrier around you.'

Poppy's eyes widened.

'What?' Andrew said. 'But that's never happened before.'

'No,' Oran agreed. 'Perhaps it only happens when the other twin is in some kind of danger.'

'Cool,' Andrew grinned. He'd heard about twin

connections before, but he'd never expected it to happen between Poppy and him.

'I got this really intense feeling that you were up here,' he said excitedly. 'But then when we got closer I knew for certain because I could hear your heavy breathing.'

'I wasn't heavy breathing,' Poppy said. 'I was trying to be as quiet as possible.'

'Then who…?' He never got to finish. A fierce growling echoed throughout the tunnel and in the darkness two green pupils appeared, staring back at them.

'Oh,' Andrew said.

'Oh indeed,' Oran whispered.

The creature stepped into the light of the torch, blinking and screwing up its eyelids. It was tall and had green scaly skin, like it had just stepped out of a swamp. Its head was a shaped like that of a tyrannosaurus rex. It had two huge horns, which at first Andrew thought were its ears. The monster didn't have any fingers, instead its arms, both as thick as tree trunks, ended in two thick claws.

They all edged backwards.

'What the hell is it?' Andrew said. As the creature turned slightly, it revealed two large wings tucked behind its back.

Oran took another few steps back. 'It's a Sepataurus,' he said. 'The single living relative of the pterodactyl. I've seen one before, you know, but this chap's only a baby.'

'It doesn't look like a baby,' Dan growled. 'It looks pretty big to me.'

The Sepataurus was probably twelve, maybe thirteen feet in height, but it stood hunched over like a gargoyle.

'You should see the fully sized ones,' Oran said with a grin.

'Thanks, Oran,' Andrew said. 'But I'd rather not. Can we leave now?'

'Wait,' Oran said, raising his unicorn horn up slowly. It glowed for a few seconds, and then went out. 'Damn,' he said. 'I was going to try and put it into a trance but I think my unicorn horn's out of power.'

'Oh, wonderful,' Dan said. 'So what are we going to do now?'

'Shhhh!' Oran said, as the Sepataurus began to creep towards them, dragging its tail along the floor. 'It probably only wants to examine us, give us a little sniff around and then be off, but you must keep silent…and very still. Any sudden movements will make the creature think you are launching an attack.'

Andrew breathed quickly as the Sepataurus bent over to sniff around his armpits like a dog. He wanted to wipe away the sweat that had accumulated on his brow, but remembered what Oran had told them: *No sudden movements*. Soon it seemed satisfied and moved onto Poppy, who stood with her eyes shut until it scuttled over to Dan. It seemed even more fascinated by him, sniffing over every part of his body.

Dan stood as stiff as a beanpole, but his bottom lip was noticeably quivering. The Sepataurus opened its mouth, a fleshy green tongue coiling outwards. Dan must have thought that the creature was about to bite him, because he let out an almighty scream and started running.

'No!' Oran shouted, but it was too late. The Sepataurus roared loudly, and raced after him like it was a game. Pouncing onto Dan, it pushed him face down on to the ground, sinking its huge fangs into his arm. Dan groaned, trying to break free, but the Sepataurus lifted its broad shoulders back, flexed its wings and dived in for the kill.

24

Oran tried his unicorn horn again. It only exuded a faint glow, but it was enough to daze the Sepataurus for a few seconds, as Dan rolled out from beneath its grip. Soon the creature was resuming control. Andrew knew he would have to act fast if he was going to save his friend from another attack. The beast roared, swinging its head about from side to side. Without thinking, Andrew took a running leap at the Sepataurus and landed on its back, gripping hold of its wings for balance.

'Andrew, catch,' Oran said, throwing a spear into the air.

Andrew caught it and quickly plunged it deep into the monster's flesh. There was a thunderous howl, and Andrew was thrown backwards onto the ground. He got straight back up again, ready to fight, but the Sepataurus roared loudly and then turned on all fours, skulking off into the shadows. Andrew let out a sigh of relief.

'Dan, are you OK?' he said, rushing over to his

friend. He felt stupid for even asking the question. Dan was still lying on the ground, wailing in pain, his arm gushing out blood.

'He's going to bleed to death if we don't do something soon,' Poppy said, pushing her way through to Dan.

Oran shook his head. 'We don't have any of the healing potion left.'

'What the hell is a healing potion?' Poppy said. She ripped a piece of material from Dan's trouser leg and wrapped it around his arm. 'This should help to stop the bleeding for a while.'

Dan smiled up at her. 'Thanks, Poppy.'

'We need to get moving,' Oran said. 'If the mother comes back for revenge, I fear we will not be so lucky.'

'Pfft!' Dan snorted. 'I wouldn't call what just happened lucky.'

Andrew helped Dan to his feet and they walked as fast as they could back along the tunnel.

'So,' he said turning to his friend with a grin. 'I think we're even now.'

Dan nodded weakly. 'I suppose we are,' he said with a fleeting smile.

They followed the chalk that Dan had drawn on the

walls, walking as fast as they could. Poppy held onto Andrew's hand, as he took the lead, still clutching the spear in case anything attacked them. Eventually a circle of light appeared as they neared the entrance of the mountain.

Andrew felt his body tense up in excitement. 'We're almost there,' he whispered.

A growling noise echoed through the mountain.

'What's that?' Poppy asked, stiffening.

'I don't want to know,' Dan muttered.

They crept forwards and saw the Flesh-gobbler. It had its wide, saggy back to them and was bent over the Sheefs' bodies, pulling bits of meat off their grisly bones.

They could have just sneaked out unnoticed, but Dan had a massive wound on his arm and Andrew knew it wouldn't be long before the Flesh-gobbler became aware of the smell of blood.

'What are we going to do now?' Dan hissed. 'I don't fancy being Flesh-gobbler dinner, or Flesh-gobbler dessert for that matter.'

Oran ran his fingers through his silvery hair, thinking hard. They all stared at him, waiting for him to come up with another genius plan.

'Just carry on as quietly as you can,' Oran said.

'Sheef blood is very poisonous. With any luck, it won't have the stomach for dessert.'

But the moment these words had left his mouth, the Flesh-gobbler looked up, sniffing the air. It stumbled towards them, huge feet pounding against the ground.

'Looks pretty hungry to me,' Andrew said, staring up at its gaping mouth. 'Quickly Oran, what's the plan?'

Oran blinked, face vacant, and then he shouted, 'Run!'

'That's it?' Poppy said. 'Just run?'

Oran nodded and began sprinting through the darkness towards the light, straight past the Flesh-gobbler. They fled outside, blinded by the sun, running for their lives. There was a huge crash from behind them and the leaves on the surrounding bushes shivered and fell to the ground. Andrew could hardly stay on his feet as the ground shook underneath him.

There was a loud grumbling sound.

Andrew spun around. The Flesh-gobbler was lying on the ground. It was clutching its stomach and rocking from side to side.

'What's it doing?' Andrew asked.

Oran stopped and stared back at it, panting hard.

'Fender's feathers! It must be the Sheef's blood. I told you it was poisonous.'

'It is going to be OK, isn't it?' Andrew asked, looking at the beast that was still rolling about on the ground, seemingly in agony. Even though the Flesh-gobbler had tried to eat him, he didn't think it deserved to die. After all, it had broken down the gate for them.

Oran nodded. 'I expect so. It's a big animal. It can take a lot. My guess is that it will just have tummy ache for a few days, which is lucky for us. It means we have time to get as far away from here as possible.'

'What about Vesuvius?' Dan said. 'Will Andrew have to disguise himself as a Luguarna person again?'

'I think we'll be OK. Vesuvius doesn't know that Andrew is with us so he'll probably be looking elsewhere, but we should all keep our wits about us, just in case.'

They carried on walking until the light faded from the sky. The past few days had taken its toll on Andrew's body, and like Dan, the skin on his feet had erupted into a million blisters, which kept on healing and then reforming again. Poppy wasn't much better. She looked pale and weak.

'You OK?' Andrew asked, putting his arm around her.

'I'm freezing cold,' she said, teeth chattering together. Oran stopped.

'I know another crevice in one of the mountains where we can rest for the night. We can light a fire and melt some snow to drink. Follow me.' They reached a small crack in the mountain, with just enough space for them to lie down. It was hardly comfortable, but Andrew was thankful for the rest all the same. He pulled the blankets over them and shared out the remaining food and water. There wasn't much left, just a few dry sandwiches and browning apples.

'So what happened once we got separated?' Poppy asked, biting into a sandwich. 'How did you send me the dream?'

Andrew began to explain all about the Dream Factory, while Oran lit a small fire near the opening of the mountain crevice, and melted some pink snow into a bottle. Andrew watched as he got out his tweezers and the strange laser device, and removed the bracelet and fear plug from Poppy's neck. She didn't complain at all, even when she blanked out for a few seconds from the pain. Andrew decided that in the last few days, she'd toughened up a lot.

'So…what kinds of creatures did you see in the mountain?' he asked, sipping from the bottle of melted snow. It didn't taste like water. It had a sweet taste, like strawberries. He licked his lips as the cool liquid slipped down his throat.

'Tons. It was terrifying,' Poppy said, eyes like big blue marbles. Andrew could have sworn he heard an ounce of excitement in her voice. 'There was this clown, not the funny kind, but the scary kind. It juggled human skulls and rode around on a tricycle. Oh and there was this beast too, even worse than the Sepataurus. It was like a cross between a werewolf and a bull. I didn't come out of my hiding place the whole time, I just stayed there watching, too frozen to move a muscle.'

'Yeah, well, at least you didn't get bitten by any of them,' Dan replied grumpily.

'How's your wound?' Andrew asked, looking at his bandaged arm.

'It hurts,' Dan replied. 'A lot.'

Oran shook his head. 'I am not surprised. What did I tell you about no sudden movements?'

Dan's bottom lip stuck out petulantly in the shadows. 'It was about to bite me, what was I supposed to do?'

'It was about to lick you,' Poppy said. 'Anyone could have seen that.'

Dan's eyes narrowed even further and he looked miserable. 'Well I didn't know that, did I?'

There was a long silence, before Dan finally spoke again. 'Erm, guys. There's something a bit weird on my arm.' He moved into the light, and Andrew saw that it was covered in green, rubbery circles.

'No way!' he whispered. 'Dan, those are *scales*.'

Oran sat up suddenly, banging his head. His expression was fearful. He didn't even seem bothered about the bump on his head. 'Scales?' he said, peering at Dan's arm. 'Oh no. This is bad. This is really, *really* bad.'

'What? Why?' Dan asked, sounding alarmed.

'I hoped this wouldn't happen. I didn't think the Sepataurus was old enough. I —'

'Spit it out,' Dan said. 'What is it?'

'When a Sepataurus reaches a certain age, it begins to release a substance in its saliva, which helps its species to reproduce.' Oran paused.

'Go on…'

'Well, whoever it infects can experience significant DNA changes, similar to the Sepataurus.'

'What?' Dan gasped. 'You mean I'm going to change

into one of those things?'

'Not exactly,' Oran replied, frowning. 'But like I said, you could develop some of its characteristic features, like scales for instance, or wings. It really depends on how your body reacts to the new DNA.' He checked through the bag of supplies, and as Andrew watched him, he suddenly remembered the book. 'I don't have any Cortizol potion with me I'm afraid, but don't worry, I've got some back at the Factory. It might reverse the effects.'

'Oh brilliant,' Dan said, with an edge of sarcasm to his voice. 'So my life as I know it depends on if this potion *might* work or not?' He tossed a rock against the floor.

'You'll be alright,' Andrew said, patting him on the back. 'And if not, well, you can always join the circus as a reptile man.'

He grinned, and Dan let out a weak laugh.

'Oh, cheers mate.'

Andrew glanced at Oran's bag again.

'Oran,' he said. 'What's in the book that you wanted to show me?'

Oran looked at him, frowning heavily. He took out the green leather book and placed it on Andrew's lap.

'Last page,' he said. 'I'm sorry I waited so long to

show you. I didn't want to burden you unnecessarily, but now Vesuvius has your fear I'm afraid I have no choice.'

What's he talking about? Andrew wondered.

He opened the book at the back and they all gasped in horror. There was a picture of Vesuvius, his mean black eyes staring out of the page at them. Andrew shivered, and began to read the handwritten text underneath.

Vesuvius – Master of the 'Nightmare Factory' is half Shadowmare, half Nusquarium and remains the most powerful creature in Nusquam. His aim is to enter the real world and create the 'ultimate' nightmare for mankind, turning people's worst nightmares into reality. He may do this by extracting the single most powerful fear available – the Releaser's fear.

'Oran, I already know all of this.'
'Keep reading,' Oran said.

Once Vesuvius has a Releaser's fear, there is only one way to defeat him. Vesuvius must be stopped by the same source that gave him this power:

the Releaser. But the Releaser's fear will not last forever, and Vesuvius must generate more in order to live on Earth. In a final battle, one of them will be defeated. The battle will end in either the destruction of the world, or in the saving of it, as stated in a one hundred-year-old prophecy.

'What?' Andrew said, staring at Oran in shock. He couldn't believe what he'd just read. 'I'm the only one that can kill him?'

Oran nodded. 'Yes. I'm afraid so. Vesuvius is going to come for you whether you like it or not. He's had a taste of your fear now, but he'll want more. It's all in the prophecy.'

'Hang on,' Dan said. 'What's all this business about a prophecy? I've never heard Vesuvius talking about a prophecy before.'

'No, that is because there are only two people that know of its existence. Myself and Tiffany Grey.'

Andrew scrunched up his face. 'But what has she got to do with any of this?'

'Tiffany is Nusquarium born, like myself,' Oran said. 'She looks about twenty to you, but in fact she is almost one hundred and twenty.'

Poppy gasped, but Andrew just nodded, his mind

flashing back to the time in the market. Tiffany had mentioned something about the prophecy then – he was sure of it.

'One hundred years ago, she had a dream,' Oran began.

'But you said Nusquarium people don't dream,' Andrew cut in.

'Exactly. They don't even have Dream Drops,' Oran said. 'So she knew at once that it must be an omen. In her dream, she was shown two possible futures. One where the world remains as it always has been, and the second where the next Releaser's fear is let loose and Vesuvius takes over the world. This eventually leads to the destruction of Earth and in years to come, the total extinction of human beings.'

Andrew sat in shock, listening to every word with a horrible feeling rising up in his stomach. He glanced over at Poppy and Dan, who looked back, ashen-faced.

'Oran, you should have told us,' Andrew said sternly.

'What good would it have done? I didn't want to worry you. You already had enough on your mind with Poppy being captured, and I thought as long as we prevented Vesuvius from taking your fear then it wouldn't be a problem. But that's no longer possible. We must begin to look at the alternatives. Or shall I say, alterna*tive*.'

'And what's that?' Andrew asked, barely daring to breathe.

Oran released a long, heavy sigh.

'You must defeat Vesuvius, like the prophecy states.'

Andrew gulped, as the weight of the world crashed down on him. 'But how? Isn't he more powerful than ever now? I'm thirteen. What can I possibly do against him?'

Oran nodded. 'He's more powerful than ever, yes, but don't forget that you've developed some of that power too. It's a part of you now, and that's exactly why we need to train you up. If you're going to defeat Vesuvius, you need to be on the same level as him. You will have to train hard in the coming days. We will help you of course. Together, perhaps we can stop him from doing any lasting damage.'

Andrew felt his brain whirl with panic. A week ago all he'd had to worry about was if his homework was going to be finished in time, but now the immensity of what he was about to face seemed almost incomprehensible.

'Do you think I stand a chance?' he asked, biting his lower lip.

'I'm not sure,' Oran said honestly. 'But what other choice do we have?'

After a restless night's sleep, they travelled up and over the mountains with even greater difficulty than the first time. They had given the last of the food and water to Poppy, and Andrew's throat had become so dry that every time he swallowed it felt like sandpaper rubbing against his tonsils. He couldn't stop thinking about what Oran had told him and the impossible task that lay ahead. How was he ever going to stop Vesuvius and his army of Shadowmares? Oran had said they were going to train him, but he knew there wasn't really enough time.

'How much further?' Dan asked again, for what seemed like the umpteenth time.

'Not long now, we're almost there.'

'I don't understand,' he groaned. 'You have magical unicorn horns and Satebite ovens, but no cars.'

'Nonsense,' Oran said. 'There is no need for cars. Humans have become lazy. Walking adds strength of character.'

'Yeah…and blisters,' Dan added under his breath.

Thankfully, this time, it really wasn't much further and Andrew could see the white building of the Dream Factory nearing into view, towering into the sky like a magnificent castle.

'Is that the Dream Factory?' Poppy asked, eyes wide in amazement. Andrew nodded, feeling a rush of relief spread through his body. Soon they would be going *home...*

Oran knocked on the door and waited for one of his little workers to come and let them in. But no one came. He tried again and they waited. Still no answer.

'That's odd,' Oran said, walking around to one of the windows. He put his hands up against the glass and peered through.

'What do you see?' Andrew asked.

Oran gasped loudly and drew back, cheeks pale.

'Fender's feather,' he said, almost in a whisper.

The creases around his eyes tightened and his lips shook.

'What is it?' Andrew said. 'What's wrong?'

'They're dead,' he said, staggering backwards. 'The Luguarna people. They've all been murdered.'

25

'Stand back,' Oran said, as he took out the unicorn horn and held it up to the lock. It began to get very windy and the door flew open with a loud thud, almost taking it off its hinges. Inside, everything was a mess. Blood was splattered across the white walls and the ceiling. The table and chairs were upturned. Crockery was smashed to pieces. The Luguarna people had obviously put up a good fight…and lost. Three of them were lying dead on the floor. Andrew looked closer and realised that one of them was Aster, the worker they had met in the Dream Drop Hall. His glasses were broken and bent and his expression was of pure horror, as if frozen on his face the moment he had died. Andrew turned away.

'How did this happen?'

Oran shook his head, eyes glassy with tears. 'After Vesuvius left the Mountain of Doom, he must have come looking for you here. When he didn't find you, he probably killed them out of rage.'

Dan looked confused. 'But I thought Vesuvius

couldn't enter the Dream Factory. Your father put a spell on it, didn't he?'

Oran shrugged. It was a hopeless shrug, full of defeat. 'He couldn't, but that was before he had Andrew's fear. Now he's more powerful than ever. I suppose he can override the spell my father put on it.'

Andrew bowed his head in shame. *So this was his fault.* So many deaths, and it was all because of him.

'It's not your fault,' Poppy said, as if reading his mind.

Oran nodded and rubbed his eyes, which were puffy and red. 'She's right. It is a great misfortune, and I am sad to have lost them but you are not to blame.'

'Will the Shadowmares come back?' Poppy asked, glancing around nervously.

'Oh yes, most definitely. As soon as they realise Andrew is here. I shall go and fetch the Cortizol potion for Dan right away, then we must go straight to the Sliders room so that you can all be transported back.'

He hurried out of the dining room, leaving them alone with the bodies of the Luguarna people.

'The Sliders room?' Dan said. 'What do you reckon that is?'

259

'No idea,' Andrew said, shaking his head. 'I guess we'll find out soon enough.' Andrew couldn't take his eyes off the door that led underground to the Nightmare Factory, half expecting it to burst open at any moment. Vesuvius had somehow managed to break in once already. What if he tried again? Andrew guessed that the other two were probably wondering the same thing.

'I think I felt safer in the Mountain of Doom,' Dan said, laughing nervously.

As they waited for Oran, an uneasy silence hung in the air like a heavy fog.

He returned carrying a green bottle of liquid. He struggled to pull the stopper off at first, but when he did, it shot up to the ceiling like a champagne cork and the liquid inside fizzled and bubbled to the top.

'Tiffany Grey gave this to me some time ago. She specialises in herbal medicines.' He turned to Dan. 'When you drink this, you'll feel as if your insides are burning, causing you to be in great pain for a while, but it will work. Go slowly with it.' He handed the bottle of liquid to Dan, who studied it carefully.

'Oh, sure, like I'm going to drink it now you've told me that.'

'Well it's up to you,' Oran said, blinking. 'But if

you don't you'll develop more characteristics of the Sepataurus. Like Andrew, your strength and ability to heal will increase, but you will have other more unwelcome side effects. You may grow a tail, you may grow wings. You may even grow a nice set of horns. You'll still look like a human being, but you will have scales all over your body. Personally, I don't think you'd be winning any beauty contests.'

Dan cleared his throat. 'Right,' he said. 'Maybe I'll give this stuff a shot then.' He took a sip from the bottle and coughed it up almost straight away.

'It's disgusting!'

'I never said it would be pleasant,' Oran reminded him.

Dan looked at the potion again, and groaned. 'OK,' he said, letting out a deep breath. 'It's just lemonade. It's just lemonade.' He tipped it down his throat, every few seconds wincing and clutching at his stomach like he'd just ingested poison. When he had finished, he handed the empty bottle back to Oran and stood up straight, burping loudly.

'Well done,' Poppy said, putting an arm around him.

'Yeah,' Andrew said, patting him on the back. 'Good on you. It looked revolting.'

Dan grinned proudly. 'Naah, it was a breeze, mate.'

Oran's lips curled into a smile. 'Good. Because you'll need to drink one every day for the rest of your life.'

Dan's jaw dropped open and he let out a loud moan. 'What? For the rest of my life? You're gotta be joking.'

Andrew couldn't help but laugh, but he stiffened as his gaze fell on the dead bodies again.

'Come on,' Oran said, his face becoming serious. 'We must get you home.'

They followed Oran up a flight of stairs and along a wide corridor, where they passed four more bodies. Andrew tried not to look, but he couldn't help but notice that there was a lot of blood around the place, sprayed against the clean white walls in a horrifying contrast. It chilled his bones to even think about what the Luguarna people must have gone through. As his hatred flared for Vesuvius, it made Andrew even more determined to learn how to use his new abilities. When Vesuvius struck again, he wanted to be able to stop him.

They came to a room marked 'Library'. Oran produced a small silver key from his pocket and opened the door. The room was full of shelves with books stacked high to the ceiling. It had an old musty smell and dust had collected on every surface.

'What are you doing?' Andrew asked. 'I thought we were going to the Sliders room?'

'We are,' Oran said, winking at him.

Poppy scrunched up her nose. 'But this is a library.'

'Hey,' Dan said, nudging Andrew. 'She's on the ball today.'

'Shut up, Dan,' she said, scowling at him.

Oran ignored them, walking over to the largest of the bookshelves and pulling out a book with 'Sliding– an expert's guide' printed on the spine. Andrew wondered what he was doing. After all, this was no time for reading a book. But then the bookshelf started to retreat, rolling back to reveal a room three times the size of the one they were in now.

'Cool,' Andrew said.

They stepped inside. Oran placed the book back on the shelf and the door closed again with an eerie creak. Andrew peered curiously around. There were no windows, just spotlights, drenching the place in an artificial glow. The walls and the floor were made from some sort of reflective surface, as if they were in a hall of mirrors at a funfair. Andrew cringed at his reflection. With his dirty skin and greasy hair, he hardly recognised himself.

He walked to the centre of the room, footsteps echoing all around him. There was a large object covered by a grey, dusty sheet. It looked like a chair was underneath it, but he couldn't be sure. Behind the object were hundreds of wires all leading to a tall metal box. He leaned in closer and noticed that a tiny man was cowering behind it. He was sitting on the floor staring back at Andrew, terror in his wide blue eyes.

It was Tarker.

26

'Tarker!' Oran exclaimed, rushing over to him. 'I thought you were dead. I thought everybody was dead!' He gave Tarker a big hug. 'I'm so happy you're safe.'

Tarker stood up and rubbed his bald head.

'I hid…in here,' he stuttered. 'It was the…only place they didn't…look.' His teeth were still chattering. 'There were…a few others that hid with me…but they've left now. I was too…scared to move.'

'Well you're OK now,' Andrew said, patting him on the back.

Tarker nodded slowly, clinging to Oran's side like a small child. Oran turned to Poppy and Dan, who were still stood by the door, and ushered them over. He pulled the sheet off the object in the centre of the room, and a cloud of dust filled the air, making Andrew sneeze. When the dust had cleared, Andrew could see what looked like a grey dentist's chair.

'One by one, I will be sending you back to Earth using this device. It's called a Slider box.' Oran tapped the metal box and Tarker jerked backwards, pink skin flushing grey. Andrew felt sorry for the little Luguarna man. He was shaken to the bone, petrified at even the slightest movement.

'It is important that once you enter the chair you completely relax,' Oran continued, spreading his hands out. 'Imagine that you are falling asleep. If you are stressed or allow yourself to feel anxious, you could end up in limbo.'

'Limbo?' Poppy said. 'What's that?'

'A very lonely place. The space between the two worlds. Nothing exists there except darkness and light. If a person gets trapped in Limbo, it is almost impossible to escape.'

Andrew's mouth turned dry. Limbo sounded worse than the Nightmare Factory.

'Try to imagine that you're floating, and like I said before, relax.' He pulled three pairs of goggles out from behind the box and handed them one each. 'Put these on. You'll need to wear them to protect your eyes. Are you ready?'

Andrew, Dan and Poppy looked at each other. Dan was frowning.

'Not really, no. But we're going to have to be aren't we?'

'Good.' Oran smiled. 'Who's going first?'

'I will,' Poppy said, stepping forwards.

'No,' Andrew said. 'Why don't I go first? You know, to test it out.'

'You've taken enough risks for me already. I'm going first, and that's all there is to it.'

Andrew nodded. He knew there was no point arguing with her.

'OK then.' Oran smiled. 'Ordinarily I would have liked to have talked you through the process a little better, but considering the circumstances…' His voice slipped away. 'Oh wait,' he said, spinning around. 'I almost forgot. You still have the key that you stole from Vesuvius, don't you?'

'Why?' Andrew said. 'Do you need it?'

'Yes, it's not only the key to the Nightmare Factory. It's the key to the Slider box too. Vesuvius wanted to make sure that no child could ever travel back. He started wearing it around his neck the same time as he built the gate to the Mountain of Doom.' His voice cracked with worry. 'So where is it?'

'Dan took it,' Andrew said. 'He was wearing it earlier.'

Oran's eyes darted to the bare skin around Dan's neck.

'Please tell me you still have it.'

Dan shook his head, looking very sheepish. 'I think I lost it in the Mountain of Doom. We'll have to go back and look for it.'

Oran's face turned the colour of a sheet, and Poppy began to tremble.

'I don't want to go back there,' she said, tugging at Andrew's sleeve desperately. 'I can't. I won't.'

Dan bit his lip. 'I guess that joke wasn't as funny as it sounded in my head,' he pulled out the key from his pocket and tossed it at Oran, who looked as if he might collapse with relief. He slotted it into the box and a fierce noise started up, like the revving of a motor.

'I hope this still works.'

'What do you mean you hope it still works?' Poppy snapped, voice as high as a mouse's.

'Well, it's been a while since I've used it, but unfortunately there's no other way back.'

'I can't believe I'm doing this,' Poppy said, walking slowly over to the chair. She looked hesitantly at it and then sat down, gasping slightly as the seat reclined backwards.

'Are you coming with us?' Andrew asked hopefully. He felt safe with Oran, like nothing could ever touch him.

'I will be soon, but I will be travelling back through one of the various portals hidden around Nusquam.'

'How? I thought you just said there was no other way back,' Andrew said.

'For you there isn't. You see, you were stolen from your sleep, so technically your body is still in the real world somewhere, and your mind is trapped here, in Nusquam. To travel through a portal, you must physically cross between the worlds, whereas sliding just transports your mind.'

Poppy sprang back up from the chair. 'So where's my body?'

Oran shook his head. 'That I could not say my dear. During your time in Nusquam, your body on Earth will have gone into a paralysed state, almost like a deep, deep coma. The likely scenario is that you will wake up in a hospital, safe and well.'

'And what's the other scenario?' Poppy asked, curling her hair around her finger nervously.

Oran grunted and shuffled his feet awkwardly.

'Well your body could have stopped breathing, in which case you'd wake up in a coffin.'

'Oh, *brilliant*,' Dan said.

'But it's highly unlikely,' Oran added quickly. Andrew wished he'd never asked.

'OK,' Poppy said quietly. 'I'm ready.'

'Are you sure? You must be fully relaxed remember…'

'Yes. Just get on with it,' she snapped, lying back down on the chair.

Oran hit the switch on the box again. All of the power in the room was shut down and they were thrown into sudden darkness. Andrew shuddered, wondering if it had broken, but seconds later an intense white light blasted out from the chair. It filled the room with a blinding intensity, and then it was sucked back in again as if by a giant vacuum. Andrew understood now why Oran had made them wear the goggles. He took them off. Poppy was no longer in the chair.

'Did it work?' he asked, looking around the room for her.

Oran grinned. 'Well it would appear that way.' He turned to Dan. 'Are you going next?'

'I suppose,' he said, shuffling forwards. 'Wait, Oran, how are we going to find each other when we get back?'

Oran took out a pen and a sheet of paper from his pocket, and then scribbled something down on it. 'Here, this is Tiffany's address,' he said, passing it to Andrew. 'I want you to promise that you'll go and see her when you get back. She can help you with your training. Do you understand?' Andrew nodded, shoving it in his pocket. He took the pen and grabbed Dan's arm, writing his phone number down.

'Just in case,' he said.

'Thanks, mate. See you on the other side,' Dan grinned, getting into the chair and closing his eyes. He wriggled around for a while trying to get comfortable. Andrew put the goggles back on and Oran returned to the box. The same bright light shot out at them, and when Andrew looked back at the chair, Dan had disappeared too.

'My turn?' Andrew asked. He slumped on the chair, feeling his body sink into the cold leather. He couldn't believe he was finally going home...he thought about seeing his mum again, and smiled. It had only been a week, but he missed her.

Oran smiled. 'I'll come and see you as soon as I have things in order here.' He walked over to the box. Are you ready?'

'Yes,' Andrew said. 'Thank you, Oran...for everything...and I'm sorry about the Luguarna people.' He turned to Tarker. 'Goodbye, Tarker. Good luck with the baby.' Tarker looked at him through puffy, tear-stained eyes and although he didn't smile, he nodded silently and patted his belly.

Oran pressed the switch on the box. Andrew shut his eyes and braced himself as he was plunged into darkness. The next thing he knew he was falling, his belly up in his chest as he plummeted downwards at an incredible speed. He didn't know where he was falling or why, he just knew that something wasn't right. He was sure he was going to die; his bones would shatter like china when they hit the – wait, what had Oran told him to do? Something about relaxing and floating…? He had been so busy thinking about Tarker that he hadn't paid any attention. Andrew tried to let his body go limp. He shut his eyes again and managed to calm down, feeling his heart rate lowering. Then, like a great wind had picked him up from behind, he began zooming forwards, purple and white light forming a tunnel of electricity around him. It was like he was flying through space – through a sort of time warp. An overwhelming feeling of safety warmed his insides and Andrew was finally able to enjoy the experience, but it didn't last long. As quickly as it had begun, Andrew felt himself falling again and he woke up with a jolt.

He opened his eyes to a bare white room. Perhaps it hadn't worked. *I must still be in Oran's Dream Factory,* he thought. Then he saw a familiar face peering over him. Rosy cheeks, curly blonde hair and a warm smile. *Mum.* He tried to reach out for her but his arms wouldn't move. It was as if he was paralysed.

'Andrew,' she said. 'Andrew, can you hear me?' The voice was distant and seemed to bounce around the room. He wanted to speak, but his throat was dry, his vision blurry. He could still see his mother's face, but it appeared to be merging into two. He felt sick, disorientated and his head was pounding like a drum. Panic flooded through him. *What was happening to him?*

The room around him began spinning, faster and faster like a merry-go-round... The machine next to him started bleeping.

Then silence...

27

He must have passed out because when Andrew opened his eyes the second time, he was still in the same white room. Except now everything was much clearer. He looked around at the white walls, the metal bed, the wires and equipment that surrounded him and realised that he was in a hospital, just like Oran had predicted. A nurse was sitting next to him, smiling warmly. She had her brown hair tucked into a neat bun and was wearing a white coat with a pocket watch.

'Hello, Andrew,' she said. 'Glad to have you back with us.'

'Hi,' he groaned, still a little groggy. 'Where am I? Where's my mum?'

'You're in Great Ormond Street Hospital. Don't worry. I'll go and fetch your mum in a second. I just need to take out your feeding tubes and run a few tests first.'

Andrew lay there for what seemed like forever, waiting while the nurse fussed around his bedside, taking his temperature and removing the various tubes and drips attached to him. She left the room, returning moments later with his mother.

'Andrew!' she gasped, rushing over and putting her arms around him. 'Oh thank goodness you're OK.' Tears were pouring down her face. She had obviously been crying a lot because her mascara was clumped, and she had more on her cheeks than on her eyelashes. She looked like Alice Cooper, the famous rock legend, Andrew thought wryly.

'What happened?' he asked. He was still so confused, and his throat felt dry and sore.

'You've been in a coma. Your sister too. It happened six days ago. I couldn't wake you up.' She blew her nose loudly into a tissue. 'The doctors are baffled. They don't understand what caused it.'

'Oh,' Andrew said, not really sure how to respond.

'How are you feeling now?'

'Fine. Where's Poppy?'

'She's in the next room. She woke up an hour ago. I still can't get over it. I thought I was going to lose you both…' She sniffed, fighting back more tears. 'And there's something else. Something even stranger,' her eyes widened and she leaned in closer. 'Another boy on the coma ward woke up, about fifteen minutes

275

after Poppy.' *Dan was here too?* 'He'd been out for almost two years! Can you believe it? I got talking to his adoptive parents. They're as surprised as me. I mean, what a coincidence.'

'Yeah…weird,' Andrew said, resisting the urge to smile. 'Can I go and see Poppy now?'

'Soon,' she nodded. 'They're moving you both to the main ward. They'll want to keep you there for a few days, while they run some more tests.'

Andrew groaned. *A few days!* He didn't have a few more days; they needed to get out of here so that they could find Tiffany Grey.

His body was still weak from being in a coma, and every time he tried walking, his legs felt like jelly. A nurse wheeled him into the main ward in a wheelchair. He didn't think he needed it, but he didn't want to cause a fuss.

It was much more pleasant in here compared to the cramped room that he'd woken up in, with loads of beds and colourful pictures filling the walls.

'Andrew,' Poppy said, eyes brightening when she saw him. She was lying down in one of the beds. 'I'm glad you're OK. Where's mum?'

'She's off getting coffee,' he said, lifting himself into the bed next to hers.

Andrew noticed a pale figure wheeling himself across the room towards them.

'Dan!' he cried. He looked different to normal. He was no longer wearing pyjamas and was dressed in baggy jeans and a blue sweater. His black hair had all been shaved off and somehow he looked even more pasty and gaunt. He still had the same cheesy grin though.

'You alright?' he said.

Mum returned, holding a tray with three steaming drinks on it.

'You know each other?' she asked. 'This was the boy I was telling you about.'

Andrew and Poppy quickly shook their heads. 'No.'

His mother raised an eyebrow. 'Then how did you —'

'The nurse introduced us when you were getting the drinks,' Andrew quickly explained.

She smiled, nodding. 'Yes of course,' she said, handing them each a hot chocolate. 'That was thoughtful of her.'

Andrew wiped his forehead. *Phew! That had been close.*

'Great. Here come my foster parents,' Dan said, rolling his eyes.

Andrew turned to see a middle-aged couple walking over, both with red hair and freckles.

'Mr and Mrs Jenson,' the woman said, moving around the beds so that Andrew and Poppy could shake her hand. 'We were just saying, we think it's extraordinary that you all woke up from your comas in such a short space of time. Weren't we just saying that, dear?'

Mr Jenson nodded. 'Yes, dear. We were.'

Mrs Jenson was wearing a floral dress and pearls and Mr Jenson had on a tweed jacket, with a handkerchief poking out of the breast pocket. They spoke quickly and accentuated their actions just like Dan did.

'Dad, what's that strange mark on your neck?' Dan asked. 'Hey look, mum's got one too.'

Andrew looked, and sure enough, both Mr and Mrs Jenson had red dots on their skin, which looked peculiarly like teeth marks.

Mr Jenson turned as red as his hair, and he laughed nervously, putting his hand to his neck. 'Oh yes, funny that. We woke up with them this morning. I expect it's an allergy to something. Either that or the cat bit us in our sleep.' He chuckled.

'It doesn't look like a cat bite,' Dan mumbled. Andrew was thinking the very same thing.

Mr Jenson glanced at his watch. 'Crikey, I'd better be going. I've got work in the morning.'

'Shouldn't you be leaving too, Mum?' Andrew asked. He wanted to spend more time with her, but they needed to plan what they were going to do about Vesuvius.

'Why don't I stay for a bit? You've only just woken up. We could chat and play a board game or something.'

'Actually, I'm feeling quite tired, Mum,' Poppy said. 'I'd rather you came back to see us tomorrow.'

She nodded. 'Yes of course, dear.'

They all said goodbye, watching their parents leave the ward, but almost as soon as they'd gone the nurse with the brown bun hurried over. 'Parcel left at reception for you,' she said, handing it to Andrew. 'From your aunt.'

Andrew studied the brown parcel suspiciously. Their aunt lived in Florida. They hadn't seen or heard from her in over two years, and this parcel was sent from a London address.

'Who's it from?' Poppy asked when the nurse had left. She knew as well as he did that it wasn't from their aunt.

'I'm not sure,' Andrew said, cautiously peeling it open. He pulled out three dreamcatchers. They were battered looking, with tussled feathers and broken beads, as if they'd been around for centuries.

'There's something else in there too,' Andrew said, sticking his hand inside. He brought out two small soul-catchers and a handwritten note.

Dear Andrew, Poppy and Dan, he read.

Great to have you back! Oran has informed me of everything that has happened these past few days. Although I am pretty sure Vesuvius won't make an appearance at the hospital with so many people around, please stay away from any shadows. The Shadowmares need the darkness to sustain themselves here, and they will use the shadows to cross over now that they have your fear. I have included two soul-catchers in case you get into any sticky situations.

Also, please find enclosed three dreamcatchers in case he tries to steal you from your dreams again. You know where to find me. Come as soon as you can.

In the meantime, stay safe.

Yours sincerely,

Tiffany Grey

'We need to go soon,' Dan said, scratching his arm through his jumper. 'Look.' He wheeled himself between their beds and pulled back a sleeve to reveal a large patch of green scales. 'I need some more Cortizol potion. I can hide this from the docs for a while, but if I grow a tail and wings, they might start to ask questions.'

'How are we going to get out of here though?' Poppy asked. 'The hospital won't let us just leave.'

They sat in silence. Then Andrew jumped up.

'It's not that hard. We'll tell them we're going to the gift shop,' he said. 'But we'll sneak out the front door and take the Tube. Mum gave us ten pounds to buy some magazines and sweets. We can use the money to buy our tickets.'

'And I've got a fiver,' Dan said. 'If that helps.'

'Can you walk though?' Andrew asked, looking at his wheelchair. 'It's going to be difficult making a getaway if you can't.'

'I think so. My legs feel stronger now. My Sepataurus healing abilities must be kicking in.'

Andrew nodded. 'Great. That's decided then. We'll need to leave first thing tomorrow morning. I don't fancy walking around London in the dark. Now that they can cross over, the Shadowmares could be lurking anywhere.'

Later that night, when the hospital staff had turned the main lights off, Andrew got into bed, pulling the duvet all the way up to his neck. He had attached his dreamcatcher to his bed and had left the bedside lamp on, but even so, he couldn't help staring into the shadows, wondering if he might see the face of a Shadowmare glaring back at him…or worse, Vesuvius. How long would it be before he started releasing Andrew's fear into the world? What kind of a world would there be once he did?

Andrew wasn't sure. But he was certain of one thing: tomorrow he could begin his training. And then, when he had mastered his abilities, he would fight Vesuvius with every bone in his body, until his very last breath…

28

After breakfast, they were allowed a bath. Andrew lay in the warm soapy water, washing the layers of dirt off him. He slipped on a pair of jeans and a T-shirt, relishing the feeling of clean cotton on his skin. He shut his eyes and breathed in the smell of washing detergent. He smiled. He'd never appreciated such simple, everyday things before.

I have to defeat Vesuvius, he thought. *I don't want to go back to the Nightmare Factory ever again.*

Nobody seemed to notice Andrew, Poppy and Dan when they strolled out of the hospital doors later that morning. Even though they were thinner than normal, they didn't look sick. People just assumed they were visitors. Of course, they were careful to make a run for it whilst there weren't any nurses in sight, sprinting the three blocks to Russell Square Tube station.

The train was packed full of serious looking business people in suits, reading newspapers. There were a few teenagers by the doors, chewing gum and listening to MP3 players, so Andrew, Poppy and Dan loitered near them, trying to look inconspicuous. The train pulled into a station. One of the men in suits dumped his newspaper on the seat and got up to leave. Andrew's eyes darted straight to the headline.

'Strange creatures – the ramblings of lunatics or genuine sightings?'

He snatched the paper before another man could sit on it, and read the article from start to finish, dread filling his stomach with every word. He passed the paper to Poppy and Dan.

'You've got to read this,' he said. 'There's been reports over the last forty-eight hours of people spotting things within the shadows. Black shadowy creatures with skeletal bodies. It's got to be the Shadowmares. What else could it be?'

Poppy frowned at him. 'You think they're already here, searching for you?'

'I know they are. The good thing is, it doesn't seem that anything else has happened yet. Maybe he's just using my fear to get into the real world, to try and bring me back so that he can get more of it.'

'I wouldn't be so sure,' Dan said, pointing to a small article in the corner.

'Some old woman in Kensington was apparently having a nightmare about monsters, and she woke up to find one standing by her bed. She said it tried to attack her.' He pointed to the picture below. Andrew leaned forwards, thinking she looked like any normal grandmother. 'The paper's making out that she's some crazy woman, desperate for her five minutes of fame.'

Andrew felt like someone had punched him straight in the guts.

It *had* started.

'I think I'm going to throw up,' he said, feeling his throat grow tight. He leaned over the seat, but nothing happened. The train stopped with a sudden jerk at Camden Town and they got out. Andrew felt glad to be back up in the natural light and the clean air again.

Camden was full of market stalls and unusual shops selling gothic clothing. There were lots of interesting people milling around, some covered in tattoos with brightly dyed hair, others with Mohawks and shoes with huge platforms. Andrew thought that Tiffany probably fitted in quite well.

'Where now?' Dan asked.

Andrew took out his map.

'Down here and then a left,' he said, beginning to walk.

They arrived at Tiffany's house, and Andrew was

surprised to find that it was quite a modern terrace, with baskets of flowers hanging from the porch. He wasn't sure what he had expected, but it wasn't this. After his time in Nusquam, her house seemed so... well, normal...

'Are you sure this is it?' Poppy asked, looking up at it.

Andrew checked the map again and nodded.

'Positive.'

He went to knock on the door, but it burst open before he could reach it.

'Andrew, Poppy!' Tiffany smiled when she saw them. 'And you must be Dan,' she said, holding out her hand. She was just as Andrew remembered. Her dark hair fell down to her waist and she was dressed in a flowing black dress. Her red lips and green eyes were the only colour on her pale face.

Tiffany hugged them. 'I'm so glad you made it back OK. Did you get the dreamcatchers I sent you? And the soul-catchers?'

'Read this, it's urgent,' Andrew said, pushing the newspaper into her hands. She studied it quietly.

'Yes, I heard about it earlier,' she said, frowning. 'It's the Shadowmares, no doubt about it, but there is a lot more trouble to come. Unfortunately Vesuvius has only just begun. There's a good chance that none of us will survive what is to follow,' she said grimly.

'I know,' Andrew said, voice shaking. 'So what are we going to do about it?'

Tiffany peered down the street. 'Come inside, it's not safe to talk here.' She opened the door wider for them. 'I'll put the kettle on. Make yourselves at home.'

The hallway smelt strongly of flowers and herbs, but as Andrew entered the living room, the source of the strange smell became clear. It looked like a jungle, reminding him of the dusting room in Oran's Dream Factory. It was crammed full of plants. There were tribal statues carved from wood along the mantelpiece and paintings of dragons and fairies on the walls. *Not so normal after all*, Andrew thought with a grin. An old television set stood in one corner, and on top of that was what looked like a Shadowmare's skull sitting in a large glass jar. Poppy nudged Andrew hard in the ribs.

'Look at this place!' she said. 'She's a nutcase.'

'She's a nutcase who can help us,' Andrew reminded her. 'So let's not forget what we came here to do.'

'Fine,' Poppy said, throwing herself into one of the chairs, and sweeping a hanging cheese plant away from her face. 'But if she starts getting all voodoo on us, I'm out of here. I'm telling you Andrew, having a Shadowmare's skull and a jungle inside your house is not normal. It's freaky.'

'Actually, I prefer to be called an herbalist if you don't mind.' Tiffany smiled, appearing from the hallway. 'I grow these plants for medicines.'

Poppy turned red. 'I'm sorry. That was really rude of me. I'm just totally weirded out by everything that's happened lately.'

'No bother,' Tiffany said, smiling. She was carrying a tray with a pot of tea, four mugs, and a plate of biscuits on it.

'That's a Shadowmare's skull right?' Dan asked. 'Did you kill it?'

Tiffany laughed. 'No. Oran gave it to me as a gift.'

Strange gift, Andrew thought, but he didn't say anything.

Tiffany sat down on one of the armchairs, studying Dan uneasily.

'You've been infected,' she said. 'By a Sepataurus.' She poured them all a cup of tea as they stared at her in disbelief.

'Yeah, but how'd you know?' said Dan eventually.

Tiffany handed Dan a mirror from the mantelpiece.

He took one look in it and let out a horrified scream. Andrew hadn't noticed before, but as he peered closer at his friend, he could see that four green scales had appeared on the side of his neck, each one the size of a finger nail.

'Luckily for you,' Tiffany said. 'I mixed up a fresh batch of Cortizol potion this morning.' She took out a small green bottle from her pocket and tossed it at Dan, who caught it in his lap. 'I made it fairly potent, so it'll last you a while. Three sips a day should be enough.'

Dan eased off the cork, and sniffed the contents. He turned away, his face screwed up into a tight ball. Then he pressed the bottle to his lips, took a swig… and gagged. Tiffany grabbed the plate of custard creams and shoved them under his nose.

'Quick, have one of these,' she said. 'It'll take the taste away.' Dan crammed a biscuit into his mouth, dropping a trail of crumbs down his shirt.

'Thanks,' he mumbled.

'So,' Tiffany said, sitting back down on one of the chairs. Her black and grey hair fell forwards, so that it covered half her face. 'It's time we started training. Vesuvius has already begun releasing your fear. It won't be long before he launches a full-blown attack.'

'But it's only me who can defeat him right?' Andrew said, looking worried. 'That's what your prophecy said. These two should go home. They don't have to help.' He was talking so fast, the words were spinning off his tongue in cartwheels.

'Don't have to help?' Poppy snapped, getting up. 'You're my brother; of course I have to help. Not to mention the fact that…oh, let's see…the whole world's in danger if we mess this thing up.'

'She's right, you know, mate,' Dan said. 'You're not getting rid of us that easily.'

Tiffany took a sip of her steaming hot tea. 'You have loyal friends.' She smiled. 'And I know you are only being proud, Andrew, but you need all the help you can get. Your fear supplies will soon run out and Vesuvius will hunt you down.'

Andrew chewed on a nail. He hated the thought of putting his family and friends in any more danger, but Poppy was right, the whole world was in danger now.

'Fine, so what do we do?'

Tiffany's smile grew and she clapped her hands together. 'I'm going to start you off on the basics. If you're any good, we can move you onto something a bit harder. I suggest we start with telekinesis.'

'Telekom…what?' Dan said, scrunching up his face.

'Telekinesis,' Tiffany repeated. 'In other words, moving objects with one's mind.'

'What, and that's not hard?' Andrew scoffed.

Poppy sat forwards on the edge of her chair. 'But why would that help Andrew kill Vesuvius?'

'Vesuvius has four main powers,' Tiffany said, putting her tea down. 'He can move objects with his mind. This means he can hurl a weapon at someone without even using his hands, which is invaluable in battle.'

'We've seen him do it before with a spoon,' Dan said. 'It was scary.'

'A spoon is the least of your worries,' Tiffany said. 'Two, as you already know, he can create light with his hands which, if it hits in the right place, can kill instantly. And three, he can create invisible energy fields in order to protect himself.' Andrew's mind raced back to the first time he'd met Vesuvius. He'd somehow created a sheet of solid air. Andrew had bashed straight into it like it was a brick wall.

'I've seen him do that too,' he said. 'He used his skull cane.'

Tiffany nodded. 'Yes, his skull cane acts as a sort of wand which he channels his powers through. It magnifies them. If you can disarm him, he'll be less powerful.'

'So what's the fourth power?' Poppy asked.

'Zip flying,' Tiffany said.

Dan snorted. 'Zipperty-what?'

'Zip flying,' Tiffany repeated, her eyes deadly serious. 'It's when someone moves incredibly fast. Like *out of this world* fast. They are usually seen as just a blur.'

'I've never seen him do that,' Dan said.

There was a short silence.

'I have,' Poppy said. 'In the corridor of the Nightmare Factory, the night we were escaping. He came up behind me so fast.'

'I wondered how he'd done that,' Andrew said. 'It was like he appeared from nowhere.' He put his empty mug on the coffee table. 'So what are you going to teach me first then?'

'We'll start with telekinesis,' Tiffany said, finishing her tea. 'You must imagine that the object you are moving is simply energy that can be manipulated. Do not think of it as a solid object. Try to merge your energy with that of the object. If you want to move it, you must become it.'

Andrew nodded, trying to understand.

He glanced around the room. 'So what should I move? What about this mug?'

Tiffany shook her head. 'Moving a mug is not going to match the power of Vesuvius. Let's see if you can move something a little heavier.' She looked pointedly at the sofa.

'Oh no,' Andrew said, shaking his head. 'There's no way I can move that thing.'

'Don't think about how heavy it is. Just concentrate on moving it.'

Andrew sighed. 'I still don't get how this is supposed to help me defeat Vesuvius.'

'Stop thinking about that. I need you to understand that everything is just energy that can be manipulated. Once you grasp that concept, you'll be able to do so much more.'

'OK.' He stared at the sofa. '*Move*,' he thought. '*Just Move!*' but the more he tried, the more frustrated he felt. 'It's no good,' he said, slumping back down. 'I can't do it.'

'I bet I can do it,' Dan said, getting up. 'Let me have a go.'

Tiffany ignored him. 'Yes you can,' she encouraged Andrew. 'Listen, haven't you ever wondered why your powers only seem to flare up when you're either angry or upset? Well it's because you've got all this pent up energy and nowhere to dispense it. Try and think of something that makes you angry, or sad, and direct that energy at the object you're trying to move.'

Andrew crouched back down on the floor again. He knew what he had to do. It was all linked to his fear.

Poppy and Dan fell silent, watching him in anticipation. This time, he took a moment to clear his mind, thinking of the one thing that always made his heart beat faster: his father. In those next few seconds, he forgot everyone else in the room.

Slowly, the sofa lifted off the ground and into the air.

'It's not working,' Poppy said, who was still sitting on it. Dan pointed to the floor and Poppy's eyes bulged in shock. 'Oh,' she said.

Andrew made the sofa float gently back down to the ground again, exhaling a lengthy sigh. He couldn't believe he'd managed it. He felt so strong and in control. *Maybe he could defeat Vesuvius after all…*

'Wow, that was awesome, man.'

'Thanks,' he said, slumping back down on the sofa. Quite honestly, it had seemed easy once he knew how. It was like he had unlocked a key to another part of his brain, and now anything was possible. He already felt like he was ready for something bigger, something better. Then a thought crossed his mind. *If he could make an object float, why not himself?*

He shut his eyes, concentrating hard, and within seconds, he was hovering inches above the ground, just like the Shadowmares. His body felt very light, as if he could be blown over by a gust of wind. He floated over to the door and then back again. Poppy and Dan sat staring in shock, too gobsmacked to move. He could see Tiffany out of the corner of his eye, mouth wide open.

He grinned, his whole body buzzing with exhilaration. 'I think I've got the hang of this telekinesis business.'

Tiffany cleared her throat, blinking. 'I've never seen anyone do that before. I thought it was a long shot asking you to move the sofa but this is amazing... truly amazing. I knew that you'd pick it up quickly.'

Andrew's smile widened. 'Thanks.'

Dan snorted. 'Alright, you'll give him a big head. Now what are you going to teach him?'

Tiffany tilted her head to one side. 'Let's see if you can put up a defence barrier.' She pulled a handful of knives from a drawer. Before Andrew could do anything to stop her, she was aiming them straight at him. The knives flew through the air towards him, and he felt a sharp stabbing pain as one of them hit him in the shoulder.

'Ow!' he cried.

The rest came flying as fast as bullets and Andrew quickly lifted his hand up. The air bent before his eyes like a clear plastic sheet. The remaining knives hit the invisible barrier one by one, and Andrew stared in disbelief as they fell to the floor.

Tiffany began clapping. 'Well done. Now that was *really* impressive. Vesuvius would have fired them back at me of course, though I'm rather glad you didn't.'

'Believe me, I wanted to,' Andrew growled. He grabbed his throbbing shoulder, and glanced at his hand, smeared with warm blood. He staggered forwards, body weak, then collapsed on the sofa.

29

'You're crazy,' Poppy yelled. 'You stabbed him!' She got up, launching herself at Tiffany. 'Why did you do that? I thought you were trying to help?'

'Relax,' Tiffany said, waving a hand dismissively. 'Andrew, check your shoulder.' Andrew pulled back his bloody T-shirt and was surprised to see that it had completely healed. It was still red and sore, but apart from that, it was flawless.

'Wow,' breathed Dan. 'You're invincible.'

Tiffany shook her head. 'No, not invincible. Not to Vesuvius. Look, I'm sorry I threw a knife at you, Andrew, but I needed to test your defences. This isn't a game. This is serious. I needed to bring out your powers.'

'But why did you have to throw *knives*? I wasn't expecting that,' he hissed angrily.

'Yes,' Tiffany said, nodding. 'But that was exactly the point. Do you think Vesuvius will tell you what his next move is? No. He will keep on hammering attacks out until you bring your guard down, which you must never, ever do. Let this serve as a painful lesson.'

Andrew thought about this, and while he still felt angry about what Tiffany had done, he understood. And he knew one thing for certain: it had worked.

'We'd better go home,' he said, getting up. 'Mum will be going insane with worry.'

Tiffany nodded. 'That's a good idea. You must leave while it is still light.'

They followed Tiffany into the hallway. 'I'll need you to come back tomorrow. There is still so much you need to learn. Oran will be here.'

'Oran?' Andrew said. He couldn't wait to see him again.

'We'll come as soon as we can,' Dan said, reaching for the door handle.

They hurried home. Andrew crossed every road, turned every corner, with a mind to attack whatever might be waiting for him on the other side. He kept on expecting to see Vesuvius standing there, staring at him with his cruel stare, but no one came. No one jumped out at him. What was taking Vesuvius so long?

Their mother was waiting by the phone when they stumbled through the door in the late afternoon.

She jumped up and wrapped her arms around them. Then she let go, and Andrew saw that her face had turned red with anger.

'Where have you been?' she shouted. 'I was worried sick. The hospital phoned and said you'd run away. I had the police out looking for you and everything.'

Andrew stared at the floor. 'We felt fine. We just wanted to come home, Mum.'

She studied them, her eyes harsh.

'Do you have any idea how worried I was? Nobody's seen you for hours. Why didn't you come straight home?'

Andrew couldn't think what to say. How could he possibly explain everything that had happened over the last few days?

'It's the summer holidays, Mum,' Poppy said sweetly. 'We'd already wasted a week in a weird coma – we just wanted to have some fun. We went to the park. We're sorry.'

Her face softened and she sighed loudly. 'You should have told someone. You can't just go running away like that. Something could have happened to you. You could have fallen into another coma or —' She hesitated, sighing again. 'Look, maybe I forget what it's like to be young sometimes. You're always off doing things, never a care in the world. But just tell me next time, OK?'

Never a care in the world? Ha, if only! Andrew thought, exchanging a knowing look with his twin.

'Sure, Mum,' he said. 'We're sorry.'

Andrew slipped his hand behind his back to give Poppy a high five. She was brilliant at getting them out of trouble.

After dinner, he went up to his bedroom, shutting the door behind him. He couldn't believe he was back in his own room again, in his own house, in his own bed! He stared around at his belongings, the comic books and horror films that cluttered the shelves, the darts board on his door, the TV with built-in DVD player. None of it seemed to really matter any more. Not with Vesuvius on the loose. He got up to attach his dreamcatcher to the window frame, yawning as a wave of tiredness crashed over him. It was then that he noticed the black figure sweep past the bushes outside.

His whole body tensed. Andrew blinked, leaning forwards, almost knocking his head against the windowpane. He stared into the darkness. The security light flashed to life, but he couldn't see anyone outside. The garden was empty, the leaves and branches swaying in the wind, the only thing moving in the garden below. But he had *seen* something. He was almost certain. The only question was, had *it* seen *him*?

30

If something was out there, he needed to be ready for it.

Andrew sat down on the bed. *I have to practise*, he thought, shutting his eyes. He thought about his father's death and the fire. Tears sprung to his eyes, and fear clutched at his insides, but he didn't stop. He put his hand in the air. A shimmering effect rippled through it, but only for a second.

He couldn't do it. It was too hard.

He looked at the dartboard on his wall, then to the darts on his bedside table. He concentrated on them instead, began to imagine them moving. Then, as if an invisible hand was lifting them, they floated up into the air, so that they were level with the dartboard.

'Yes,' Andrew whispered, careful not to lose concentration. He was doing it. All by himself. Without anyone to guide him!

Then, one by one, he fired them into the bullseye.

The door burst open. Poppy screamed. The last

dart froze in mid-air, inches away from her face.

'Oh my God, Poppy, I could have killed you! Are you OK?'

Poppy smiled. 'I came to say goodnight. What are you doing? Are you practising?' she plucked the dart from the air and handed it to him. 'Is it going well?'

Andrew shrugged. 'I guess. I thought I saw something moving outside. Something in the shadows.'

Poppy frowned, and pulled the curtain back to take a look. 'There's nothing out there now. Maybe it was next door's cat?'

'Maybe,' Andrew said. 'Have you put your dreamcatcher up yet?'

'First thing I did when I got home.'

'Me too. Make sure you leave the light on tonight.'

'I will,' Poppy said, and then she smiled. 'It's going to be OK, Andrew. You were amazing today. You can defeat Vesuvius. I know you can.'

I really hope you're right.

'Goodnight, Poppy,' Andrew said. 'Sleep well.'

He climbed back into bed, pulling the duvet up to his neck. His whole body ached with exhaustion. The second he closed his eyes he fell into an uneasy sleep.

In the early hours of the morning he awoke to his mobile phone ringing. He didn't recognise the number. He'd almost forgotten he even had a phone.

'Hello,' he said, groggily. 'Who is it?'

'It's Dan,' said a worried voice on the other end. 'Look, I think you had better get over here fast. God, something really bad has happened.' He was speaking so fast, Andrew could barely make out what he was saying.

'Calm down,' he said. 'Where's your house?'

'Ten, Park Road. Hurry!'

The line went dead.

For a moment Andrew just sat in bed, frozen, wondering what could have possibly happened. Had Vesuvius shown up? Was Dan in trouble? Springing back to life, Andrew grabbed a pair of jeans and a T-shirt and hurried to wake Poppy up. It was 6 o'clock in the morning, and the sun had only just risen in the cloudy sky. They ran downstairs, as quietly as they could.

'Wait,' Poppy said, as Andrew reached the door. 'We'd better leave a note for Mum.'

Andrew nodded. 'You're right. Be quick though.'

Poppy grabbed a pen from the phone shelf and scribbled something down. Then they rushed outside and hailed a cab.

It pulled up outside a white house with a black gate and red door. Before they had even knocked, the door flew open, and Dan was standing there, face gaunt. He had a thick scarf wrapped around his neck, covering his scales.

'Come in,' he said, frowning. 'They're in the living room.'

'Who's in the living room?' Andrew said, but he needn't have asked because as they made their way into the hallway Mrs and Mr Jenson stepped out, pale as two ghosts. Mrs Jenson's eyes were a pearly white colour and Mr Jenson appeared to have turned three shades greener.

'Andrew, Poppy,' Mrs Jenson said, ushering them inside. 'How lovely to see you both.' She was smiling, but Andrew couldn't help but notice that she was *frothing at the mouth.*

'Are you alright?' he asked.

'Fine, fine. We're just feeling a bit under the weather that's all.' Andrew watched uneasily as Mr Jenson wiped the beads of sweat from his forehead with a spotted red handkerchief.

'They've been like this since I got home last night,' Dan whispered. 'But I think they're getting worse.

Mum just tried to bite me. I don't know what's wrong with them.'

'We're fine,' Mr Jenson insisted, although he was swaying from side to side like a sinking boat.

Suddenly, there was a loud moan.

'What was that?' Andrew whispered, peering upwards.

'I don't know,' Dan said, tensing up. 'I've heard it a few times now, but I haven't gone upstairs to investigate. I wanted to wait until you guys got here.'

Another moan. And then a grating noise from overhead, like someone dragging a body across the floor.

'Right.' Andrew swallowed. 'That was thoughtful of you.'

He began climbing the stairs. The others followed quietly behind him.

Andrew stood still, holding his breath. A fierce growl rattled through the house. They were getting closer. He turned a corner of the stairway, a sense of dread creeping over him.

'What do you think it is?' Poppy asked.

'No idea. It doesn't sound human though does it?'

They crossed the landing.

'It's coming from in here,' Poppy said, pushing her

ear up to one of the doors.

Dan glanced over his shoulder. 'That's my parents' bedroom. I'm not supposed to go in there.'

'I think we can make an exception,' Andrew said, pushing open the door. He peered around the bedroom. There was a double bed, a wardrobe and a chest of drawers, but apart from that, the room was empty.

'That's strange. I could have sworn it was coming from in here.'

Another groan filled the air.

'It's coming from in *there*,' Poppy said, pointing to another door.

'That's the en suite bathroom,' Dan whispered.

Poppy took a step towards it.

'Wait. Let me,' Andrew said, pushing her behind him and reaching for the door handle. He took a deep breath, counting to three in his head, and then opened it.

Bath. Toilet. Sink.

He sighed, relaxing. 'It's fine, there's nothing there,' he said, turning around. But the moment the words had left his mouth, a man with sickly yellow skin stumbled out of the shower, ripping back the curtain. He was wearing a suit, which was torn at the front and splattered with blood. He had pearly white eyes and a vacant stare. Andrew blinked, trying to decide whether he was imagining it or not, but when he looked again, the man was still there, dribbling and staggering towards them like a…

'Zombie,' Andrew whispered.

He slammed the door shut again and put his weight against it.

'There-there's a zombie in my parents' bathroom?' Dan said, moving quickly away. 'What are we going to do?'

'We're going to kill it,' Andrew said. 'But for now, we need to lock this door.'

Dan nodded, and pulled out a key from the chest of drawers, slotting it into the lock. 'How did it even get there?'

'I think we know how it got there,' Poppy said. '*Vesuvius.*'

'One of your parents must have had a nightmare about zombies and dreamt it into existence,' Andrew said. He remembered the strange marks they'd seen on them at the hospital. 'And then the zombie bit and infected them.'

Poppy's eyes were the size of golf balls. 'Oh my God. But then that means…'

'Yes,' Andrew said. 'Dan's parents are going to turn into zombies too.'

Dan's mouth dropped open.

They turned to see Mr and Mrs Jenson staggering into the bedroom, furiously scratching at the wounds on their necks. Their lips were pale blue, their movements stiff and sluggish. Andrew felt a horrible sickness creep into his stomach. It was one thing killing the zombie in the closet, but what were they going to do with Dan's foster parents?

Dan shook his head, throwing himself down on the bed. 'I knew they weren't cat bites. Felix is never that vicious.' Andrew stared at the black cat brushing against his leg, and then to Mr and Mrs Jenson stumbling towards them.

'No,' he said. 'So, what are we going to do?'

'We're going to have to kill it aren't we?'

'Obviously we're going to kill the zombie. I meant about your parents.'

'Well, we can't kill them.'

'No, but they could bite and infect other people. We're going to have to do something. Come on,' Andrew said, hurrying towards them. 'Help me tie them up.'

'Tie them up? What, as in so they can't move?'

'That's generally the idea, yes.'

'But they'll kill me,' Dan said.

Poppy ignored him. 'What are we going to use?'

Andrew looked desperately around the room. 'Dan, do you have any rope?'

'Rope? Why would I have rope?'

'It doesn't matter,' Andrew said, spotting a rack of ties. He grabbed a handful of them. 'We'll use these.'

'Ready?' he said. He couldn't believe what they were about to do. Poppy nodded. On the count of three they raced towards Mr and Mrs Jenson, grabbing them by the arms. Dan hesitated by the bed, as if his feet wouldn't move.

Mr Jenson stared at them wildly. 'What are you doing? Release us this instant!' he shouted. The vein on his head looked as if it were about to explode. 'Dan, what are they doing? Get them to stop this circus.'

Dan bit his lip, looking sheepish. 'I'm sorry Mum and Dad, but this is for the best.' He stepped towards them, helping Andrew and Poppy drag them onto the bed, kicking and screaming, where they tied their wrists and ankles together.

'This is an outrage!' Mrs Jenson cried. 'You three are

going to be in so much trouble when I get my hands on you. Dan, you're grounded, and you…' Her neck snapped round to Andrew and Poppy. 'When your mother hears about thisssss…' Her words turned into a horrified squeal as the zombie burst out of the bathroom, throwing the door off its hinges. The pale-faced creature staggered towards them, salivating at the mouth.

'Oh,' Dan said, waving a hand. 'Don't worry about him, Andrew's going to kill him for us, aren't you, Andrew?' Mr Jenson let out a small squeal, which sounded like a little girl, and Mrs Jenson fainted. Andrew flexed his fingers, and moved towards the zombie.

*Here goes…*he thought, swinging his fist and punching it hard in the face.

The zombie groaned, opening its jaws to try and bite him. Andrew put his hand up automatically. The air rippled around him like stones hitting water. The zombie smacked into it, face hitting the solid air as if it was a sheet of glass, and tumbled to the floor.

He'd done it! Without even trying, he'd created a defence barrier.

There was no time to wonder why, or how. Andrew kicked the zombie in the stomach. It didn't feel like he'd kicked it that hard, but the zombie groaned and its guts exploded everywhere. Its blood was luminous green, and looked like gunge in a game show, splattering the walls in a thick slime.

Cool, Andrew thought. Perhaps his strength had increased just as Oran had said it would.

Mr Jenson had been watching the spectacle in disbelief, and his eyes rolled slowly into the back of his head.

'Have they both fainted?' Poppy asked. Neither of them appeared to be moving.

'What if they're dead?' Dan said, checking his mum's pulse. 'Or what if they never go back to normal? I won't have any parents left.'

'They'll be fine,' Andrew said, pulling the duvet over them to keep them warm. 'They're just unconscious. And that's probably a good thing. We're going to be in so much trouble when they wake up…'

'We need to get to Tiffany's,' Andrew said, checking his watch.

The three of them raced to the Tube station through floods of rain-swept wind and thunder. The sun had completely disappeared from the sky and the streets were cast in ominous looking shadows. *Was this down to Vesuvius?* Andrew wondered, running further down the flooded streets.

A sudden crack of thunder made them stop in their tracks. It was as loud as a gunshot. A huge branch fell into their path from above. Andrew grabbed Poppy and pulled her back, out of the way of a swinging power line that followed.

'Thanks,' Poppy said, catching her breath.

Two people sprinted past them.

'What do you think's going on?' Dan asked. 'What are they running from?'

'No idea. Come on, quick,' Andrew said, setting off at a sprint himself.

When they arrived at Tiffany's, they were exhausted and soaked through.

'Where's Oran?' Andrew panted as Tiffany opened the door.

'He'll be here soon,' Tiffany said, ushering them in. She gazed anxiously out at the street. 'He had to attend to some urgent business. Are you alright?'

'Dan's parents have turned into zombies,' Andrew said. 'It's madness out there. Have you seen the weather? I think it's Vesuvius.' He paused, letting Tiffany's words float through his head. 'Wait. What urgent business?'

She pushed them into the living room and gestured to the TV.

It was an old black and white set that looked as if it might blow up at any moment. The skull on top of it was missing. *Weird*, Andrew thought. He was about to ask Tiffany where it was, when the news report made him stop short.

'Scientists are baffled by the strange phenomenon sweeping the world where people are reportedly waking up to find their nightmares are real. The latest case was reported in New Jersey, where a twenty-six-year-old woman claimed she was having a nightmare where she was drowning, and woke up to find her house completely flooded.' Andrew's eyes were glued to the screen as the lady appeared on camera, hair and clothes dripping wet.

'Flooding. It's my biggest fear. It's a nightmare I regularly have, but when I woke up, it was actually happening.' The camera zoomed out to show the woman's house completely destroyed by water. The news reporter returned to the screen. 'Breaking news just in from another incident in Knightsbridge, London, where a group of vampires have reportedly been caught on CCTV attacking a man outside a butcher's shop. Many experts have branded it a "hoax", but others are saying it is a sign that the supernatural really does exist. Take a look and decide for yourself.'

'No way,' Andrew said, as the grainy footage appeared of three vampires ripping chunks out of a man's neck.

Andrew turned away, unable to watch. He couldn't speak. He couldn't even think straight. His mind was like a whirlpool of thoughts all fighting to get to the centre. It was happening, the world was becoming like Oran had said it would. And it was *his* fear that had given Vesuvius the power to achieve it.

There was a sudden bang, and a gush of icy air rushed through the living room.

Poppy jumped up. 'What was that?'

'Maybe we didn't shut the door properly,' Dan suggested. 'It's blown open in the wind.'

'No, I definitely shut it.' Poppy crept out into the hallway.

'What are you doing?' Andrew whispered.

'Sshh,' she hissed. Andrew could feel his heart pounding against his chest.

He walked to the end of the passage and put his head around the kitchen door. It appeared to be empty, so he tiptoed through, making sure he kept as quiet as possible. He stopped dead when he felt someone lurking behind him. It caught him completely off guard. He didn't even have the time to scream before a cold hand grabbed his mouth and pulled him backwards into the shadows.

31

Andrew scrambled free and turned to face his attacker. He put up a defence barrier. With his other hand he felt around in one of the drawers. *Yes!* He pulled out a large carving knife, but a familiar voice made him freeze in his tracks.

'Fenders feathers! Andrew, it's me.'

Andrew blinked and peered into the darkness. A tall figure with a top hat stood before him. 'Oran?'

'Yes.'

Andrew switched on the light. 'What are you doing creeping around like that? I was about to kill you.'

Oran chuckled. 'Yes I know. I was testing how good your defences are, and it appears they're coming along. That defence barrier you put up was impressive.'

'You people have got to stop doing that!' Andrew sighed. 'It's good to see you, Oran, but perhaps next time you could just greet me with the normal hello?'

Tiffany crept into the room clutching a baseball bat.

'Where is he?' she hissed. 'I'll get him round the skull.'

Oran turned around, beginning to chuckle.

'Tiffany! Feisty as ever I see.'

Tiffany grinned and she dropped the baseball bat. 'Oran!' she said, running to hug him.

Poppy and Dan appeared in the doorway.

'Dan's eyes brightened. 'We didn't think you were coming. How is the Factory, you know...since... what happened there?'

'It's OK,' Oran said, sweeping his grey hair off his face. 'Tarker can't really do much now, he's too heavily pregnant. But three other Luguarna people survived, and they help me a fair bit. Is the Cortizol potion doing its job?'

Dan shrugged awkwardly, and pulled the scarf tighter around his neck. 'It's fine.'

'Aren't you hot in that?' Tiffany asked. 'Why don't you take it off for a while?'

'I'm fine,' he repeated irritably, mopping the sweat from his forehead with the back of his hand. 'I've still got a few scales left, though.'

Tiffany stroked her chin. 'I thought they would have all disappeared by now. Perhaps I made the Cortizol potion too weak. I'll make you some more before you go.'

Andrew turned to Oran. 'Are you going to be staying long?'

'As long as I need to. My duties are here with you now. Come,' he said. 'We must train more.'

'How long have we got?' Andrew asked.

Oran frowned, rubbing his eyelids. 'There is no way of knowing. That's what worries me. Although Vesuvius has started releasing your fear, he is only doing so in dribs and drabs. It's as if he's releasing just enough to let us know that he is here. But not enough to do any real damage.'

'But that's good, isn't it?' Poppy said. 'I mean, surely the less he's releasing the better?'

Oran nodded. 'Yes, but it doesn't make any sense. Vesuvius has half a cylinder's worth of Andrew's fear. I don't understand why he's not using it.' He stroked the stubble on his chin, the furrows on his forehead deepening. 'It's as if he's saving it up for something.'

Andrew took a deep, shaky breath.

'But what for?' he asked.

'That,' Oran said, 'is a very good question…'

They spent the rest of the afternoon practising in the living room. Andrew used Oran's unicorn horn to fire sparks at the wall, and then had a go without it, trying to create the same effect with his finger. At first nothing happened, but the more he practised, the better he got. He pointed his finger at the fireplace, gathering all his energy. There was a loud bang, and then a cloud of dust. When the air had cleared, Andrew saw that he had made a huge hole in the wall.

'Wow!' Dan cried. 'That was unreal, mate. You're like Harry Potter, or something.'

'Did that just come from *you*?' Poppy said. She got up and grabbed his index finger, which was smeared with black soot. 'Amazing.'

Andrew stared at the hole in the wall, eyes wide. He couldn't believe how powerful he was becoming. A week ago, he hadn't been able to control his abilities, now he was doing things that even Oran was impressed by. But it scared him…this power wasn't his own. It had come from Vesuvius…surely that could only be a bad thing?

Oran chuckled. 'He's getting good Tiffany, admit it.'

'Yes,' Tiffany said, raising her eyebrows ever so slightly. 'A little too good. I think that's enough for today, or else I'm not going to have a house left.' She glanced worriedly at Dan, who was busy scratching his neck.

'I'll fetch you that Cortizol potion,' she said, going into the kitchen. Dan nodded, but Andrew noticed that he looked shaken and anxious.

'I have to leave now,' he said, voice cracking, as he rushed out of the door. Andrew raced after him, but by the time he got outside, Dan was nowhere to be seen. *That's odd*, Andrew thought. *What's up with him?*

Tiffany came back into the room, carrying the bottle of potion. 'Where did he go?'

'I don't know, he just ran off.'

'That was a bit sudden. I hope he's alright.'

Poppy shrugged. 'I don't know, maybe he wanted to go and check on his parents.'

'That makes sense,' Andrew said. 'Don't you think we should go after him though? Check that he's OK?'

Oran nodded. 'That's a good idea.' He pulled out two flashlights from the cupboard. 'Be careful. It's getting dark outside. You may need these.'

Andrew glanced out at the street, feeling a shiver slide down his spine. Oran was right – it was unusually dark. It was 4 o'clock on a summer's afternoon. Something wasn't right. In fact, as Andrew left to go and find Dan, he had the distinct feeling that something was very, very wrong.

32

Andrew and Poppy raced all the way to the Tube station, icy rain lashing down on them. The streets were deserted, but many of the houses had lights on, as if people were afraid to go outside. The wind was whistling and groaning as it whipped around the trees and buildings, and thick, grey clouds hid the sun.

'It'll be pitch black by six o'clock,' Andrew said. 'We'd better be quick checking on Dan. We don't want to run into any Shadowmares.' He still had the soul-catchers that Tiffany had given him in his pocket, and he kept his hand over them the whole way.

Andrew knocked on Dan's door, but there was no answer.

He knocked again.

Still no answer.

'That's strange. I thought he would have come straight home.'

'Unless he's ignoring us,' Poppy said. She pointed to a twitching curtain.

'Why would he do that?' Andrew said, banging on the door even harder. 'Dan, open up, we know you're in there.'

There was the sound of footsteps, and then the letterbox flicked open.

A groggy voice answered from the other side. 'Go away, I'm sick.'

'We just want to see if you're alright. You ran away so fast… Let us in,' Andrew said.

'I said go away!' Dan growled. 'I don't want to see anyone.'

'Charming! We come all this way and that's how you treat us? Come on, Andrew, let's go home.'

'Wait,' Dan called out. 'You can come in.' They heard the lock turn from the other side and then Dan scurrying away again. Andrew and Poppy smiled at each other and stepped inside. The curtains were drawn, and the house set in darkness. Dan was sitting on the sofa hidden under a big duvet.

'What are you doing under there?' Poppy said. 'And turn on some lights. You know that the Shadowmares can cross over in the dark. Do you want to get yourself killed?' She went to switch on the light.

'No, don't,' Dan said, sounding desperate.

'Why not?' Andrew asked, staring dubiously at the

323

big lump under the duvet cover.

'Because I don't want you to see me like this.'

'Like what?' Andrew said, starting to feel annoyed. There was much more for them to worry about than a few spots.

There was a long pause and then Dan slipped out from under the duvet cover, eyes fearful. 'Like this,' he whispered.

At first Andrew thought that his friend was wearing a mask, but as he peered closer he realised that it was his own flesh. Dan's face was covered in green scales.

'Why? When?' Andrew stuttered.

'You haven't been taking the Cortizol potion have you?' Poppy said, folding her arms.

Dan shook his head, staring down at the floor. 'Not for some time now, although the transformation happened pretty quickly. That's why I ran off so fast. I could feel it beginning. I was ashamed.'

Poppy spread her hands in a helpless gesture. 'But why not? You know you need to drink it every day.'

He looked up, his green eyes focusing on them both. They were the only things recognisable about him apart from his spiky black hair.

'I wanted to be able to help. I wanted to be useful in the fight against Vesuvius. Don't you get it? I'm so much stronger now.' He held out his arm, green scales glistening in the light. 'Look, I've got muscles I never had before. Huge, bulging muscles, like an action star.'

'Yeah, you also look like The Hulk,' Poppy said.

Andrew stared at his friend's rippling muscles and waxy skin. 'You did this for me?' He sat down on the sofa next to Dan. He couldn't believe it.

Dan nodded. 'But not just for you. If Vesuvius wins, he'll eventually lead the world to its end. The prospect of having green scales didn't seem too terrible a price to pay.'

'I suppose…' Andrew said, understanding.

'That was a brave thing to do,' Poppy said. 'Stupid, but brave.'

'You have to promise to call me when Vesuvius shows up,' he said, handing Andrew a piece of paper with his number on.

Andrew nodded.

'I promise.'

'Actually, there's something else I want to show you.' Dan shuffled around and pulled his T-shirt over his head to reveal a brawny green back. From the centre sprouted two rubbery bat-like wings. 'I woke up with them this morning,' he said, like it was as normal as growing a new tooth. 'Pretty cool, huh?'

'Cool?' Poppy said, unable to hide the disgust in her voice. She pulled her hands through her hair. 'I mean, yeah, they're great.'

Andrew reached out to touch the rough edges around the wings. It was like feeling the bark of a tree. 'Woooh,' he breathed. 'Can you fly with them?'

'I'm not sure. I don't think they're big enough yet.' He flapped them up and down a few times. 'They feel really sore. I think they're still growing.'

Poppy was gazing at him with a stunned expression. 'I can't believe you actually think this is a good idea, Dan. What if your foster parents see you like this?'

'My foster parents are zombies,' Dan reminded her. 'I don't think they'll care.' He looked glumly at the ground. 'Anyway, when this is all over, I can start taking the Cortizol potion again. I'll be back to normal within a few days.'

'What if it's too late by then? What if it doesn't work? You might never be the same again.'

An uncomfortable silence hung in the air. Dan sighed. He stared at the wall, stroking his scaly chin. 'That's a risk I'll have to take.'

33

Andrew and Poppy hurried home, darkness pressing in on them. Andrew glanced nervously at the shadows, and for a split second, swore he saw the glowing red eyes of a Shadowmare watching him. *But why were they waiting? Why didn't they attack?*

When they stumbled in through the front door, drenched in rain and sweat, Mum was waiting for them.

'You look like two drowned rats. So much for summer.' She laughed, ushering them into the living room where she had the fire burning. 'So you're certain you're both feeling OK now? No dizzy spells or anything?'

'We're fine, Mum,' Poppy said, smiling. 'Honest.'

Andrew crouched down on the sheepskin rug, drying himself off with a towel. He kept thinking about what Oran had said to him about his fear. *It's as if Vesuvius is saving it up for something…*

When he went up to bed, he still couldn't shake the troubling thought from his mind. Lying under the covers with the light on, the house still, Andrew could hear the wind banging against the windows and the letterbox, howling and whistling, trying to get inside. He lay awake into the early hours of the morning, until he couldn't keep his eyes open any longer and he finally drifted off to sleep.

A crack of thunder shook him awake at a quarter to three. He was sweating from head to toe, lying on a soaking wet mattress. It was so hot he could hardly think straight. Then he realised why – the room was on fire! Andrew sat bolt upright in bed, staring at the flames blazing around him, clawing at him like a sea of giant orange hands. Fear paralysed his body, and suddenly he couldn't breathe. He glanced up at the window, the dreamcatcher diminishing into a cloud of smoke and flames.

Billowy grey smoke was filling the room, thick and fast.

He had to move quickly else he was going to die.

Heart pounding, Andrew got onto the floor and grabbed a T-shirt to cover his mouth with. He crawled over to the door and eased it open, careful not to create a draught that might cause the fire to spread. In the hallway the fire was not as bad, but smoke still thickened the air.

'Poppy!' he screamed. 'Mum! Where are you?' He crawled into Poppy's bedroom. She was crouching in the middle of the bed, head in hands. 'It's not real, it's not real, it's not real,' she kept on repeating.

Andrew felt something soft and squelchy underneath him.

'Urgh!' he cried, jumping to his feet. The floor was covered in tiny wriggling maggots. All kinds of creepy crawlies were filling the room, spilling out of the dresser drawers, the waste-paper bin and from the sink in the corner.

Poppy was rocking back and forth, eyes fixed on a black and red snake that was coiled around the bedpost, its tongue dancing energetically from its mouth.

'Come on!' Andrew yelled, grabbing his twin's arm. She looked up at him, face filled with terror. 'I can't, Andrew. I'm too scared.'

'I know, but we've got to get out of here. It's happening. Vesuvius is here.'

He shook the creepy crawlies off, and made a run for the door, over the wriggling maggots and cockroaches and into the smoky hallway. The fire had reached the edges of Andrew's bedroom door, flowing underneath like a waterfall in reverse. He knew that by now it must be an inferno in there.

'Outside,' he told Poppy, pushing her towards the stairs. 'I'll go and get mum.' He made his way back along the landing, coughing and choking from the smoke, his heart hammering inside his chest.

I can't go on, he thought. But he didn't need to get as far as his mother's bedroom door. She was already rushing towards him, yelling and screaming.

'Run!' she cried, urging him to follow. 'Vampire!'

'Vampire?' Andrew said.

His mum grabbed him by the arm and together they fled down the stairs and out the front door, where Poppy was waiting on the porch. Slamming the door shut behind him, all Andrew could see through the frosted glass was the dark shadow of a man running towards them.

'Quickly,' Andrew said, pulling them into the bushes. 'Keep still. I don't want it to see us.' The vampire opened the door, pale face and sharp fangs glowing in the moonlight. It darted off into the street looking for them.

'Are you OK?' Andrew whispered to his mum.

'He was…in my…dream, and then…in my… room. We need to…call the police.' Her breath came in short bursts. She raised her eyebrows. 'Oh my God – is the house on fire?'

Andrew glanced at Poppy, hoping that she might know what to say, but when he looked again at his mother, she was slumped against the hedge.

'Great, she's fainted. What are we going to do now?'

Poppy didn't seem to be listening. She was staring at the street in a daze. 'Look at it all.'

Andrew looked.

It was still pouring down with rain and the roaring thunder was crashing all around them with blasts of lightning, illuminating the street like a flare. Andrew shivered. There were countless people, running about in a panic, still in their pyjamas. Mrs Churchill from across the road was being chased by a bull except that it wasn't a bull; it had wolf-like fangs and red eyes. Mr Green from next door was on the roof of his bungalow hanging onto the chimney for dear life.

'He's afraid of heights,' Poppy said. 'The poor man. He must have woken up like that.'

Another neighbour stumbled out of his house. 'Help!' he yelled, as a dentist chased after him with a needle in one hand and a drill in the other. The dentist was laughing wickedly and his white coat was covered in blood. He revved the drill again.

And then Andrew saw the Shadowmares.

He froze, heart pounding.

They were standing in the middle of the street, their black cloaks billowing menacingly in the wind, glowing electric purple in the night air.

They're feeding off my neighbours' fear, thought Andrew, as he watched them getting brighter and brighter.

Andrew shivered, and came back to his senses. He remembered his promise to Dan. He had to let him know that Vesuvius was here, but his mobile phone was in his bedroom. By now, it would surely be reduced to useless melted plastic. There was the landline in the office though. He could run in and use it and be out within seconds. He took a step towards the house.

'What are you doing?' Poppy asked, tugging at his pyjama top. 'You're not going back in there are you?'

'I've got to call Dan. We said we would, remember?'

'But it's too dangerous.' Her face was contorted with worry.

'Poppy, we made a promise.'

She bit her lower lip. 'Do you want me to come with you?'

Andrew shook his head. 'No. Stay here. I can defend myself, but I think Mrs Sparks could use your help.'

Three doors down one of their elderly neighbours was trying her best to fight off the vampire with a saucepan. She was doing quite well, and had bashed it over the head once already, but the creature with the pale face and hooked fangs was not easily deterred and was moving in for another attack.

'I'll handle it. Be careful, bro,' Poppy said, rushing over to her.

Andrew peered at his mother who was still unconscious in the bush. He hoped she would be safe.

He eased open the door to his house. Creeping into the hallway, Andrew could already feel the heat from the fire as he ran up the stairs, deeper into the smoke. His eyes were stinging and he could barely keep them open. He stepped into the office, choking and spluttering. Luckily, the smoke wasn't as bad in here. He closed the door behind him and ran over to the phone. Quickly, he pulled out Dan's number from his pocket and dialled it. He waited, feeling as if it was ringing forever. A groggy voice answered, weary from sleep.

'What do you want?'

'Dan, he's here. Vesuvius is here!' Andrew shouted down the phone. There was a slight pause on the other end, and then a loud gasp. Then the line went dead. Andrew leapt back to his feet. He had to get out of here as soon as possible. He sprinted back into the hallway. He had just reached the top of the stairs when he heard a familiar voice calling his name.

'Andrew, help.'

Andrew felt the insides of his stomach knot up. The voice sounded exactly like his father. But his father was dead. It wasn't possible that he could be here. Andrew shook his head and carried on down the stairs. The smoke must have affected him more than he had thought.

'Andrew, please don't leave me here to die, not again.'

Andrew froze, feeling tears spring to his eyes. What did he mean, *not again*? Suddenly, images began scrawling through his mind as he returned to the night of the fire; Andrew in his bedroom shielding himself from the flames, the shape of his father coming through the door and sweeping him up into safety… being wrapped in a big fleecy blanket and passing through the small opening in the window…falling… caught in his mother's arms, staring up at the smoky house, expecting his father to come flying out of the window after him at any second. Then the almighty bang that followed…the ball of fire blasting out at them and showering the street in glass and rubble. Andrew's mother screaming, Andrew screaming… The realisation that he'd never see his father again.

Andrew collapsed to the floor, blinking back the tears that were streaming down his cheeks. The guilt, the anger, the fear… Then, he didn't know why but he started running back up the stairs. Andrew had never believed in ghosts, but after everything that had happened to him these past few weeks he just didn't know what to think any more. He couldn't take any chances – if it was his father, he needed to know.

Flames licked the edges of his bedroom door and a deep fear punched at his chest. There was no way he could make it in there and survive. He froze, not knowing what to do.

'Andrew, I'm trapped. Help me!' The voice cried out, more desperate this time. Before Andrew had time to decide, the door burst open. Andrew threw his arms over his face as heat and flames lashed at his body. Overhead, the smoke alarm was blaring. Andrew could just about make out the shape of his dad at the other end of the room, but he had his back to him, shielding his face from the flames.

'Dad!' Andrew cried out, tears pouring down his face. He gasped for air, but his lungs convulsed, sucking on nothing. 'Dad, I'm here!' he croaked.

His dad cocked his head at the sound of Andrew's voice and slowly turned around to face him. But it was not the figure Andrew had been expecting. Instead, an old man with crumpled skin and white hair stared back at him. He had jet black eyes and was holding a cane with a skull on top. And he was laughing – a cruel, wicked laugh.

Vesuvius.

34

Vesuvius clicked his fingers and the fire disappeared. Andrew's bedroom was completely normal again. He blinked. Everything that had previously been ablaze, the curtains and the bed and his wardrobe, it was all untouched. *How could I have fallen for such an obvious trick?* Vesuvius was still cackling with laughter as he moved forwards at lightning speed and grabbed Andrew by his T-shirt, pulling him into his icy grasp.

Andrew tried to struggle, but he couldn't move. His eyes fell on the dartboard on his bedroom door. *I could use them as a weapon...* he thought, focusing all of his energy on the darts. They began to float through the air.

Vesuvius's head snapped round. 'I wouldn't try that if I were you,' he said, holding his skull cane up, and the darts shot into the carpet, narrowly missing Andrew's feet.

Who was he kidding? His strength was nothing compared to Vesuvius.

Vesuvius cackled again. 'It's time to go back, Andrew.'

Suddenly, the door to his bedroom swung open and Tiffany, Poppy and Oran appeared. Relief flooded through Andrew; Oran was brandishing his unicorn horn.

'Aaah,' Vesuvius said when he saw them. 'My dear brother.' He was still smiling but his voice was laced with sarcasm.

'You're not my brother,' Oran spat. 'You're not even half the man that he was.'

Vesuvius stopped smiling and his black eyes narrowed. 'Really, Oran, you should have more respect for your family.' He raised his skull cane and light came flooding out of it. He was about to kill Oran!

'No!' Andrew shouted, but Oran drew his unicorn horn just in time, firing it back at Vesuvius. There was a burst of purple light as the two flares met in the middle and a moment later, Andrew was temporarily blinded. He felt Vesuvius's grasp loosen on his shoulders, and when he could see again, realised that he had completely disappeared.

'Where'd he go?' Andrew asked, peering around. 'Is he…dead?'

Oran shook his head. 'No. He is toying with us. Come, we must find him.' Oran turned and headed for the door.

'Andrew, this is it. You must find your courage. Are you ready?'

No, not really, thought Andrew wryly, but he nodded.

They raced down the stairs and outside, where Andrew's mother was still lying unconscious in the bush. People were still running wildly through the street. Beasts with horns and multiple limbs were chasing people out of their houses. Cars were upturned like toys. Windows were smashed, but there was no sign of Vesuvius. Andrew stared into the darkness of the trees, wondering where he could be hiding.

There was a thunderous noise, loud and repetitive like a drum.

Tiffany stiffened. 'Where's it coming from?'

Something heavy landed on Andrew's head. THUD. Then something else. THUD, THUD, THUD.

He jerked back.

'Ow! What is that?' He stared up into the moonlit sky, and saw that millions of small brown objects were falling from the clouds.

'Rats!' Poppy shrieked. 'Millions of rats!'

Several more rats hit the roof and tumbled onto the ground. Soon, there were rats everywhere.

'Whose fear is this?' Andrew shouted, trying to shield himself from the flurry of rodents that were falling down on them.

'Don't look at me,' Tiffany said, crouching under the gutter. 'I used to keep one as a pet. My fear is heights.'

Andrew didn't need to question the strange downpour for long. He looked around, his eyes having adjusted to the darkness, and saw that Madam Bray was cowering in the garage, her face pale, body trembling.

Andrew smiled.

'Who would have thought it? The mean old hag is afraid of cute furry rats.'

Just then a crack of lightning whipped down beside him. He turned quickly, and saw that Vesuvius was standing where the lightning bolt had hit.

The rats scurried across the lawn in a sea of brown and white.

'I want your fear,' Vesuvius said, moving towards Andrew. His white hair was soaked, his black eyes gleaming like the water droplets that clung to his suit.

Oran stepped in front of Andrew.

'You'll have to fight me first, Vesuvius,' he said, holding up his unicorn horn in front of him.

'And me,' Tiffany said.

'Me too,' Poppy added, stepping forwards and folding her arms.

Andrew felt a rush of pride, and suddenly, he didn't feel so alone, but he didn't want anyone to die for him.

'This is my battle,' he said firmly. 'Go back inside where it's safe.'

Poppy shook her head. 'No way. We're staying.'

Vesuvius merely shrugged. 'Very well,' he said, his icy breath chilling the air. 'What are three more bodies compared to one?' He smirked and raised his cane.

A black coil of cloud shot out from it and swayed above their heads like a snake. Wait. It actually was a snake – a giant black snake with a long red tongue! It slithered over to Poppy, who froze instantly, and began coiling itself around her. Andrew leapt forward, charging at the snake, but Vesuvius pointed his cane at him. A great white light shot out and Andrew was catapulted through the air. He landed on his back, pain ripping through his body like a tidal wave.

Vesuvius smiled and pointed his cane at Tiffany, who he blasted up so high into the air that she landed on Andrew's roof with a thud. She slid down the wet tiles and managed to grab hold of the drainpipe, which she clung on to for dear life. Poppy had somehow managed to wriggle free from the snake and was charging towards Vesuvius. He sneered at Madam Bray, who was still quivering in the garage.

'Don't just sit there you insolent fool. Fight!'

Madam Bray shot to her feet, and darted towards Poppy, drawing something from her coat. At first glance Andrew couldn't make out what it was. Then he realised it was some sort of bladed frisbee.

'Run, Poppy,' he shouted.

But it was too late. She launched it in the air. Andrew watched it fly towards Poppy, as if in slow motion. He was too far away to reach her, so he latched onto the frisbee, moving it in the air so that it swung back around to Madam Bray. She squealed as it spun towards her, slicing off the top of her bun.

She cowered in shock, putting her hands to her severed hair.

'Call that a close shave,' Andrew said. 'But you won't be so lucky next time.'

He looked over at Oran and Vesuvius, who had both drawn their sticks. It was like a fireworks display, as the sparks burst between the two of them, breaking into a million shards of light. Andrew was just about to run in and take over, when he felt a sudden coldness engulf him. He yelled out in pain and collapsed to the ground. Dazed, he turned and looked up to see Kritchen standing over him, the scar on his skeletal cheek was more prominent than ever in the lightning-swept sky. He jumped to his feet. Kritchen opened his mouth, and blew another breath of cold air over Andrew. He could feel the life draining out of him, but Andrew mustered one last piece of energy to produce a defence barrier. The air around him rippled silver. It had worked! But Andrew knew that if he allowed himself to drop concentration for even a second, he would lose all power. He was about to shoot light at Kritchen, when a wailing scream filled the air. Andrew swung his head around.

It was Oran – he'd been hit.

He was clutching his left shoulder with one hand, and fighting with the unicorn horn with the other. Andrew felt his knees buckle and he fell to the ground. Kritchen knelt over him, holding a Glow Knife, and grinning like a hyena. Andrew groaned miserably – eyeing the blade inches away from his face. He had allowed himself to lose concentration and now he was going to pay the price with his life. He grabbed hold of the Shadowmare's arms and tried to wrestle him off, but it was difficult to keep a good grip –Kritchen's bones were slippery and wet like a fish's. And Andrew was too weak. Too cold. He spotted something in the air. It was small and green and getting bigger as it nosedived towards them.

'What the?' Andrew whispered, as the green object got closer. Andrew blinked. *Oh my God! It's Dan!* He came streaming through the sky and straight into Kritchen. The Shadowmare was thrown on his back, the glowing dagger flying out of his hand.

'You learnt to fly,' Andrew said in amazement.

Dan grinned, getting up off the floor. 'Yep. Luckily for you.'

Andrew scrambled to pick up the dagger that was stuck in the grass. Without thinking, he brought it down onto the Shadowmare's chest. There was a sound of cracking ribs, and Kritchen let out a painful howl.

Andrew quickly reached into his pocket for the soul-catcher, but Kritchen disappeared into thin air, before his very eyes.

'Where'd he go?'

'Back to the Nightmare Factory before you could finish him off. He's wounded!' Tiffany yelled. They looked up. She was still holding onto the drainpipe, which was bending with the weight of her and threatening to come loose at any second. 'What about some help up here?'

Dan nodded and flew up to the roof so that he could bring Tiffany back down to safety. She seemed a lot calmer when she had two feet on the ground. They glanced over at Poppy, who was trying to fight off Madam Bray *and* a giant snake with her bare hands.

'I'll help Poppy, you two deal with Vesuvius,' Tiffany said, pulling a spear out from her leather coat.

The two of them turned to see Vesuvius and Oran battling it out. The bone in Oran's shoulder was jutting out at an awkward angle, and his face was contorted in pain.

'Andrew, I've held him back all I can. It's up to you now.'

The power of Oran's unicorn horn was diminishing. It was only emitting a faint glow and more and more light was reaching Oran, making him crumple in pain. Andrew knew what he had to do. This was it. This was the moment that the prophecy had talked about…

He stepped towards Vesuvius, and Dan flew over

his head, holding the Glow Knife tightly in his hand.

But they were too late.

There was a howl of pain as a spear of light hit Oran in the chest. He grabbed his heart, collapsing to the ground.

'No!' Dan screamed, raising the Glow Knife and plunging it deep into Vesuvius's neck, catching him off guard. A wail of pain cut through the night air. Andrew expected him to keel over, but he simply stood there, fury twisting his pale face. Then, just like Andrew's shoulder, the huge gaping wound on Vesuvius's neck began to seal itself up again.

His mouth curled into a smile and he lifted his cane up, pointing it at Dan, who was still hovering in mid-air. A tunnel of bright light burst out and Dan was thrown to the other end of the garden. He crashed against the brick wall with a dull thud, and rolled onto the lawn.

He didn't get up.

'No!' Andrew cried. Anger raged inside him. He wouldn't let Vesuvius get away with this. He fixed his eyes on his skull cane. In one quick movement, it sprang from Vesuvius's hands, falling to the ground and snapping in two.

Vesuvius laughed.

Andrew stared at him, confused. He couldn't understand what was so funny.

'You think that's going to stop me?' Vesuvius asked in a patronising tone.

He cackled even louder as he moved his finger in a circular motion, and before Andrew could do anything to stop him, an almighty ring of fire shot up from the ground, surrounding them.

Andrew turned, searching for Tiffany, but he couldn't see her. Huge dancing flames blocked his view, rising high into the night sky.

'Your friends won't be able to help you now,' Vesuvius said, scowling. Andrew's heart raced. Vesuvius was right. It was just Andrew alone with the master now and he knew that only one of them would be walking away from this battle alive. He tried to put up a defence barrier, but the heat of the roaring flames was draining his concentration. Vesuvius was too strong. *He couldn't do it.*

Andrew raised his hands and used all his energy to fire a stream of light at Vesuvius, but the master deflected it, shooting it back at him. Andrew screamed as the light hit his skin, burning like oil on a pan. His head throbbed. His body ached. He felt so weak… Vesuvius stepped towards him, arms outstretched, and Andrew prepared himself for the coldness to embrace him.

But something inside him snapped. As he stared at the flickering orange and blue glow of the fire, he realised that he wasn't afraid of it any more. Not like he had been. The power came back to him. Vesuvius must have been able to read something on Andrew's face, because he paused for a moment, watching him carefully.

This time it was Andrew's turn to smile. 'It's too late, Vesuvius. I'm not afraid any more. Even if you do manage to take me back, you'll never get hold of my fear again.'

Vesuvius looked at him, eyes thinning into black slits. 'I'll *make* you afraid, Andrew, no matter how long it takes. Now, it is time to leave,' he said, coming closer. 'We must return to the Nightmare Factory.'

'No,' Andrew said firmly, moving out of the way. 'It's time for you to leave.' He focused all of his energy on the surrounding fire. Up until now, he'd only ever tried to move solid objects with his mind, but he was sure he could manipulate the fire itself. He let his mind and energy merge with the flames until his entire body felt as if it was ablaze. The burning sensation was so intense he could hardly stand it, ripping through his muscles and filling his head with an unbearable heat, but he knew that he must carry on.

Slowly, the flames parted behind Andrew, and he was able to step back out of them. He knew that he had to keep concentrating on making the fire obey his commands. Andrew forced the fire closer to Vesuvius until it began to singe the edge of his cloak.

'What are you doing?' Vesuvius bellowed. He looked at the fire spreading up his cloak and his black eyes flashed an angry red colour. He raised his hand in the air, but it was too late. Andrew had created a protective barrier around himself, and Vesuvius's light bounced straight off it.

'So,' he said, sneering. 'You are going to kill me like you murdered your father now? How *valiant* of you.'

'I didn't murder anyone,' Andrew said, lowering his finger slightly. 'My father was killed in a house fire. It was an accident. You're the only murderer here.'

Vesuvius laughed wickedly. 'Is that what you think?' he said, cackling even louder now. 'It wasn't *an accident*. It was you, Andrew. You started the fire. You killed your father.'

'No!' Andrew shouted, shaking his head. Once again he felt the wave of guilt rising around him like a tide. Tears welled up in his eyes. Had he really started the fire? Killed his father… He couldn't bear the thought…

'Andrew don't listen to him,' Tiffany cried. 'He's lying. He's twisting your mind.'

'Murderer!' Vesuvius taunted.

Andrew couldn't take it any more. He wanted to collapse to the ground, let Vesuvius have him. If he really had started the fire that had killed his father, he didn't deserve to live.

'Andrew!' Tiffany shouted. 'Listen to me. You need to carry on fighting. Think of Poppy, Dan, your mother. Do it for them.'

Andrew looked up, Tiffany's words drifting into his head, slowly starting to make sense. She was right. It wasn't about *him* any more.

He felt the strength return to his body and he forced the fire to rise back up. He took a deep breath, lifting his hands up above his head, summoning the fire even higher so that it formed a wall of dancing blue and orange flames.

He'd never felt so powerful.

'No,' Vesuvius cried, pointing his finger at him. But Andrew brought his hands together, and in one great rush, the flames swallowed Vesuvius. A deafening scream filled the night air. It was so piercing that Andrew had to cover his ears. Vesuvius staggered towards him, a ball of flaming fire, yelling and shooting light out from his whole body in a desperate attempt to take Andrew down with him.

Andrew ducked from a mass of blinding flares.

The orange blaze stopped moving and collapsed to the ground.

Andrew let out a long sigh. He felt nothing. Vesuvius had ruined too many lives for sympathy.

He turned and stumbled towards Tiffany and Poppy, who had just finished killing the snake. The giant serpent was lying lifeless on the floor, a spear lodged in its side. Madam Bray was slumped up against the garage door, unconscious.

'Andrew, watch out,' Tiffany shouted.

Andrew swivelled around just in time to see a blazing skeletal hand shoot out from the flames. Vesuvius grabbed Andrew around the neck, trying to pull him inside. Andrew screamed as he was dragged backwards, hot flames clawing at his body. He felt the fire melting his flesh. His vision began to blur. Terror came flooding back. Then all the pain disappeared, as a numbing sensation drifted over his body. He shut his eyes, too weak to move.

This was how we was going to die...
His fear had finally killed him.

'Andrew!' Poppy screamed. He felt her yanking him towards her, out of the flames. He collapsed onto the cool, wet grass. Suddenly, the pain came flooding back, intensified, ripping through all the nerves in his body. The next thing he knew, Poppy and Tiffany were rubbing some sort of cold ointment all over his skin.

The pain faded away again. He sat up, head spinning. He held out his arms. There wasn't a single burn on them. *How could that be?*

He felt the gooey ointment on his skin. 'Hey, what is this stuff?'

'Don't worry about that now,' Tiffany said. She pulled something out from her leather coat. It was the Shadowmare skull in the glass jar. 'Here, quickly,' she said, passing it to him. 'I know you're tired, but you need to get this over with. Open it. Hold it up in the air.'

Andrew took the stopper out, and Tiffany began chanting in a strange language that he had never heard before.

'Sheeeeee Mon Laaarr Vesuvius! Maska Van be

gone!' She carried on repeating this, as Andrew held the jar up. Screams filled the air as a black cloud began to rise up and out of the fire. It drifted all the way over to Andrew, hissing and wailing as it was sucked into the bottle like some kind of spiritual vacuum. When all the black smoke had been pulled inside, Andrew jammed the stopper back on the jar. It began to swirl around, until all that remained was the Shadowmare skull and two jet black eyes staring back at them. The screaming noise continued, and then all fell silent.

Andrew breathed a sigh of relief.

It was over.

He turned to see Oran getting up off the ground.

Andrew rushed over to him. 'Oran. You're alive!'

Oran rubbed his head like he had just woken up from a long sleep. His eyes travelled to the glass jar.

'Andrew, you did it,' he said, a smile creeping over his worn face.

'We all did it,' Andrew corrected him. He smiled, but his heart plummeted when he spotted Dan lying crumpled at the other end of the garden. He still hadn't moved. Poppy was leaning over him, sobbing. Andrew raced over, the others following closely behind. Dan was lying in a twisted position, his wings broken and burnt.

'Is he...dead?' Andrew asked. He didn't think he would be able to forgive himself if he was. Oran bent down to check his heartbeat.

There was a long, tense silence.

'He has a faint pulse,' Oran said, sitting up. 'But it's going to be touch and go whether he'll make it or not. He needs treatment immediately.'

Andrew heard Oran speak the words but he didn't *really* hear them. It was like he was in a movie, watching his life unfold before his eyes. Dan couldn't die, he just couldn't.

35

'I've got plenty of potions at home,' Tiffany said. 'We just need to get him there.'

They all helped lift Dan into the back seat of Tiffany's car.

'I hope she can save him,' Andrew said, watching the car speeding up the road.

Poppy nodded. 'Me too. I wish we could go with him.'

'Don't worry. He's in good hands. And we'll go and visit him soon enough,' Oran said. 'But we've got things to clear up here first.'

The grass outside Andrew's house was black and dead from the fire. The street was still a mess. Cars were upturned and glass and rubbish littered the pavement.

All the monsters and Shadowmares had vanished now that Vesuvius was gone, but the residents of Seymour Road were asleep in the most unusual places. A few were lying on the pavement. Andrew's neighbour was still on the roof next door. And his mother was still unconscious in the bush. They carried their mum back up to bed, and then one by one, Oran, Poppy and Andrew helped get the rest of their neighbours back inside their houses. At least this way, there was a chance they would all think it was a strange dream.

Andrew froze when he spotted Madam Bray still lying unconscious on the ground. Poppy and Oran appeared behind him.

'Ooops,' Poppy said. 'I forgot about her.'

Oran shook Madam Bray by the arm. She stirred slowly, and looked up at them, confusion etched on her face. Then she growled unhappily, putting a hand to her sheared off hair. She scowled at Andrew, face as sour as a lemon.

'You,' she hissed accusingly. 'You did this to me.'

'You're lucky he didn't kill you,' Poppy said. She turned to Andrew. 'What are we going to do with her?'

'After everything she did to us, I could think of a few things.' He sighed. 'But none of them would be right. We have to let her go.'

Oran smiled. 'Did you hear that baldy? They're letting you go. I'd say you got off pretty lightly compared to what they did to Vesuvius.'

Madam Bray didn't say anything. She just glared

up at them and then scurried off down the road.

'She looked pretty upset to see us,' Poppy said, watching her leave. 'You don't think she actually wanted Vesuvius to win do you?'

Andrew shrugged, shaking his head. 'Who knows? She's a crazy old bat.'

'But where do you think she'll go now?'

'As long as she never bothers any of us again I don't care,' Andrew said. 'Come on, we've got more important things to worry about. Like Dan.'

Poppy, Oran and Andrew made their way onto the night bus. Oran stood at the front, staring at all the buttons like it was some kind of alien spaceship.

'Come and sit down,' Poppy hissed at him. 'You're drawing attention to yourself.' He was so tall that he had to crouch to avoid hitting his head. All of the other passengers kept staring at him.

'I'm sorry,' he said, taking a seat. 'I've never been on a bus before. What's this?' he asked, moving his hand towards the stop button.

'Don't do that,' Poppy said, slapping his hand away, as a beeping noise filled the bus.

Andrew laughed. He was glad Oran was taking his mind off Dan.

When they arrived at Tiffany's, Andrew rushed straight through the front door and into the living room, where Dan was lying on the sofa.

'Is he going to survive?' Andrew asked, watching his friend's shallow breathing. Dan still had his eyes closed.

'He's been drifting in and out of consciousness for a while now,' Tiffany said. 'I've given him nearly a whole bottle of Cortizol potion and other herbal remedies. He should make a full recovery.'

Andrew smiled, feeling his body turn weak with relief. It was the best news he'd heard in ages.

'You're amazing, Tiffany,' Poppy said, giving her a hug.

'I'll second that. What was that stuff you were rubbing on me after Poppy pulled me out of the fire? I haven't got any burns.' He paused. 'Apart from the ones I already had of course.'

'A concoction of rare Nusquarium plants,' Tiffany said. 'I brought it with me because I had a feeling we might need it.'

'I'm glad you did,' Andrew said.

Poppy bent over Dan. 'He looks normal again,' she mused. There were green scales on the carpet, but his skin was clear.

Tiffany smiled. 'Almost,' she said. 'His wings have shrunken, but they're still there. He should be fully recovered in a few days.'

Andrew frowned. 'What about his parents? Are they still zombies?'

Tiffany laughed. 'No, thankfully not. I'm going to go and check on them later. They should have returned to normal when Vesuvius was defeated. Although they might want to know why they woke up tied to a bed.'

They all laughed.

Oran entered the room, carrying the skull in the glass jar. Andrew shivered as the skull's black eyes stared back at him.

'I thought you said that Vesuvius couldn't be killed with a soul-catcher,' Andrew said.

'Not a normal one, no. Vesuvius required a very special type of soul-catcher. One meant just for him.' She pointed to the Shadowmare skull inside the bottle, and suddenly Andrew thought he understood.

'That's Vesuvius's skull? Before he took over Burtrum's body?'

Oran nodded.

'Oh my God,' Poppy said, backing away. 'That's creepy.'

'I gave it to Tiffany to keep safe. I knew that one day you'd need it.'

Andrew froze, feeling his head swim with panic. 'But, if his spirit's trapped in there, that means he's not actually dead?'

Tiffany sighed. 'It is more complicated than that. He has no body to live in so technically he is dead. But Andrew, such a large amount of evil cannot just disappear. All energy continues to exist, whether good or bad. His soul would have travelled the world until Vesuvius found someone else to re-attach himself to. Thankfully, now he won't be able to do that.'

Andrew nodded, finding it somewhat hard to take in. Then he remembered something.

'Before Vesuvius's spirit was trapped in the soul-catcher, you started speaking in some sort of foreign language. It sounded…weird. What was it?'

Tiffany smiled. 'An ancient Nusquarium language. It means "I order you, Vesuvius, to leave." She paused, face turning serious. 'The powers that you developed from Vesuvius are greater than I imagined, Andrew. You managed to move the strongest element with your mind.'

Andrew grinned despite himself. The fire had saved his life. It was ironic really.

'And the way you dodged Vesuvius's light spears like that. I've never seen someone zip-fly so fast.'

Poppy jumped up. 'What? He was zip flying?'

'I had no idea,' Andrew said, unable to believe it.

Tiffany laughed. 'I told you it cannot be taught.'

'So, what are you going to do with that now?' Poppy asked, pointing to the soul-catcher.

'I'm going to hide it,' Oran said. 'Somewhere no one will ever find it. After all, we can't take any chances.'

Andrew shivered just looking at it. He was glad that Tiffany wasn't going to be keeping it on top of her television any longer.

Andrew and Poppy slept in late the next day. They were both exhausted and couldn't seem to open their mouths without yawning, but they tried their best to act normally when their mother stumbled into the kitchen at a quarter past ten. She yawned as well, wiping away the crusts of sleep from her eyes and staring wearily at the clock.

'I overslept!' she gasped, her eyes widening. 'I've missed work.'

Andrew laughed. 'Mum, it's a Saturday.'

'Oh,' she said, yawning again. 'Good.'

'Do you want some coffee?' Andrew asked, getting

up. His mother stared at him suspiciously.

'Why are you being so helpful?' she asked, eyes narrowing. 'What are you both up to?'

Andrew laughed. 'Nothing, Mum. You just look tired that's all. Didn't you sleep well?' His mother's face softened and her suspicion was replaced with an odd look of confusion.

'I didn't actually. I had the most awful nightmare. It was so vivid. You were both in it, and a man with a knife. The house was on fire. There was a snake on the landing...' she stopped talking, probably realising how silly it all sounded.

Andrew couldn't help but grin. 'Sounds bizarre,' he said, winking at Poppy. 'Perhaps you need a dreamcatcher.'

'Don't be so ridiculous.' his mother laughed.

Later that evening Andrew and Poppy went to visit Dan again. He was back at the same hospital where they'd woken up from their comas.

'Andrew, Poppy!' he shouted when he saw them heading though the doorway. He tried to sit up but screamed out in pain. He had a broken leg, his left arm was sprained and he was bruised from head to toe. Apart from that, he looked fine. All of his scales had completely dropped off, and if he had any wings left, you couldn't tell. 'Tiffany told me you killed Vesuvius!' he said, eyes bright and full of excitement.

Andrew shrugged. 'As good as.'

'Andrew was *amazing*,' said Poppy. 'You should have seen him.'

'You two were great as well. Dan, I had no idea you'd learnt how to fly.'

'I didn't know I could until I tried. I just jumped out of my bedroom window, flapped like hell and hoped for the best. Luckily for me it worked out OK.' He grinned.

'Still as crazy as ever then,' a familiar voice said. They all spun around. Oran was standing at the foot of the bed, smiling widely. 'I wanted to say goodbye before I left.'

Andrew raised his eyebrows. 'Why? Where are you going?'

Oran chuckled. 'Home. I do still have a Dream Factory to run you know. Plus I've just talked to Tarker. He's had the baby. It's a little boy weighing in at two stone.'

'Two stone!' Dan cried. 'That's not a baby!' He laughed. 'Tell him congratulations.'

Oran nodded. 'Oh, I almost forgot. Tiffany told me to give you this. It's your favourite drink.'

Dan's eyes lit up. 'Lemonade?' he said.

'You'd be so lucky.' Oran smiled, pulling out a bottle of Cortizol potion from behind his back.

'Great,' Dan said. 'I almost forgot about that too.' He took the bottle off Oran and took a swig, pulling a nasty face. 'Yuck. That stuff never tastes any better!'

Oran chuckled. 'I must be off now. I'll come and visit again soon, but in the meantime, go and see Tiffany if you need anything.'

'Oran,' Andrew said, just as he was turning to leave. 'Yes?'

'What will happen to all of the children in the Nightmare Factory…now that Vesuvius is gone?'

'I'll let them go of course. Now that I have the key to the Nightmare Factory and to the Slider's box.'

'Will the Shadowmares not try and stop you?' Poppy asked.

'Probably, but I have my unicorn horn. And I doubt they'll be very strong without Vesuvius ordering them around.' He smiled. 'I really must be off now. Take care you three. Maybe you can come and visit some time?'

'What, at the Dream Factory?' Dan said, sitting up. He screamed out in pain again. 'Man, I really gotta learn not to do that.'

'Of course at the Dream Factory. Where else did you think I meant?'

'Cool!' Andrew said.

They said their goodbyes and Oran left. Andrew sighed, feeling a bit sad that he wouldn't be seeing him for a while. He'd really grown fond of Oran this past week.

'My parents are coming to visit in a minute,' Dan said, breaking the silence.

'What did you say happened?' Poppy asked.

'That I fell off my bike. I don't think they believed me. And they kept asking questions about why they woke up tied to the bed. I don't think they remember much.'

'Good,' Andrew said. 'But maybe we'll leave now, just in case they suddenly do.'

Dan grinned.

'Yeah, maybe that's best. See you at school?'

'What do you mean?' Poppy asked, confused. 'You don't even go to our school.'

'I do now.' Dan grinned. 'My school wanted to move me down two years, because I'd missed so much from being in a coma. I asked if I could just transfer to your school instead because I'd be in your year then.'

'That's wicked!' Andrew said. 'Hopefully we'll be in some of the same classes.'

Poppy smiled. 'When do you think you'll be starting?'

'The principal said I can start as soon as my leg heals, which will be in about six weeks' time. Hopefully sooner if my Sepataurus genes kick in. Maybe I'll stop taking the potion for a while and…'

Poppy opened her mouth to speak.

Dan grinned. 'Only joking.'

Andrew went to bed that evening feeling exhausted. The past week had completely drained him of all his energy. He walked over to the window and took his dreamcatcher down.

He opened his chest of drawers and hid it under a pile of clothes. He didn't need it any more. Vesuvius could never harm him or anyone else again. *He was free.*

He got into bed, but there was a knock at the door. His mum popped her head around.

'I just wanted to say goodnight.'

'Night, Mum,' Andrew said. Then he sat up. 'Wait. Mum. I need to ask you something.'

His mum pushed the door open wider and came

and sat on his bed.

'Oh?' she said, frowning. 'Are you OK? What is it?'

'I was wondering…about Dad. How did he die?'

'You know how he died, Andrew. In the house fire, when you were five.'

'I know. But *how* did he die? Was it my fault?' He couldn't stop thinking about what Vesuvius had said to him.

Tears began to flow from his mum's eyes.

'Of course not,' she said, hugging him. 'You didn't cause the fire. It was an accident. Why would you think such a thing?'

Andrew shrugged. 'No reason. I was just being silly I guess.' He realised that as his mum hugged him, tears were running down his face too. But they weren't tears of sadness any more. He felt like a huge weight had been lifted off his shoulders. Finally, he could put the past behind him. The fire, the guilt, his fear, *everything*.

That night, he fell into a peaceful sleep. He dreamt that he was back at school. He dreamt that he was made captain of the football team. He dreamt that everything was normal again… Then he was thrown into darkness.

'Andrew,' a familiar voice hissed.

Andrew looked up. 'Who's there?' he shouted.

But he already knew.

Vesuvius.

How was that possible? Nightmares didn't exist any more. Vesuvius didn't exist any more. But the voice seemed as real as ever, cutting through the darkness like a scream.

'I'm coming back, Andrew. I've already found a way, and when I do, I'll be coming for you…'

TO BE CONTINUED…

Read on for an exclusive extract of
The Nightmare Factory:
Rise of the Shadowmares!

Quentin Bane stood transfixed.

He knew that he was dreaming because everything was slightly hazy. The tall figure with a black cloak and top hat hovered in front of him, his thin grey hair cascading down his shoulders. His nose was shaped like a hook. His eyes were as black as coal and as narrow as the slits on a money box.

'Are you ready?' Vesuvius asked in a scratchy voice. He crept towards Quentin, raising his cane with a human skull on top.

Quentin felt a shiver run down his spine. He peered around his grimy cell. Graffiti covered the walls and damp and mould poisoned the air. *What am I doing?* he wondered. *I'm a rebel. A hardened criminal. I've never taken orders from anyone. Why now?*

'I hope you're not having second thoughts?' Vesuvius hissed, as if reading his mind. He raised his skull cane again, and Quentin flinched.

'No, Master. I am at your command.'

Vesuvius's lips curled into a smile. 'Good,' he said, lowering the cane. 'I have visited you in your dreams every night for the past six months. You were all alone, Quentin, and I was there for you. Me. The only one.'

'I know, Master. I owe you my life.'

'Indeed you do. Is everything still in place for tomorrow?'

Quentin nodded, hands trembling by his sides.

'You had better not disappoint me, Quentin.'

'I won't let you down. You can count on me, Master,' Quentin said, with a hint of desperation. He wanted to please Vesuvius, more than he'd ever wanted to please anyone before, but he had no idea *why*. It was a burning desire deep in his soul, which had grown stronger every night, like some sort of disease. Sometimes he wondered if he was going insane. But he couldn't ignore it anymore. The voice, the dreams, what they were telling him to do…

Quentin's eyes snapped open.

He climbed out of bed and slid his hand underneath the mattress. He glanced through the bars into the dimly lit corridor.

No guards. Good.

He pulled out a knife and a small rock and begun

sharpening the blade. He smiled. It was almost time. Tomorrow the bloodshed could begin.

Andrew, his twin sister Poppy and their mum sat staring at the TV, robotically shoving forkfuls of spaghetti Bolognese into their mouths. Happy Families was on, the worst show *ever*.

Andrew cleared his throat. 'Pass me the pepper, will you?'

'Shhh!' Poppy hissed. 'Doug's about to reveal that he's having an affair!'

'Oh wow, highlight of my day,' Andrew muttered, rolling his eyes. He leaned over the table, reaching for the pepper pot, but a searing pain cut through his head.

'*Hurry up*. I'm waiting,' a chilling voice rasped.

Andrew stiffened, dropping the pepper pot. Its contents spilled all over the table.

'Did you hear that?' he asked, looking around.

'Hear what?' his mum said, not taking her eyes off the television.

It was so loud… Why hadn't she heard it?

'A voice,' Andrew said. 'It sounded like…' He knew what he wanted to say. *It sounded like Vesuvius…* But that was impossible. Vesuvius was dead.

Wasn't he?

'Like who?' Poppy asked. She turned away from the TV. Her eyes were locked on Andrew's, full of concern. 'Who did it sound like, Andrew?'

'I don't know,' he lied. 'It was nothing. Probably just my imagination.'

'Are you OK, dear?' Mum asked. 'You look pale.'

Andrew nodded. He picked up his fork again. His mouth felt as dry as sawdust, and the spaghetti stuck to his throat as he tried to swallow it. What if Vesuvius had found a way back, just like he'd dreamt he would six months ago?

Andrew pushed his plate away. 'I'm not hungry,' he said, getting up from the table. 'I'm going to bed.' He hurried upstairs to his bedroom and reached for the chest of drawers. He pulled out a bundle of clothes until he found the dreamcatcher hidden underneath them. He held it up, tracing his finger over the willow hoop, decorated with beads and feathers.

Tiffany Grey had given it to him as a gift. It was supposed to protect him from Vesuvius, so that he couldn't steal Andrew from his nightmares again.

Andrew walked over to the window, searching for a place to hang it. He had a feeling that he was going to need it.

'What are you doing?' Poppy said, making him jump. He turned around to find his twin sister standing in his doorway.

'It's just in case,' Andrew said, tying the dreamcatcher to the curtain rail. 'Maybe you should do the same with yours.'

'Why?' Poppy said, grabbing him by the arm and staring deep into his eyes. 'You think he's coming back, don't you? Why did you run away from the dinner table like that? What did you hear?'

Andrew sighed, and sat down on his bed.

'I heard Vesuvius. I think it was him anyway. He sounded so angry.'

'Well, what did he say?'

'He said, "Hurry up, I'm waiting." What do you think he meant by that?'

Poppy sat down next to Andrew, frowning heavily.

'I think it was all in your mind. You defeated Vesuvius. He's gone. You locked his spirit in a soul-catcher. Oran hid it—'

'I know, I know, somewhere it could never be found. But what if somebody's discovered it and let him out? What if Vesuvius has a new body to live in and—'

'Listen, bro,' Poppy said, putting an arm around

him. 'I realise this is hard for you. It's hard for me too. But what happened six months ago, is now in the past. You've got to learn to put it behind you.'

Andrew nodded. But that was the problem – he *had* put it behind him...until today. Until he'd heard the voice... Then all the fear and worry had crept back in. Didn't Poppy understand that it was different for Andrew? He was The Releaser. If Vesuvius got hold of Andrew's fear again, nightmares would become real. The whole world would fall into chaos.

He shuddered, trying not to think about it. 'Well, I'm going to leave the dreamcatcher up anyway...just in case,' he said, laying back and pulling the covers over him.

Poppy shrugged, rising to her feet. 'Whatever makes you happy bro, but honestly, you've got nothing to worry about. Trust me.'

'I hope you're right,' Andrew muttered when she'd left the room. 'I really hope you're right...'

The next morning, a knock at the door rattled all the way through the house.

'I'll get it,' Andrew said, running down the stairs with his toothbrush between his teeth. He opened the door. Dan was leaning against the porch, grinning widely from ear to ear.

'What are you so happy about?' Andrew said through a mouthful of toothpaste.

Dan stepped inside. 'It's my first day at Fairoaks, man.'

Andrew walked into the kitchen and spat into the sink. 'Oh yeah, I forgot. Better get ready for the head-flush!' he grinned, rustling Dan's hair.

'Huh? Head-flush?'

'Yeah, didn't you hear? All the new Fairoaks kids get their heads flushed down the toilet. It's sort of an initiation thing.'

Dan's face dropped.

'He's joking.' Poppy laughed, running down the stairs. 'Don't listen to him.' She slung her school bag over one shoulder.

'Oh,' Dan said, folding his arms. 'Yeah 'course, I knew that.'

'Hadn't we better get going?' Andrew said, glancing at his watch. 'We'll be late if we don't hurry.'

They stepped outside into the early morning light. A thick layer of frost coated the ground. Andrew tugged open the garage door and they grabbed their bikes from inside. They cycled down the street, cutting into a muddy lane, sparsely sheltered by skeletal trees. In the distance, the white school building rose into view.

'Last one there buys snacks at break time,' Andrew yelled, whizzing down the hill. He turned to see how far the others were behind him. But a splitting pain sliced through his head, as if it was being ripped in two.

'Ow!' he yelled. His mind whirled. The trees and the pavement merged together, melting into a blurry watercolour of shapes and patterns. Seconds later, he was spinning head first over the handlebars and hurtling straight for a brick wall.

When his vision came back to him, he was in a room surrounded by metal bars and dusty brick walls. A stale smell lingered in the air. *Where the hell am I?* His heart was pounding against his ribcage with the force of a drum. *Am I in hospital? Oh god,* Andrew thought, a wave of fear flooding through him. *I'm back in the Nightmare Factory.*

But wait. There was a man dressed in blue, lingering outside the bars. He was wearing some sort of a guard's uniform, with a ring of keys attached to his belt.

'Belmarsh Prison,' Andrew read on the man's badge.

So I'm in a prison. But why? The last thing he remembered was crashing his bike.

He took a step forwards. The walls were covered in drawings of skull and crossbones and hundreds of nametags.

Never pick up a dead man's gun, someone had written with a black marker pen. *Three days until freedom*, another had carved into the brickwork. Andrew's eyes flitted to the next piece of writing.

Free Vesuvius. Free Vesuvius. Free Vesuvius. Free Vesuvius. Over and over, the name was scrawled with terrifying clarity. For a second, he couldn't breath. His heart was frozen inside his chest. Surely it was just a coincidence.

But what if it wasn't?

A rasping voice filled the room, making Andrew jump.

'Wake up, Quentin. It is time.'

Andrew spun around. *Vesuvius.* He was sure of it. There was no mistaking that deep and foreboding tone. He glanced around the room, scanning the empty shadows. But nobody else was there.

A loud cough echoed against the stony walls. A stocky man ripped back the blanket and sat up in bed. At first Andrew thought it was Vesuvius, but then the man turned towards him, and he could see his greasy black hair, draped like wet seaweed over his muscular shoulders. He was wearing a bright orange jumpsuit, with the sleeves rolled up to show off his faded tattoos.

'Use the knife, Quentin. Kill him,' the voice boomed. It was inside the room. Inside Andrew's head, louder than his own thoughts.

Impossible. Yet the prisoner, Quentin, cocked his head as if he'd heard the voice too. His eyes were fixed firmly on the wall, as if he was in a trance, as if he was…*sleepwalking.*

Quentin moved his hand down towards his pocket. Tiny beads of sweat trickled down his forehead. Slowly, he pulled out a knife.

Acknowledgements

In every bookstore, behind every title, there is not just an author, but also many people who have helped put that book on the shelf.

A huge thank you to everyone at The Darley Anderson Agency, particularly my wonderful agent, Madeleine Milburn, who believed in me from the very start. Somehow, this small mention doesn't seem enough for everything she has done for me.

My editors, Sarah Lilly and Matt Ralphs who together shaped *The Nightmare Factory* into the book that it is today. Thanks also to the entire team at Orchard Books for their hard work and for an awesome cover!

A massive thank you to Daniel Bage for an amazing author website (I owe you quite a few drinks!). To my Mum and Dad, for their constant support (financially and emotionally!) and to my English teacher Mr O'mahony, who encouraged me to start writing in the first place.

To Smeg, for always being there for me, and whom I love dearly.

Also thanks to: Emma and Paul Knee, Gavin Jones, Sarah Moass, Mark Murphy, Jenna Haws, Christina Bulmer, Charlie Measures, Luke Mason, David Westley, Reema Huzair, Gemma Daniels, Samantha Phillips and Amy Hodges...because every writer needs great friends.

About the Author

Lucy Jones is twenty-five years old but has been writing stories since she was twelve. *The Nightmare Factory* is her first novel. She is fascinated by all things supernatural, and has a huge passion for reptiles, especially snakes. In her spare time she enjoys watching horror films and going to rock festivals. She currently lives in Exmouth, Devon, with her dog, Boo.

www.Lucyjonesbooks.co.uk